Dear Reader,

The summertime temperatures here in Boise, Idaho, have been in the high nineties and low hundreds for several weeks now. It's our hottest summer on record! Sure makes me long for the seaside—and not just any seaside, but Marble Cove, Maine. It's been many years since I planted my feet on a sandy beach or dodged ocean waves, but as I wrote *Ringing True*, I could easily imagine the cool breezes blowing in from the waves as I jogged along the boardwalk with Beverly (and that's really stretching my imagination, since I don't jog!) and sitting around a bonfire on the beach, toasting marshmallows for s'mores. Makes me want to pack up and move thousands of miles to that lovely coastal town.

Of course, I couldn't move away from Boise. As much as I've fallen in love with Marble Cove, Boise—hot as it is today!—holds a special place in my heart. This is where my own good friends live. I'm a pretty independent person, but I'd feel lost without my nearest and dearest friends. As I'm writing about our Marble Cove friends, I use bits and pieces of my friends' personalities to create situations and dialogue. They help me make Margaret, Beverly, Diane, and Shelley come alive in my mind. I hope that, as you read *Ringing True* and all of the other books in Miracles of Marble Cove, you'll see one or more of your special friends reflected there.

And I hope this story of good friends and a town full of miracles will capture your imagination and transport you to Marble Cove, if only in your heart.

Blessings,
Patti Berg

MIRACLES *of*
MARBLE COVE

RINGING TRUE

PATTI BERG

Guideposts
New York

Published by Guideposts Books & Inspirational Media
110 William Street
New York, NY 10038
Guideposts.org

Acknowledgments

Every attempt has been made to credit the sources of copyrighted material
used in this book. If any such acknowledgment has been inadvertently
omitted or miscredited, receipt of such information would be appreciated.

"From the Guideposts Archive" originally appeared as "His Mysterious
Ways" by Judy H. Armstrong in *Guideposts* magazine. Copyright ©1991 by
Guideposts. All rights reserved.

Cover and interior design and cover photo by Müllerhaus
Typeset by Aptara, Inc.

Printed and bound in the United States of America
10 9 8 7 6 5 4

CHAPTER ONE

The first hint of Tuesday's early morning light slipped through the window of Beverly Wheeland's office and streaked across her computer screen, highlighting the list of campaign slogans she'd been working on since long before dawn. Running for mayor of Marble Cove had seemed to be such a manageable endeavor when she'd entered the race. Now she was faced with the most daunting task: searching for a slogan. The words that would describe her cause—her campaign platform—could make or break her efforts to win the election.

With the mayoral race on her mind and the sound of the surf whispering through the open window, she quickly saved her file and swallowed her last few drops of now-cold coffee. Slipping her feet into her running shoes, she tied the laces, did a few routine stretches, and jogged down the stairs.

The aroma of sausage frying on the stove drew her to the kitchen. She hadn't expected her father to be up already, but he was standing at the counter slicing a Red Delicious apple, still dressed in his pajamas, the robe her mother had given him the Christmas before she'd passed away, and his favorite, well-worn slippers.

"Good morning." She pecked him on the cheek and he greeted her with a smile.

"Want some turkey sausage and make-believe eggs, with one of Shelley's sugar-free oatmeal cookies on the side?" He gave her a wry smile.

"Thanks, but I had a yogurt earlier."

"You don't eat enough to keep a bird alive," her father admonished, shaking his head.

Beverly ignored the comment, one of her father's favorite refrains, and plucked a wedge of apple from her mother's pink Depression glass fruit bowl. "This'll tide me over until I get back from my run."

A moment later, she slipped out the front door, standing in the midst of her father's beautifully landscaped garden. Earlier in the year, she'd helped him nurture the hydrangeas he and her mother had planted years before, and their blooms were once again amazingly large and a deep, dramatic blue. A hummingbird darted among the rosy mauve blossoms of the clematis climbing up and around the porch, and the flowers cast off a light, sweet scent that mingled with the salty sea air. She took a long, refreshing breath, realizing—not for the first time—just how much she had come to love living in Marble Cove.

Beverly did some more stretches and then began her run. She started out slowly, warming up, then gained speed as she made her way to the boardwalk. She had the place all to herself this morning. It seemed ages since that had happened. Vacationers had flocked to Marble Cove over the summer, but the past three days—Labor Day weekend—had, she hoped, seen the last of the summer rush.

She'd recently managed to thwart a land developer's efforts to build a major resort complex in Marble Cove, and she'd won, at least temporarily. Now she had to fight that same developer—Dennis Calder—for the job of mayor. She was determined to win, not just for herself, but for her community.

A cool breeze blew in off the Atlantic, whipping up and around the lighthouse. As she had many times in the last ten days, she wished Jeff Mackenzie was in town. She missed talking with him. Bouncing ideas off him. Feeling his hand in hers. The warmth of his smile. His kiss . . .

Russia was such a long way away, but that's where he'd gone this time: a photographic tour along a portion of the Trans-Siberian Railway. It was a good contract and nice money. He couldn't have turned it down. Still, she wished he were here.

She stopped running and sat down for a moment on one of the benches that had been installed for sightseers so they could look out over the rocky coastline and the Atlantic. Pulling out her cell phone, she hoped to find a message from Jeff, but she hadn't had one in days. Nothing said she couldn't send him a text message, though.

Her fingers started to punch in letters on the very small keyboard.

Hello! Any new pictures of St. Petersburg? The Kremlin? Something that will win you a Pulitzer Prize?

The ring tone announcing she had a text message sounded light and airy. Suddenly a photo of the golden domes of St. Petersburg's St. Isaac's Cathedral, with the purple-and-red glow of sunset as its backdrop, popped up on the screen, followed by Jeff's message:

Heading home tomorrow. See you soon.

She closed her eyes and thought about their past, their present, and...and whatever the future might hold in store for them. Smiling, she stood, tucked her phone back into her pocket, and twirled around, not caring if anyone was watching. She came to a stop with the view of Marble Cove stretching out before her. Its quaint houses. Its church spires. Its cobbled Main Street, planned and built well over a hundred years ago.

As Beverly began to run again, she spotted Silas Locke, the pastor of her church—Old First—walking in the opposite direction along the water. She slowed down, but he hadn't seen her, and she didn't call out. The almost always staid middle-aged man, with a nearly bald head, wore a windbreaker over a dark shirt and his clerical collar, and the bottoms of his black slacks were rolled up to his knees. With his head bowed and his shoulders slumped, he looked deep in thought, as he had since the fire had damaged Old First's roof and the town authorities insisted the sanctuary be closed until repairs could be made.

If only she and her friends could find the treasure they'd been hunting the past few months.

She slowed again to a walk and took in some deep breaths, watching Reverend Locke walk up the beach, at last looking up from the sand toward the high cliffs and a rugged stretch of coastline where not all that long ago he, his sister, plus Beverly, Margaret, Shelley, and Diane, had taken metal detectors and found little more than rusty hinges, a lock, remnants of what could have once been a box—and one intriguing gold piece.

The treasure they'd sought the past few months seemed to have disappeared over the centuries. Whether it had been found years ago by someone strolling the cliffs, they might never know. Maybe the box had rotted and the rest of the gold coins had slowly worked their way down to the rocks below, then washed out to sea. Or maybe Reverend Thorpe—the eighteenth-century minister and founder of Old First Church, as well as the town of Marble Cove—had truly absconded with the money, as some centuries-old legends seemed to imply.

Beverly sighed. It would be so easy to think that they'd wasted their time looking for the treasure. But they'd heard the old church bell ringing as they searched the cliffs; softly, miraculously. The ringing was a sign; they'd been sure of it. A sign that the church was calling them back, letting them know that they needed to continue their search.

Beverly looked toward town off in the distance, spotting Old First's bell tower, a stoic sentry above Marble Cove. It was silent now. The congregation had been meeting at Diane's church since the fire. And yet she and her friends sensed—no, *knew*—that *something* of value had to be there in the church.

Running faster now along the beach, she turned her attention back to her campaign. Slogans again paraded through her head. She'd been told to keep them snappy and succinct, to tap into the core of the community's values. She'd skimmed every book and Web site on how to run a campaign, but all her slogans felt lifeless and drab.

She had run to her turnaround point and was heading back up the boardwalk as she recited the slogans, thinking they might sound better out loud. "Beverly Wheeland—For You; for Marble Cove; for the Dream." Too cheesy, she decided, as she slowed her pace again. Another slogan came to mind. "Looking Out for Everyone, Not Just Number One!"

Beverly shook her head. That was awful. Definitely not right for her campaign.

"Talking to yourself?"

Beverly recognized the familiar voice and looked up to face Dennis Calder. Observing his attire—a business suit, tie, and shiny black tasseled loafers—she assumed he wasn't out for a morning jog.

"Hello, Dennis." She ignored his comment. "Beautiful day, isn't it?"

Dennis nodded and held up a small camera. "Perfect for capturing a few good photos of the sunrise. My campaign Web site's about to go online, and I want to include a few pictures of our community, you know, what we have to offer...what we could offer."

Beverly's eyes narrowed. "Still trying to overdevelop Marble Cove, I see."

He sighed. "Look, Beverly. You might have succeeded in destroying my plan to build a resort complex here in Marble Cove," he said, "but I assure you, that's only temporary. Once we have a new mayor and like-minded town council members, I'm sure the complex will find its way back on the drawing board."

"But I'm going to be the new mayor, Dennis." She gave him what she hoped was a confident smile. "I'll have veto power, and I will not let the quaintness of Marble Cove be destroyed. I don't want that; neither do our citizens."

He'd chuckled throughout her argument. "Sorry to disappoint you, Beverly, but there is no way you can beat me in the mayoral race."

"You're sadly mistaken. But on the off chance you do win—and that would take a miracle—you'd have a serious conflict of interest on your hands if you try to get the resort approved."

He frowned, deep in thought. Hadn't the conflict-of-interest issue even crossed his mind?

She looked at her watch as she began to jog in place. "I'd best get going," she said. "I've a telephone conference in an hour, and—"

"Here. Take this with you." Dennis thrust a colorful red, white, and blue trifold campaign flyer at her. She could see his name in big print, followed by the words "Prosperity and Progress." Though she didn't like the sentiment, she had to admit that, as campaign slogans went, it was pretty catchy. It spelled out Dennis' platform in three short, succinct words.

No doubt it would make a lot of citizens of Marble Cove take notice. Could hers do the same?

Dennis turned away from Beverly and snapped another photo, just one more iconic shot of the Orlean Point lighthouse, before offering her a hasty salute and disappearing.

It seemed useless to argue with Dennis Calder. He had his ideas for Marble Cove and she had hers, and apparently the twain would never meet. Suddenly she had a deplorable vision of a Marble Cove of the future if Dennis had his way, a town awash in gaudy neon signs and her beloved Newport Avenue plowed under to make room for a casino.

She couldn't let that happen. She had to win. Suddenly her slogan—her platform—came to her. It was perfect!

Embracing Marble Cove's Heritage.

Chapter Two

Diane Spencer plucked what she hoped was the last of the just-emerging dandelions and other assorted weeds from the rose garden that bordered a portion of her white picket fence. They could easily take over the yard if she'd let them, but gardening was her delight, never a chore. This morning, the first Tuesday in September, with the sky a brilliant lapis, she paused to enjoy the butterflies flitting around, along with the pair of hummingbirds that had made her home theirs, and let her creative juices flow. She had another mystery to write, and she was determined to work on it even while gardening.

"The man was dead."

Diane clasped a gloved hand to her chest. In her mind's eye she could clearly see the victim in the book. Her heart beat rapidly. She drew in deep gasps of air, as if she were living her heroine's tale, then continued to dictate the story into the electronic gadget one of her critique partners had insisted she try. She could dictate now, then plug it into her computer and the words would end up as text. It was all so amazing; it gave her a newfound freedom and eased some of the horrendous writer's block that had hit her a couple of months ago.

Again she dictated: *"The butler walked silently to the old-fashioned phone and dialed 9-1-1 with a bony finger. 'This is Higgins, at Bonforte Manor. There's been an incident.'"*

Rocky, her yellow Lab/golden retriever mix, nudged her left hand, then nosed his way under her arm. His warm brown eyes looked up into her face.

"I've been ignoring you, haven't I?" She pulled off her right glove and ruffled the fur on top of his head. "Ever since I got this gizmo"—she adjusted the electronic miracle wrapped around her ear—"I tell my stories to it, not to you."

Rocky dropped down on the grass and rolled over on his back, exposing his belly for a hearty rub. "You know, Rocky, I think we need a little more intrigue in this book. Something a little different. What do you think?"

Rocky barked once, rolled over again, jumped up onto all fours, and ran off, chasing a monarch butterfly into the pink and blue hydrangeas. Smiling to herself, Diane pulled on her gardening glove again before picking up the clippers to trim a tangerine-colored Lady Emma Hamilton rose. She inhaled the sweet, fruity fragrance, and went back to work, gardening *and* writing.

"Off in the distance, she heard a foghorn. Somewhere down the beach a dog barked. Classical music—Mussorgsky's Night on Bald Mountain, *she was sure of it—blared through an open window, the mixture of woodwinds, brass, strings, and percussion blending with the sound of the tide, becoming an eerie companion to the dark. It was such a fitting soundtrack for the moment, for something sinister had been at work."*

"Diane?"

Diane nearly jumped out of her skin, startled by the voice that seemed to come out of nowhere. Tilting her head up, she saw Beverly standing on the other side of the picket fence, wearing periwinkle blue spandex jogging shorts and matching tee. Beverly grinned; Diane smiled back. With her knees starting to ache from too much time kneeling on the grass, she rose and pressed her hands against the small of her back to stretch out the kinks.

"Were you talking to yourself?" Beverly's question echoed the one Dennis had asked her.

"Actually, I'm learning to write—hands free—while I garden. A little trick I learned from one of my writer pals."

Beverly frowned, and Diane pointed out the gadget fastened around her ear. "It's pretty much the same concept as a hands-free phone."

"And it actually works?"

Diane nodded. "So far so good. Of course, I have no idea how much sense my words are making, but it's all somehow freeing. Makes me feel like I can conquer the world and still whip out a few thousand words a day."

Diane clipped one of her most fragrant English roses, a Lady of the Mist, its petals ranging from a soft violet pink to a coppery buff, and a few others to go with it, and handed the small bouquet to Beverly. "These have the loveliest scent, and they'll look gorgeous in one of your mom's Depression glass vases."

Beverly held the vibrant bouquet close to her nose and inhaled. She smiled and thanked Diane.

"You're still planning to come over for dinner tomorrow night, I hope." Diane said. "Margaret and Shelley are definitely going to make it, and I've found this wonderful recipe for fettuccine Alfredo with shrimp that I want to try out on the three of you."

"I'll be there, but please tell me that isn't the same recipe you told me about a few weeks ago, the one that you've planned to use to kill off a character in your new book."

"Just for you"—Diane grinned—"I'll leave out the arsenic."

Beverly laughed just as the phone in the house rang.

"Gotta go," Diane said, backing away from the picket fence. "If I don't see you before, I'll see you tomorrow night. Seven o'clock."

Diane turned on the second ring and jogged up the steps and through the front door, anxious to get the phone, nearly tumbling over Rocky in her rush. She hoped it was her editor or her agent with good news of any sort. She could always use a boost. Or maybe it was the movie producer who'd optioned her first book, a miraculous event that still amazed her.

After grabbing the phone and saying hello, she heard her sister-in-law Jeanette on the other end, sounding bright and cheerful. She'd recently been promoted to head up the English Department at Portland College, and with the new

school year starting any day—if it hadn't started already—
she seemed quite calm.

"How on earth could you possibly find time to call?"
Diane asked. "Hasn't school just started?"

"Next week, thank heaven. I've spent the past month
inundated by paperwork and there's still much more to do,
but we haven't talked in ages and, well, it seemed high time
I give you a call."

Diane knew she should have done the same. She and her
late husband Eric's sister, Jeanette, had been close from the
first moment they met. Jeanette was the first one to graciously
welcome Diane into the family, making her feel at home
during the early years. She'd been there for Diane when Eric
had died, offering support in every imaginable way.

They'd stayed close until Diane packed up and moved to
Marble Cove a year and a half ago; sadly they'd drifted apart
since then.

"I admit I'm not the best when it comes to picking up
the phone to call friends and family," Diane admitted. "The
busier I get with my writing, the worse I get, and lately, my
writing seems to have consumed my life."

"At least you don't have to leave home to work."

Diane's jaw tightened. That was a line often used by
people who didn't understand all the energy it took to write.
Somehow she tossed off Jeanette's words, and shared her
latest success. "You'll never believe this, but *The Lighthouse
Goes Dark* was optioned by WMN—the Women's Movie
Network."

"That's wonderful," Jeanette said, and then laughed. "I hope that doesn't mean you're too busy to have company for a couple of days."

"You're coming to Marble Cove?" Diane loved the idea of seeing Jeanette again. "You really have time for that?"

"I need a couple of days of downtime before the school year begins. That doesn't mean I won't be bringing my laptop and cell phone along in case there are fires to put out. But I really do want to see you, as long as you have an extra bed and can put up with my OCD."

Jeanette always claimed she had an obsessive-compulsive disorder, and Diane had been unable to overlook the way Jeanette straightened books and knickknacks in everyone's home. Jeanette's own home had always been immaculate. Her library was alphabetized and there wasn't a speck of dust anywhere. Her sister-in-law was a woman of many accomplishments—not only an English professor, but an art historian.

"I've got plenty of room, and you're more than welcome, anytime," Diane said. "There's so much in Marble Cove that I'd love to show you. The lighthouse and Old First…"

"I've something I want to show you too. Remember Dr. Standish?"

"Of course." Dr. Standish was the archive curator at Portland College who'd been so helpful when she and Beverly trekked to the college to find information about Reverend Thorpe and his elusive treasure.

Jeanette chuckled. "He's pretty hard to forget. Well, you'll be thrilled to know he's found a few documents about your Bandit Preacher."

Diane felt her heart pick up speed. "Diaries? Old letters?"

"Newspaper clippings, actually. I haven't had a chance to look at them yet, but he's given me photocopies. You are still interested in learning more about Reverend Thorpe, aren't you?"

"Very much!"

"Then I'll bring them with me this weekend and you can show them to your friends. Dr. Standish doesn't know if they're all that revealing; I don't either, but reading through them definitely couldn't hurt. I also think these documents have piqued Dr. Standish's curiosity enough that he'll keep looking for more documents about Old First and Reverend Thorpe."

"Bless him."

Jeanette laughed. "I must admit, my curiosity's been aroused by this hidden treasure and the supposed Bandit Preacher too, and I'm dying for you to show me the church that's at the center of so much intrigue. For such a little town, it certainly has its share of mysteries."

Diane laughed. "You don't know the half of it!"

Chapter Three

D o they have a playground with monkey bars and swings?" Aiden asked Shelley, skipping alongside his sister Emma's stroller. The three were taking a walk along Main Street that first Tuesday after Labor Day.

"You'll find out soon enough. I'm sure you'll get to do all kinds of fun things in pre-K," Shelley told her four-year-old son. She was thrilled that he seemed excited about his first day of school, but she dreaded the fact that she'd be leaving her little boy in the company of strangers. All morning long she'd fought off the tears, trying to forget that he was growing up way too fast.

"Like what, Mama?"

"Oh, I imagine you'll have snack time and singing and story time."

"Will Teacher read my favorite books?"

"If you tell her the names of your favorite books, she might put them on a list and read them when and if she can."

"I'll ask her as soon as we get to school."

"You might want to wait a day or two."

"Why?"

"To see what the teacher reads to you and to find out what other stories she'll be reading. Maybe some of her books will become your favorites too."

Aiden peppered her with questions as he skipped along, full of energy, looking handsome in his first-day-of-school outfit—a short-sleeved plaid shirt with a button-down collar, brand-new blue jeans, and big-boy tennis shoes.

They were only a block away from the renovated Craftsman-style house that had been turned into a bright and cheerful place for learning. She was happy that Maine had adopted the universal pre-K system; without it, she and Dan would have had to pinch even more pennies to find a way to enroll Aiden in preschool.

School was going to be great for her precocious son. And, for a change, she'd have at least a couple of hours, on the days Aiden was in school, to spend bonding one-on-one with Emma. They had just had a wonderful birthday celebration for Emma with Dan's family, and her two-year-old was becoming more engaging by the day.

Of course, as soon as she got back home today, she would have baking to do. She began going down her orders for the day in her head.

"Look at the swing set and the slide, Mama!" Aiden hollered, interrupting her mental inventory. He ran ahead toward the schoolhouse door. "Wait for us, Aiden," Shelley called out, and he turned back. "We should all go in together." Finding a place in the shade where she could leave Emma's stroller, she picked up the two-year-old, fluffed her golden curls as well as her pretty pink ruffly dress, and set the toddler on the sidewalk. "Come on, princess." She took Emma's hand. "We're going to meet Aiden's new teacher."

"Hurry up, Mama." Aiden jumped up and down at the foot of the schoolhouse stairs.

"Let me tie your shoes first." Shelley knelt down in front of Aiden, realizing that she was stalling, suddenly coming up with all sorts of excuses to keep from going inside. Was she doing the right thing by sending him off to school when he was only four years old? Did she really want him leaving her sight for several hours a day? With strangers?

Shelley cradled Aiden's face in her palms, looking deep into his bold blue eyes, at the freckles dotting his nose and cheeks, and sandy-colored hair that had been neatly combed less than half an hour ago and now seemed to shoot out in all directions. She kissed his nose.

He giggled. "Mama! You're treating me like a baby."

She couldn't tell him that she'd miss him. He was a tough yet sensitive little guy and she wasn't about to make him feel that there was anything he should worry about—like leaving his mom.

"Come on, big boy. Let's go meet your new teacher."

Emma held them back, bending down to reach for a ladybug. They could easily dawdle all day, but they had to get going. "Come on, sweetheart," Shelley said, taking her daughter's little hand before she could capture the red-and-black-spotted insect, and led both children up the stairs, opening the door at the top.

Aiden escaped Shelley's hold, running inside quickly, only to be caught in the arms of Miss Davidson, whose name was printed in big block letters on the name tag she wore just above the pocket on her turquoise blue polo shirt.

Aiden stumbled backward out of Miss Davidson's hug and clutched Shelley's leg. The teacher offered her hand to Shelley. "Hi. I'm Leila Davidson."

Shelley introduced herself, smiling at the petite brunette, who couldn't have been much over twenty-five.

"And this must be Aiden." Miss Davidson knelt down, her hand extended toward Aiden, who was now clinging even more tightly to Shelley's leg. Not the least bit put off by his hesitance, the young teacher stayed at Aiden's eye level and talked to him in a soft voice. "What's your favorite thing in all the world?" she asked him.

Aiden looked up at his mom, and Shelley said, "This is your new teacher, Miss Davidson, Aiden. It's okay for you to answer her."

"I have a favorite thing," Miss Davidson said. "Want to know what it is?"

Aiden nodded gently.

"My puppy. Her name's Honeysuckle, but I call her Honey."

"I have a dog," Aiden said, but still he didn't let go of Shelley's leg. "She was a surprise from my dad, so we call her Prize."

"What a perfect name." Miss Davidson smiled. "We're going to have a bring-your-pet-to-school day in a few weeks. Won't that be fun?"

"What if your pet's a snake or a rat?" Aiden asked.

"We're going to invite all creatures great and small."

"Even an elephant?"

Miss Davidson winked up at Shelley. "Even an elephant, although we might have trouble fitting one into our classroom."

Miss Davidson rose. She talked to Shelley for a moment or two, then snapped a photo of Shelley and Aiden. When she went off to talk with another family, Shelley took a stroll around the classroom, with both Emma and Aiden holding on tight. The walls were painted a soft blue and decorated with enormous, brightly painted flowers, birds, bees, and butterflies. It was like stepping into Wonderland.

They marveled at the bins filled with toys, papers, crayons, chalk, and jars of paint. They looked out the windows across the back wall at the playground filled with swings and teeter-totters and other equipment, all as brightly colored as the room.

Aiden at last began to smile.

Even more children came into the classroom with their moms or dads, and Miss Davidson greeted each in her own special way.

When Shelley was one hundred percent positive that Aiden could settle in just fine, she walked with him and Emma to the door. "I'm heading home now," she said, "and I'll be back at two o'clock to pick you up."

The smile on Aiden's face turned upside down and his lip quivered. A fat tear slipped from the corner of each eye.

He opened his mouth as if to cry, and Shelley quickly knelt beside him. "I wish I could stay, because I know it's going to be a lot of fun here. But your new school is for boys and girls, kids your age, not for grown-ups like me."

"Mama! Please don't go!"

Shelley fought to hold back her tears, but before she had a chance to say anything more to Aiden, Miss Davidson swept in. "Do you like computers, Aiden?"

Aiden thought about the question a moment, then nodded. "Mama and Daddy have a laptop and sometimes I get to play games on it."

"Well, why don't you let me show you our computers? We've got some of the very best games, and I know you're going to love them."

Aiden looked at Shelley for approval.

"Go on, honey." She blew him a kiss, and as Miss Davidson led him away, she lifted Emma into her arms and slipped out the front door as quickly as she could. Tears already filled her eyes, ready to spill, and she couldn't help but wonder if she and Dan had made the wrong decision to send Aiden off to prekindergarten. He was so young.

Her babies were growing up much too fast.

Chapter Four

Margaret Hoskins dabbed a few brush loads of blue iris oil paint onto the canvas set up in a corner of her studio's showroom, adding depth and dimension to the hydrangeas that were the focal point of the Marble Cove landscape she was painting. She was titling this painting *Endless Summer,* after her favorite hydrangea, the ones that grew in profusion around her home on Newport Avenue. They were at their height of beauty right now, and at long last she had time to pay homage to one of the star attractions of their town.

The Shearwater Gallery had been open all of Labor Day weekend, like all of the shops and entertainments in Marble Cove, and her gallery had overflowed with tourists looking for a souvenir to take home after a wonderful stay.

Now that Tuesday had arrived, she felt free. Relaxed, even. For the moment, she had the gallery all to herself. She could paint to her heart's content. As luck would have it, of course, the chimes at the shop's front door rang. She peered around the edge of her canvas to see a couple—both in the best upscale southern-climes coastal wear: crisp white pants with navy blue-and-white shirts. The woman was wearing a big straw hat over her white hair.

Definitely tourists. People in Marble Cove didn't dress that way.

Margaret put down her brush and palette and wiped her hands before rising from her stool to greet them, tugging on the hem of her silky blue tunic. "Good morning."

"Good morning," the man said. His hair was the same snowy hue as that of the woman he was with—his wife, Margaret imagined. The expensive-looking gold watch he wore on his left wrist glittered in the sunlight streaming through the large plate glass window, as did the mass of diamonds the woman wore on the ring finger of her left hand. "My wife and I were in here the other day and a gentleman—I believe his name was Allan—showed us a painting of one of the quaint streets in Marble Cove."

"We weren't sure at the time we wanted to buy it," the woman said, "but I haven't found anything else in Marble Cove that quite compares with the quality. I'm hoping it's still available."

"We did sell quite a few pieces over the holiday weekend," Margaret said. "Do you remember the artist's name?"

"No, but I know exactly where it was." The woman strode purposefully across the gallery, stopping in front of one of Margaret's paintings of Newport Avenue, depicting Diane's cottage and picket-fenced yard, spilling over with flowers. The woman's hand flew to her chest and she smiled. "It's still here, Ben. And it's even lovelier than I remembered."

Margaret couldn't help but smile. "That's one of mine," she said a little less modestly than normal. "And that's my neighbor's home, with some of her English roses in full bloom."

"It's beautiful," Ben said. "Reminds Joyce and me of our once quaint little beach town in California."

"It's not so quaint any longer," Joyce stated bluntly. "Hasn't been quaint since the developers moved in forty-plus years ago. Now the beach is littered with resorts, and cozy galleries like yours have been taken over by high-end boutiques selling designer fashions and art that only millionaires can afford."

"I know exactly what you mean." Margaret nodded in understanding. "It wasn't all that long ago that a lot of our citizens banded together to fight off the advances of a developer who wanted to build a resort. I hope we don't have to go through that again in my lifetime. I like Marble Cove just the way it is."

Ten minutes later, Margaret had completed the credit card payment for Ben and Joyce's purchase, put a sold sign on the painting, and walked them out to the Main Street sidewalk, promising to ship the painting to their home in a week, when they'd be back in California, ready to accept delivery. She waved good-bye as they walked up the street and ducked into the Crow's Nest, Marble Cove's bookshop.

Main Street looked especially lovely today, a light breeze keeping clouds away, leaving the sky a gorgeous cerulean blue. She could hear the clang of bells from boats just off the wharf and the screech of circling seagulls scouting out an easy meal. The scent of the sea was always present, always loved, and with very few cars going up and down Main today, she could easily hear the murmurs of the surf, a sound that lulled her to sleep most every night.

She was just about to step back inside when she saw her neighbor and friend, Shelley Bauer, pushing Emma's stroller down the street, with Emma toddling at her mother's side, holding Shelley's hand. Margaret waved, catching Shelley's attention.

Were those tears in Shelley's eyes? She was on the verge of running toward her friend when the gallery's phone rang. "Gotta catch the phone," Margaret called out. "Everything okay?"

Shelley gave her a damp smile. "I dropped Aiden off for his first day at pre-K."

Margaret knew those pangs of a mother being separated from her child all too well. She'd experienced them many a time with her daughter Adelaide, who'd been born with Down syndrome. Even now, when Adelaide was in her midtwenties, Margaret still worried herself sick when Adelaide was allowed to strike out on her own—like tomorrow, when she'd board the bus all by herself to spend her second day on a college campus. Thankfully Allan had accompanied her today.

Margaret dashed into the gallery and headed for her office. She grabbed the still-ringing phone. "Shearwater Gallery," she said breathlessly.

"Margaret?" The voice at the other end of the phone sounded familiar. "It's Karen Donahue, over at the community center."

Margaret ceased to breathe. Her heart raced. "Has something happened to Adelaide? Has she been hurt?"

"No, no, nothing like that. I'm sorry to have scared you."

Margaret took a deep breath, only then remembering that Adelaide wasn't at the community center today. She was in her early-childhood education class.

In college.

"It is sort of an emergency though," Karen continued, "and I do hope you'll say yes."

Margaret laughed. "You'll have to give me a little more information before I commit myself to anything."

"As I'm sure you know, since it's been announced in every newsletter the community center has sent out for the last few months, we're offering a month-long beginner's art class for preteens."

Margaret knew full well about the class, and had wondered why they'd chosen an out-of-towner—a woman named Montana Phipps—to teach it. She'd wondered about the instructor's credentials, but it wasn't really her concern. Now, from the worried sound in Karen's voice, the community center director was having some misgivings.

"The class sounds wonderful, Karen, and I imagine you have quite a number of registrations."

"Well, that's just it. We have fifteen signed up, and no instructor. She had to back out for health reasons, which is such a shame. The program she put together was what sold us on the idea of offering the class, and our enrollees—especially their parents—are looking forward to what Miss Phipps had to offer."

"Surely you've found someone to take over the class," Margaret said. "It starts this week, if I'm not mistaken."

There was a long silence at the other end of the phone. Finally, Karen Donahue said, "It was just this morning that we learned that the instructor had to bail out, which is, of course, late to completely cancel a class. Thank goodness I thought of you. You're the only person I know with the skills to take over."

"Oh no, that's impossible. Did you ask some of the others at the community center for recommendations?"

"I did, and they all stated that you were the best. We all know the quality of your work. We know that you've won awards, that your art is now gracing greeting cards, not to mention the mural you painted at the Cannery. We know you're reliable; we know you adore children. Please, Margaret. The salary isn't exorbitant, but it's a nice little sum, which will be detailed in the contract we'd have to sign with you. So . . . will you do it?"

Margaret hesitated.

"Please?" The desperation in Karen's voice was obvious.

"This is all so sudden."

"Probably more than you think, I'm sure," Karen said. "The class starts Wednesday evening at seven."

"That's tomorrow. Only a little over twenty-four hours from now."

"I know it's short notice. I'm so sorry. But the class is just one hour long, two days a week—Mondays and Wednesdays—for four weeks. This week, because of the holiday, we're meeting Wednesday and Thursday."

That's *if* they found an instructor.

"I suppose you need an answer right now?"

"We're hoping you can give us an answer now, and if you agree, I'll e-mail you the contract and the class outline that's already been put together, which we'd like you to follow, since it's what the parents and students expect. If not, I'll have to call other artists, and I doubt I can find anyone of your caliber." She paused. "Margaret, the students and their parents are so looking forward to this class."

Karen Donahue was trying to butter her up, saying all the right words, but Margaret hadn't taught a gaggle of ten-, eleven-, and twelve-year-olds before. Well, not really. She'd mentored Caleb Wadsworth last year, right before Christmas, and that had been not only fun, but illuminating. But what about her own art projects? The free time she'd hoped to have now that the summer rush was over?

And then she thought about the kids. What about them? They'd be terribly disappointed if the class was canceled.

After a long sigh, Margaret said. "All right. I'll do it."

CHAPTER FIVE

Diane hunched over her desk not more than an hour after talking with Jeanette, sending a quick text message to Shelley, Margaret, and Beverly, telling them about her sister-in-law's visit and the documents she'd be bringing with her. *Who knows? We might learn something more about the treasure,* Diane typed, and hit Send.

An instant later, Beverly replied. *Or maybe the truth about Jeremiah Thorpe.*

That would be great! Shelley added. *Might as well kill two birds with one stone.*

Diane didn't want to kill any birds or throw any stones. But she did want to get to the bottom of this Marble Cove mystery so she could fully concentrate on the one she should be writing right now.

When the phone on her desk rang, she jumped. Just as she had earlier, she hoped it was her agent or editor delivering news of the positive sort.

She grabbed the phone, hastily said hello, then heard the female voice on the other end. "May I speak with Diane Spencer?"

The voice wasn't at all familiar, and she quickly looked at the caller ID. Augusta Oncology Group. Fear struck her, keeping her from responding.

"Hello. Are you still there?"

Through the lump in her throat, she finally managed to respond. "This is Diane."

"This is Rhonda Howard at Augusta Oncology Group. I'm Dr. Crowley's assistant. How are you doing?"

"Fine, thank you." She'd been fine since the cancer disappeared miraculously almost four years ago. Why was someone calling her now?

"I'm sure you're not aware of this, but Dr. Crowley moved from Boston to Augusta six months ago."

What was she supposed to say? Congratulations?

"To make a long story short, Dr. Crowley was checking up on some of the patients he'd cared for in Boston, and was told that you'd moved. He was also told that you'd canceled—or missed—your last two appointments."

"Boston was really too far to travel to see the doctor." That was a better excuse than saying she was too scared to see the doctor again.

"Did you find another oncologist locally?"

"No, I didn't see the need. I've been perfectly fine for years."

"Your story is the kind of story we'd like to hear from all of our patients, Diane. Nothing short of a miracle, from what Dr. Crowley tells me."

Diane pictured Rhonda smiling at the other end of the phone. She still smiled when she thought of God's miracle. She'd had cancer one day, and the next, there wasn't a trace.

"Still," Rhonda added, "we believe it's wise to continue having checkups. It's unlikely that there's any cause for concern, but it is in your best interest to come in to see the doctor."

She didn't want to be poked and prodded. She was being absolutely childish, but she'd had her fill of doctors.

She spun around in her desk chair and saw a picture of Eric hanging on the wall, Eric who might not have died of a heart attack if he'd gone to the doctor regularly. Their daughter Jessica, who'd stood by Diane's side through all her treatments, smiled down from the picture just to the right of her dad's. Her son Justin's photo hung to the left. Her children didn't have a father any longer; they still needed a mom.

"We have an opening next Wednesday at 11:00. Could you make it?"

Diane heard a knock at the front door and peered through her office window to see Beverly on the front steps.

"I need to go. Could I call you back?"

"Certainly, Diane. But I'll go ahead and pencil you in for the appointment. We don't often have cancellations, and the sooner we see you, the better." Diane absently wrote the date and time down, along with the address and the doctor's phone number. She wasn't going to go, but she didn't want to argue with the assistant.

"I look forward to meeting you."

Diane wished she could say the same. As soon as she hung up, she raced for the front door, only then realizing that her eyes were filled with tears. She wiped them off with the backs of her hands, pasted on a smile, and opened the door.

"Mind a little company?" Beverly asked. "I'm in a quandary about the campaign and I really need someone to talk to."

"Sure, come on in." Diane opened the door wide, and Beverly, dressed in a sunflower-yellow shift, slipped inside. She was such a contrast to Diane in her denim capris and old maroon–and-gold Boston College T-shirt, yet somehow their personalities had clicked, and they'd become the best of friends. "Would you like some iced tea or lemonade?"

"I'm fine, but thanks."

I'm not, Diane wanted to tell her friend. She really didn't want to talk politics, especially the mayoral election, but Beverly, who was always so calm and cool, looked completely stressed out. Beverly wouldn't turn her away in a time of need; Diane couldn't turn Beverly away now.

Diane dropped down on the sofa, curling her legs beneath her. Rocky, who'd been asleep under the desk in her office, came lumbering out, hopped up on the couch beside her, and dropped his head in her lap. "How can I help?"

"I'm embarrassed to say this, but I have no idea why I decided to run for mayor. I'm not qualified—not really, I've only lived here a year, something Dennis Calder would be only too happy to use against me." Beverly shook her head, whether in disgust over Dennis' tactics or in sheer consternation, Diane couldn't tell. "In the beginning I thought my chances were good, because my platform of preserving the quaint nature of our town seems to be what most of the citizens of Marble Cove want. But now I have to wonder. And besides, who on earth wants to vote for a newcomer in town, when two men are running who've lived here all their lives?"

"First of all, I'm going to vote for you. Second, you are qualified. Evelyn Waters is a nice woman, but the only qualification she had for the job the first time she ran—or so I've been told—was that her father had been mayor before her. Lee Waters owns a pet shop, for heaven's sake. Not that there's anything wrong with that, but he'll be running on his mother's record—not his."

"But there's far more going on—or not going on, I should say. I don't have a campaign manager to take care of the bigger details or even the more mundane ones. My old friend, Senator Charles, whom I worked with at the State House, told me just this afternoon that I really need a campaign manager. He also strongly suggested I hire an accountant, someone to keep me from commingling my campaign contributions with my personal finances."

Beverly let her head fall back on the sofa. She looked almost defeated. "How could I possibly commingle campaign contributions with my personal finances when I hadn't given any thought to raising campaign money in the first place? I'd planned to run the whole show on my savings. I mean really, Diane, how could I possibly ask people in town to contribute to my campaign when I've been hitting them up for months now, asking them to contribute money to save Old First?"

Diane couldn't help herself. She laughed at her friend's dismay. "You don't need a campaign manager. You definitely don't need an accountant. You might want to think about putting a Please Contribute button on your Web site, because the whole thing's bound to cost more money than you plan on. But you'll do quite well without a bunch of professionals backing you up. And you know you'll have a little help from your friends."

Beverly kicked off her sandals and curled her legs up under her, just as Diane had done. "Then you don't think I've made a big mistake? You don't think I should drop out of the race before things go any farther?"

"Not on your life. You're just having a crisis of confidence. How that happened is beyond me, since you're the most confident person I've ever met. You have more smarts and savvy in your little finger than Dennis and Lee could ever dream of having."

"Dennis talks a pretty good game."

"Dennis is all show. You know that as well as I do. As for Lee—well, Lee has his mother pushing him and that's all he's got. I don't think he's at all serious about campaigning and I don't really think he wants the job. Face it, Beverly, you're going to be the next mayor of Marble Cove"—Diane grinned—"so buck up."

Truth be told, Diane thought ruefully, she needed to buck up too. It was only a doctor's appointment. Simply a checkup, and she really did feel perfectly fine. God was watching over her and had been for a very long time. She had to put all her faith in Him. She had to let go of her fears and let God take the burden on His shoulders.

Certainly nothing could go wrong.

* * *

Margaret worked late at the gallery, going over the course outline for the art class she'd be teaching starting tomorrow night. "Stick to the plan," Karen Donahue had said emphatically. But the plan was all about teaching technique, how to blend colors, how to hold a brush.

How to hold a brush?

What about inspiration and sheer creativity? What about the passion? Not that you could teach those most important aspects of painting, but she worried that starting out teaching youngsters all the techniques would stifle them and take the fun out of the artwork.

She wasn't a rebel, exactly, but tomorrow night she would not start the class by teaching technique.

"Hi, Mom!"

Margaret peeked out of her office, a smile building rapidly at the sound of Adelaide's voice.

Spinning around in her desk chair, she stood, feeling the long day of work and stress in her joints, especially her knees. Before she could take a step out of the office, Adelaide stepped in and threw herself into Margaret's open arms.

"Today was so much fun. Riding the bus was fun. Finding my class was fun. Meeting my teacher was fun." Adelaide tilted her head to look at Allan. "You had fun too, didn't you Daddy?"

Allan nodded at Margaret and a moment later he eased himself down into one of her office chairs.

"Long day?" Margaret asked.

"There's a good reason the biggest percentage of people in this world go to school when they're young. My feet hurt. My back hurts. My head hurts." He grinned at Adelaide, then turned to Margaret again. "Seventy-one-year-old men should start thinking about rocking chairs, not attending college with their daughters."

"Seventy-one-year-old men who start talking like that grow old real fast." Margaret cradled her husband's beloved face in her palms. "So no more talking like that. I don't plan to grow old until I'm at least ninety. Ninety-five if the good Lord lets me, and I need you here by my side as I inch toward that age."

"Me too." Adelaide stepped behind Allan and wrapped her arms around his neck. "You did real good, Daddy. You got lost only once."

"Only because you steered me in the right direction."

Had she really heard those words? Margaret wondered. Margaret had worried for twenty-five years about her daughter and how she'd get along on her own—if she had to. But apparently Adelaide could find her way just fine.

CHAPTER SIX

"Aren't we waiting for Margaret?" Beverly asked, taking a seat next to Shelley at Diane's dining room table, surprised to see that it had only been set for three.

"Didn't you hear?" Shelley carefully unfolded a sea-foam green linen napkin and laid it across her lap. "She's teaching an art class at the community center."

Beverly frowned. "Really? I thought she was planning to kick back now that summer's over. Take more time for herself."

"This teaching assignment came up unexpectedly." Diane set a wooden salad bowl and tongs on the table and took her seat, leaving Margaret's usual place looking rather forlorn. "The original teacher dropped out yesterday morning, and Margaret agreed to fill in, with just one day's notice."

"I stopped by the gallery after picking up Aiden from pre-K this afternoon," Shelley said, "and Margaret looked totally harried, as if the weight of the world had dropped down on her shoulders. She was told this was to be a beginning class, but Margaret says there's far too much to cover in just one hour."

"And she was specifically asked not to change the course outline," Diane added, "since the parents are expecting exactly what they paid for."

"I can't imagine Margaret bucking the rules," Beverly said.

"I can, especially where art's concerned." Shelley reached for the salad bowl, then passed it on to Beverly.

"How did Aiden enjoy his first two days in preschool?" Beverly asked as she scooped some salad onto her plate.

"He was excited at first, then put up an absolute fuss when I had to leave him. I guess that's expected the first week of school."

"Justin had a penchant for pitching fits, and not just at the beginning of school," Diane said. Beverly watched Diane as she spoke. She was laughing on the outside, but something was troubling her, something she didn't want to discuss. Had Beverly been so preoccupied with her own fears that she'd turned a blind eye to Diane's? Maybe—hopefully—Diane would confide in her and Shelley before the evening was over.

"It's not just a matter of him pitching fits." Shelley shook her head and sighed. "When I dropped him off this morning he was calling me Mama. When I picked him up, I was suddenly Mom."

"That was bound to happen sometime," Diane added.

"I'll always remember when and why." Shelley stabbed a tomato. "His newfound best friend—and according to Aiden, this is his best friend in the whole wide world—

teased him this morning. Told him only babies say Mama. Nearly broke my heart."

"He'll slip up," Diane told her, smiling as she put a comforting hand on Shelley's arm. "At least every once in a while."

"I certainly hope so," Shelley said. "I'm just not ready yet to be plain old Mom."

"Other than that," Diane asked, putting down her fork and pushing her nearly untouched salad away from her, "how did *you* survive his first two days at school? I remember it being awfully tough for me when both Jessica and Justin left home."

"I was unbelievably lonely, which doesn't make sense. I've been looking forward to him going off to school so I could have a little time with Emma, you know, just the girls. Instead I felt guilty for enrolling him in pre-K, for dropping him off with a bunch of strangers, for leaving him to fend all on his own."

"That's just another part of growing up—for all of you," Diane said gently, and Beverly thought once more that Diane had missed her calling. She was so good at passing on wisdom, at making people feel better about themselves, that she could or should have been a counselor. "It'll get easier as each day goes by, but I don't think mothers can ever completely not worry about their children."

Shelley took a sip of tea. "I don't know if you're making me feel better, or making me wonder how I'll survive all this worry I'm going to experience the rest of my life."

Diane laughed. "I can't believe I'm spending my evening consoling you, so soon after spending nearly an hour consoling Beverly."

Shelley frowned as she stared at Beverly. "You're the most put-together person I know. What could possibly be troubling you?"

"I'm not always totally put-together. Just like everyone else, I have my moments of sheer panic. I just try not to show it."

"So what got you so panicked that you needed Diane's counseling?"

"She's gotten cold feet about running for mayor," Diane offered, picking a pecan off her salad plate and popping it into her mouth.

"That's crazy, Beverly. You're the best candidate," Shelley stated, a fork full of salad poised in midair. "Not a one of us wants Dennis Calder getting the job."

"We need a strong candidate to run the town," Diane added, "which includes fighting developers like Dennis Calder and his ilk."

"I couldn't agree more," Shelley said. "You fought him once, but it'll be easier to fight him when you're mayor. Heaven forbid that he should turn our town into something we don't want it to be."

Diane stood, taking the salad bowl from the table and walking the few steps into the kitchen. "I know Dennis helped with the fund-raiser for Old First, but I imagine if he'd had his druthers, he would have torn it down so he could build a modern cathedral or something else that doesn't fit into Marble Cove."

"He's definitely running on a platform of growth. Look at this." Beverly pulled Dennis' campaign brochure from the back pocket of her navy blue pants.

"What is it?" Diane asked from the kitchen, where she was mixing together the pasta and sauce.

"One of Dennis' campaign brochures," Beverly told her. "He made sure I took one when I ran into him up by the lighthouse yesterday morning."

Shelley looked at the brochure. "*Hmm*, Prosperity and Progress." She turned up her nose. "Prosperity is fine, and so is progress, and I suppose it makes a great campaign slogan, but Dennis' idea of prosperity and progress is more like slash and burn. I like Marble Cove just the way it is; I don't want him messing with my town."

"I haven't lived here all that long," Diane added, carrying two plates full of scrumptious-looking pasta to the table and setting one in front of each guest. "But I moved here *because* Marble Cove is quaint. Because if you could time travel back to the Marble Cove of 1901, you'd find there hadn't been much change in over a hundred years."

"I just had a thought," Shelley said. "If we could time travel, we could go even farther back in Marble Cove history."

"I like that idea!" Beverly twirled her fork around in her fettuccine Alfredo, getting prepared to take a generous bite. "Maybe we could go back to the night the original Old First burned—"

"Or to the day Jeremiah Thorpe hid the treasure," Diane noted. "So we could follow him, and we'd know what became of it."

"And *why* he hid it, exactly," Shelley added. "I mean— why all the cryptic notes and even ciphers?"

"I know what you mean. But if we could go back and dig it up—and then come back to the present…" Beverly held a forkful of pasta close to her mouth. "We could cash in the doubloons or whatever—"

"And restore Old First!" Shelley finished triumphantly.

"Of course," Diane said, "time travel might not be necessary at all. Every answer we're looking for might be in the papers Jeanette is bringing with her this weekend."

Beverly smiled. "One can only hope."

* * *

"Pablo Picasso, one of the all-time greatest artists, said, 'All children are artists. The problem is how to remain an artist once he grows up.'"

Margaret stood in front of her students, each ten-, eleven-, and twelve-year-old fidgeting, finding it difficult to sit still at their worktables while she introduced them to the world of art. That wasn't on the original teacher's course outline, but Caleb, the young boy she'd mentored last winter, had balked at the mundane. Margaret imagined these children would throw a fit if she just gave them an art project—especially the one she'd been instructed to teach.

"Picasso wished he could paint like a child, because he truly believed children are the most original, unique, and free-spirited members of society. Their responses are honest and imaginative, because children see the world with fresh eyes."

Danny Wharburton yawned. Cecily Springfield rubbed her eyes. Felicity Monroe blew out a loud sigh. And Margaret scratched her forehead. It seemed pretty obvious that her students hadn't grasped the meaning of what she'd just said. Worse still, they appeared to be bored to tears.

"I imagine all of you have painted before. Right?"

Her question received a few nods, a few more sighs and yawns, and absolutely zero enthusiasm. It was impossible for Margaret to search back nearly fifty-some-odd years to remember how her art teachers had instructed. Things had changed a lot since she was a preteen. These kids were used to computer games, where colors were wild and everything moved fast. Their minds were constantly stimulated, but they were stimulated by games and activities that had already been created for them.

A sudden sense of urgency came over Margaret. She had four weeks—just eight classes—to help them find their own creativity.

"Danny and Felicity." Margaret pointed to the two children, who looked at her with little interest. "Would you please each come up front and take a piece of watercolor paper, a paint palette, and brush?"

The two pushed up from their seats, walked lazily to the front of the class, and latched on to a piece of paper, a brush, and an empty palette.

"Now, Danny, please walk over to that side of the room"—she pointed off to the left—"and Felicity, I'd like you to stand as far away from Danny as you can get, while still staying in the room."

"I can't go outside?" Felicity asked, laughing.

"You could." Margaret smiled at her. "But then you'd miss out on this creativity project."

"And then your mom would have a fit," Danny said, a sly grin on his face. "I heard her telling you to create something beautiful tonight—that she expected nothing less from you."

Oh dear. Margaret didn't expect anyone to paint anything beautiful. Not tonight. And not at the rate they were going. But she'd give it her all.

"Now, I want the rest of you to come up here, take your piece of paper and box of crayons, and find a place in the room to stand."

"Does it matter where?" Taylor Holmquist asked.

Margaret shook her head. "Not to me. It only matters to you. I want you to find a place that feels comfortable to you. A place—in this room—where you feel you can be the most creative."

"Mind if I move?" Danny asked, with Felicity echoing his question.

"Actually, I'd love it if the two of you would stay right where you are."

Danny frowned. "But this is where *you* told me to stand, and I don't think it's my most creative spot."

Margaret grinned. "Exactly."

Danny and Felicity were both looking annoyed now.

"Why don't you think you can be creative in that spot?" Margaret asked, walking about the room, but focusing her attention on Danny and Felicity, who both looked extremely uncomfortable, as if they'd been put on time-out.

"Because there's no sunlight over here," Felicity said, "and because I feel like you're going to keep on telling me exactly what to do and how to do it, when everyone else—except Danny—gets to do their own thing."

"Yeah," Danny agreed. "I kinda feel like I'm in prison."

Margaret laughed. "You'd probably also feel like you were in prison if I told you to paint an apple sitting on a table, when I told everyone else to pick something that made them happy or sad or just plain bored."

Margaret walked to the front of the classroom where she'd set up three easels, and slowly turned around each painting so what she'd painted faced her students. "These are three of my painting styles—landscape, seascape, and abstract. I always let my mood dictate what I'm going to paint. I believe we should paint the way Pablo Picasso felt we should paint—like children—with imagination and honesty."

"Does that mean I can move somewhere else?" Danny asked, one dark eyebrow raising in question. The gesture hinted at a challenge.

"You and Felicity may move wherever you like. That goes for the rest of you too. Grab your table and chair and push them to a spot in the room that feels comfortable to you, where you think you can be the most creative—just don't fight over a spot."

The next minute or two were pure chaos, the sound of chairs and tables scraping across the floor nearly deafening, giving Margaret a headache. She wasn't following the original teacher's plan, but she was doing what she felt was important. Now all she could do was hope this would work.

"Now what?" Jake Morris asked, doing a handstand. Whether he was trying to show off or just feeling creative, Margaret didn't know, but she wanted her class to be loose. That's what pure artistry was about, and she didn't want to stifle her students.

"We're going to paint a kaleidoscope."

"The outside?" Charlemayne Carr asked, and Margaret hoped the rest of her students would have gotten a clearer vision from that one simple word. Kaleidoscope meant so much more to her, and she wanted it to mean a conglomeration of things to her students.

"If that's what you think of when I say the word *kaleidoscope*," Margaret said, "then fine, paint the outside, the twisty-turny thing that you put up to your eye so you can see a starburst of colors. Or you can paint that starburst, in whatever shape or form you envision."

Walking around the room, Margaret looked at each student's paintings, happy with the creativeness she saw from nearly everyone. Poor Charlemayne, however, was drawing the kaleidoscope device itself. She'd found a ruler somewhere and was painting straight lines, measuring to make sure everything was perfect. She was analytical, definitely more left-brained than right.

The hour went by quickly, but Margaret had already been there two. Her feet and back were tired and her head hurt, but all in all, she thought the first session had gone pretty well. Still, the thought of doing this again tomorrow night made her temples throb, and the pain snaked its way behind her eyes.

"What are we going to do tomorrow night?" Felicity asked when parents started filing into the room to pick up their kids.

"It's a surprise," Margaret said. And it would be; she wasn't sure yet what they'd do. Right now, she was taking this class day by day. "Just be prepared to have fun, and to let your imagination rule what you do."

When the last student and parent left the room, she looked around at the mess, then collapsed in her chair. She'd clean the paint brushes and spilled paint in a little while, after her feet had a rest and her head stopped pounding.

A nagging thought bubbled to the surface: if she was this tired now, what would she feel like after a whole month of this?

Chapter Seven

I've heard Lee Waters is running for mayor," Beth Levesque, manager of the Crow's Nest, said as she rang up Beverly's book purchase Thursday afternoon. "Goodness knows Lee's a nice guy, and he recommended the best organic dog food for my little dog Cuddles, but between you and me, Lee's just not mayor material."

"I hear Dennis Calder's running too." Beverly waited to see Beth's reaction.

Beth's dark brown eyes rolled. "I suppose the whole town's heard by now." She reached under the counter and pulled out a stack of Dennis' Prosperity and Progress postcards, with his good-looking face smiling up from the glossy campaign cards. Beth slapped them down next to the cash register. "He dropped these off just yesterday. Asked me—as pretty as you please—to hand them out to everyone, shook my hand, and asked me if he could please have my vote. Said the Crow's Nest would grow by leaps and bounds, and I'd make money hand over fist once he is in charge of Marble Cove."

"And what did you tell him?" Beverly asked, knowing that garrulous Beth would be more than forthcoming with her answer.

"Oh, I just smiled. Told him the Crow's Nest, and a lot of other stores here on Main Street, would grow by leaps and bounds if he'd invest some of his money in us, instead of just his words." She shook her head. "I don't quite think he understood what I was getting at, but no matter. I wouldn't vote for him for love or money."

Beth rested her elbows on the counter and leaned forward. She whispered, "I hear you're running too. That you got your paperwork in right at the last minute."

Beverly nodded. "Yes, I'm definitely running."

"That's good to know. That husband of mine—you know Ham—we liked the stance you took on the resort complex Dennis-the-Menace-Calder wanted to build. We liked the way you got the town council to take a second look at the project and put it on hold. We don't want that kind of progress here in Marble Cove. Personally, I wish it was still 1960. I don't want change."

"I don't want to change a thing," Beverly agreed. "We've got a good thing going here in Marble Cove. It's the quaint feeling of our town that brings people here during the summer and that keeps people of all ages living here. As long as we can maintain or maybe even strengthen the health and safety of our citizens, that's what's important."

The bell above the door jangled, and two customers entered the store. Beth thanked Beverly for her purchase, excused herself, and stepped out from behind the counter to help the couple.

Beverly exited the Crow's Nest and turned south, planning to drop by and see Margaret at her gallery, and nearly crashed into current Marble Cove mayor, Evelyn Waters.

"Good morning, Beverly." Evelyn's smile was nearly as bright as the silk scarf tied loosely around her shoulders. Marble Cove wasn't a fancy place by any stretch of the imagination, but as mayor, Evelyn always dressed to impress.

"Couldn't be a lovelier day." Beverly tucked a breeze-blown strand of her shoulder-length hair behind her ear.

"If you haven't had lunch yet, perhaps you'd like to join me." Evelyn's invitation caught Beverly completely off guard.

"I'd love to, but I've just had lunch with Josie at the Quarterdeck Inn. Have you been there lately?"

Evelyn nodded. "You helped her design a new Web site, didn't you?"

"We worked on a business plan together and a new Web site was part of that," Beverly said proudly. "She's such a nice woman, and I'm so glad I was able to help her and her business."

"You know, you might have to curtail some of the work you do for your clients when you start actively campaigning for mayor. And, of course, if you were to win the election, time for your business would decrease exponentially," Evelyn told her. "A lot of people believe that serving as mayor of Marble Cove is a cushy job, that I'm more of a figurehead than an active administrator."

Beverly maintained her smile. Was Evelyn offering friendly advice, or was there an undercurrent of warning in her words? After all, Evelyn didn't want to be just the second in the line of her family members who'd been mayor of Marble Cove. She now wanted her son to carry on the family dynasty.

"I've watched you at work in town council meetings—"

"There's much more involved than that," Evelyn interrupted Beverly.

Then her smile brightened. Her eyes twinkled in the sunlight. "Oh, I'm not trying to frighten you off, of course. Marble Cove needs a strong mayor. That's why my son Lee is running, and he'll be giving his all during the campaign."

"Dennis Calder's already started to campaign. He's going to be a force to reckon with too."

Evelyn's face soured for a moment. She seemed to have caught herself in the midst of thinking the worst of Dennis Calder, and thought better of it. "Yes, he's a strong candidate too, which should make this election highly competitive."

Evelyn looked at her watch. "I'd best be going. Perhaps we can have lunch another day."

"I'd like that," Beverly said, but Evelyn Waters was already marching up Main Street, turning left at the wharf, no doubt ducking into the Pet Place to see Lee. Beverly imagined they were strategizing together, thinking of all the right ways to beat his competitors and become the next mayor of Marble Cove.

She'd need to pull out all the stops if she was going to win. And a strong campaign Web site would be one of them. An idea came to Beverly, and Margaret was just the person she needed to see. She turned and walked to the Shearwater Gallery and paused for a moment in front of Margaret's window. A beautiful necklace sparkled from its perch on a bleached piece of driftwood—and Beverly knew just the outfit she would wear it with. She would have to ask Margaret about it.

She entered the gallery, where she found Margaret in the back, dusting. "We missed you at Diane's dinner last night," Beverly said in greeting.

Margaret rolled her eyes. "I suppose you heard that I'm teaching a children's art class at the community center."

"I heard you'd rescued them from disaster." Beverly smiled at her friend, who seemed a little harried.

"It's nice to know that I'm the first knowledgeable artist who came to mind when the community center needed a teacher, but I really needed more prep time. I'm teaching yet another class tonight, since the Labor Day holiday forced them to jiggle the schedule, then every Monday and Wednesday for the rest of the month." Margaret chuckled. "Ten-, eleven-, and twelve-year–olds are far more active than I remember. More mouthy too, or at least more opinionated."

"Would you mind if I stopped by this evening to take some photos of you and your students?"

Margaret's eyes widened. "Whatever for?"

"My campaign Web site. I'm not going to win the mayoral election on the fact that I've lived in Marble Cove all of my life, or even for several years. I want to win over the voters by showing them that I know the *real* Marble Cove, what our citizens do in their daily lives, how people help each other, come what may."

"Great idea, not that I love having my photo taken, of course. Thanks for the heads-up anyway, so I can dress up a little." She paused. "But I'm not sure you can take photos without the parents' permission."

"I thought about that. If I bring release slips when I stop by, could you ask the parents to sign them when they drop off their kids? I know that's a bit of an imposition—"

"Isn't that what friends are for?" Margaret moved on to the next painting, using her dust cloth to get into the nooks and crannies in its frame. "Besides, I—we—need you to be our next mayor. I'll do anything I can to make sure that happens."

Before Beverly could say another word, she heard the chime from her cell phone that announced a text message. She pulled the phone from her purse and smiled when she noticed the sender's name.

Plane landed Boston. Pick you up for dinner six tomorrow night.

Beverly frowned. Jeff's text message was too short, too impersonal. He never wrote notes like that. He didn't say "I love you" or even "Miss you!" He'd been out of the country for more than two weeks. Had he met someone else? Had he changed his mind about where he wanted their relationship to go? Or worse?

"Everything okay?" Margaret asked, concern in her eyes.

Beverly shook her head. "Oh no, everything's fine. Jeff's back in the States and he'll be in Marble Cove tomorrow night."

"That's good. I know how much you've missed him."

Beverly nodded, then absently said, "I'll see you tonight, camera and permission slips in hand."

With a wave, she headed out of the gallery, the necklace completely forgotten.

CHAPTER EIGHT

The house couldn't have felt emptier, Shelley thought. A dull ache of loneliness had settled into her heart with Aiden gone. She stood in the middle of her state-of-the-art kitchen Thursday afternoon, feeling lost and trying to keep focused on the baking she needed to do before heading to Aiden's preschool to pick him up. Emma was napping. Prize was lying on the floor, halfway between the kitchen and the living room, her dark brown eyes watching Shelley's every move, although she hadn't been moving all that much in the past hour.

Dragging in a deep breath, she pounded a dust-covered fist into a large ball of gingerbread dough, sprinkled it with a little more flour, and squished it down with her rolling pin. Back and forth she worked until the dough was only a quarter of an inch thick, just right for her seashell gingerbread cookies.

She glanced at the clock on the wall. It was only 1:15. She had time to bake this entire batch and put them on cooling trays before heading uptown. They'd be cool by the time she got home, and she could get them decorated with pale pink and lavender icings, the colors her client had requested, and pack them up tonight to ship off first thing in the morning.

She'd just shoved two trays each into her double ovens when the phone rang. She jumped, immediately worrying that something had happened to Aiden. Or maybe Dan was going to be home late from work. Snatching a towel, she quickly wiped her hands and grabbed the phone, surprised to hear her sister Susannah at the other end. She normally didn't call in the middle of the day, but then again, Susannah hadn't been big on calling at all for years. They hadn't been terribly close since they were teenagers, and they'd slowly drifted apart, first when their parents divorced, then Susannah married, had a baby, and she too divorced.

But lately they had been calling more often.

"Hi, sis. Hope I didn't call at a bad time," Susannah said, her voice a little shaky.

"I have to go pick Aiden up from pre-K in a few minutes. Is everything okay? Is Hailey okay?"

"I'm…okay. Hailey's fine too. She's been kind of a handful this summer."

Shelley waited. Something was going on, but Susannah seemed in no hurry to bring it up.

"How are you and the kids?" Shelley's sister asked.

"Dan'll be working in Bangor next week, so it's going to be extra lonely around here."

"You have Aiden and Emma and all your friends. How can you be lonely?"

"Not having Dan around is a different kind of lonely. There are some things you just can't share with your children or even your closest friends. I can share everything with Dan."

Susannah let out a hollow laugh. "I can't imagine sharing everything with anyone. No one would believe half of my secrets."

Shelley didn't want to ask this next question, but she did. "Sis, I need to pick Aiden up. Is there something you wanted to tell me? Are you really okay?"

Maggie, their father's girlfriend or fiancée—Shelley wasn't quite sure which—had mentioned once that she wasn't all that crazy about some of Susannah's friends. Maggie felt that Susannah was hanging around with the wrong crowd, people who could get her in trouble. Was that the case now? Had she gotten herself into a jam?

In the silence that rested between them on the phone, Shelley could easily imagine her petite, blonde-haired sister, a near carbon copy of herself, massaging her temple, trying to ease away a headache. "I told you, Shel, everything's fine." Susannah's words were abrupt. "I've got to get going. I just wanted to touch base. Talk later."

Without another word, Susannah hung up, and Shelley was left with nothing but the dial tone ringing in her ear.

The oven timer went off and Shelley quickly pulled her gingerbread seashells out. The timing had to be perfect, otherwise the cookies were too hard or the centers weren't quite cooked. She set the cookie sheets on cooling racks and stared at her phone a moment, then dialed Susannah back. She needed to know what was going on. But there was no answer. The phone rang and rang, and there was no voice mail so she could leave a message.

Shelley sighed, then punched in Maggie's phone number. She and her dad's friend weren't close, but Shelley respected and appreciated her. And right now, she needed to talk with someone.

As soon as Maggie answered the phone, Shelley could hear the jangle of the dozens of bracelets Maggie wore on her wrists. They shared a few words of greeting and talked for a moment about Shelley's dad and about Aiden and Emma. Then Shelley asked, "Maggie, have you talked to Susannah lately? She called me a little while ago and, I don't know, she seems upset about something, but all she'd say was that everything's fine."

"I wish I had better news, Shelley, but both your father and I have tried calling Susannah and the phone just rings and rings. We haven't heard from her in maybe a month or more."

Again Shelley wished Dan was in town so she could talk with him about this, instead of sharing her concerns with her father's girlfriend, but she had to talk to someone.

"You don't think she's in trouble of some kind, do you?" Shelley asked, leaning against the gleaming kitchen cabinet.

"I hope not. Your father and I have both been concerned about the man she was—or still is—dating. And, of course, we're worried that Hailey might not be getting all the attention she needs."

"Susannah can be awfully immature at times, but she'd never put Hailey in harm's way."

"I know she loves Hailey. Your father knows that too, but for a while there, she was having friends watch Hailey after school and late into the night…a lot. I'm afraid there might have been times when Hailey would be left home alone in the evenings, with only the television to keep an eye on her."

Maggie's words made Shelley sick to her stomach. How could a mother neglect her children or foist them off on someone else? Even though she knew better, she still felt she had abandoned Aiden by shipping him off to pre-K.

Looking up at the clock, she realized it was a little past time to leave the house if she wanted to be at Aiden's school as soon as it let out for the day. And she still had to wake up Emma.

"If you hear anything from Susannah, please call me," Shelley told Maggie.

Five minutes later, she and Emma were rushing out the door. She couldn't—wouldn't—be late to pick up her son. He'd been so anxious to see her at the end of his first two days of school, and his face had lit up with excitement when she walked through the door. Heaven forbid she should ever be late and let him think that she no longer cared about him.

That was something her own mother and father had done to their children. Shelley would never repeat that behavior with hers.

* * *

Margaret stood outside the gallery's front door, soaking up the warm afternoon sunshine and freshness of the ocean. She laughed at Shelley, who dashed by pushing Emma's stroller, with only enough time to breathlessly tell Margaret that she was late, and if she didn't hurry, Aiden might never forgive her. What brought that on Margaret might never know. Shelley had seemed excited at the thought of sending Aiden off to preschool, but now she looked completely distressed.

Margaret knew the feeling. She still felt it even now, on her daughter's second day of classes, with Adelaide taking the bus to and from school all on her own. And not just any school: college. Never in her wildest dreams did she, or Allan, think that Adelaide would attend a real college, but she was. Margaret was not only proud as could be, but anxious too. Adelaide had been given a cell phone to call home if she needed help of any kind, Margaret reminded herself, or if she simply needed some cheering on as she made her way to and from the bus to her class. She would call if she needed anything.

A hand landed on her shoulder, and she nearly jumped right out of the clogs she was wearing. Jerking around, she saw Allan smiling. "She's going to be just fine, you know. Standing here watching for the bus to arrive isn't going to make it happen any sooner."

"What if she doesn't get off the bus?" Margaret asked, turning back to stare at the bus stop at the corner of Main and Waters, right at the edge of the wharf. "What if she got lost with so many other students running this way and that, trying to get to their cars—" A terrible thought hit her. "What if she got into a car with another student? A kid who drives too fast or takes corners like a madman? What if—"

She stopped and took a deep breath. "Would you listen to me!" She laughed. "Will I never learn?"

Allan chuckled. "You're going to worry yourself sick if you keep this up."

"I know, I know. But I know you worry too."

"All right, I admit to a few ounces of worry."

Allan kissed the top of her head as he did so often, and gripping her shoulders lightly and pulling her back against his chest, he held her tight as they waited for the bus.

It seemed as if an hour went by before it arrived, but it had barely been minutes. Margaret was sure she'd stopped breathing as she waited for passengers to disembark, first one, then another, and finally Adelaide stepped down carefully, found her footing, and looked toward the gallery. She waved at her mom and dad, looked both ways to see if any cars were coming, as she'd been told to do time and again since she was little, and at last crossed the street, her honey-colored hair pulled back into a ponytail that bobbed up and down as she walked.

Margaret caught her breath and started to walk toward her daughter, but Allan held her back. "I know it's hard to let go, but Adelaide's got to do this on her own. We've got to stop coddling her."

Margaret sighed. She knew Allan was right, and Adelaide had successfully made it to college and back all on her own. It was one of many new steps they had to let her take, no matter how difficult they were for mom and dad.

"I had fun today, Mom," Adelaide said, throwing her arms around Margaret and squeezing her tight. "Miss Stewart, my teacher, told us about nu—" Adelaide's brow wrinkled. She sighed. "Oh yeah, *nutrition,* and how important it is for little kids."

"Maybe you can teach your mom and me a thing or two about what we should and shouldn't eat." Allan slipped Adelaide's backpack off her shoulders and held the gallery door open for Margaret and Adelaide. "I'm not all that crazy about apples, but I'm sure they're good for kids."

"Oh, Dad!" Adelaide laughed. "Apples are good for everyone. I don't like the skin, but Teacher—"

"Call her Miss Stewart," Margaret corrected.

"Miss Stewart says the skin is good. And did you know that apples have lots of vitamin C?"

"I'd heard that," Allan said, he and Margaret taking in every word Adelaide spoke, smiling at her exuberance.

"I have a whole bunch of papers to read before school next week. You might have to help me with some of them, and I have to do some homework on the computer, looking up things on the Internet. Oh, and I get extra credit if I babysit. I told...I told Miss Stewart that you're teaching an art class and she said I could get extra credit if I helped you. She gave us papers you can fill out saying what we've done. So can I help you tonight?"

Margaret smiled. "I don't see why not." She looked at her watch. "Maybe you should take a nap before class starts." Margaret could've used one too, but there'd be little to no rest for her the entire month of September. "And you and Dad should make us some dinner before we go. I imagine you're hungry. It's been several hours since lunchtime."

Adelaide's shoulders bunched up and she looked down at the floor, as if she'd done something wrong. "I ate my lunch on the bus."

Margaret frowned. "Why didn't you eat at lunchtime?" All sorts of scenarios ran through Margaret's mind. Had Adelaide gotten lost trying to find the cafeteria or a place to eat? Had she wandered away from campus? Gone exploring?

"I didn't want to wait until I got home to read the papers Miss Stewart gave us, so I went into the library to read, and you can't eat in the library. Was that okay?"

Margaret smiled, relief flooding through her. "It was okay today, but one thing you need to remember about nutrition—and I'm sure Miss Stewart will tell you this—is that you shouldn't skip meals. It's not healthy for anyone."

"Okay, Mom. I'm excited I get to come help in your class."

Two days in college and Adelaide was already eager to apply the things she was learning. Her daughter was stretching, reaching for her full potential.

Now if Margaret could just step aside and let it happen.

★ ★ ★

Diane pushed her shopping cart through the produce section of the grocery store, stopping beside a bin piled high with cantaloupe. She lifted one that was much too soft, put it down, picked up another, and held it close to her nose to inhale its sweetness. It seemed perfectly ripe, just right for the breakfast she wanted to serve Jeanette on Saturday morning. She selected a carton of ripe blueberries and bananas that were bright yellow, without a tinge of green on them anywhere. Already the fruit in the cart was making her hungry.

Out of the blue she thought about next week's doctor's appointment. She hadn't called to cancel. Of course, she'd never officially said she'd be there. Dr. Crowley's assistant had only penciled her in. She still wasn't sure if she'd go. It seemed like such a waste of time.

Then again, not going made her worry. If they didn't find anything, great. If they did . . . She didn't want to think about it.

She was on her way to the checkout counter, softly singing along with an old Buddy Holly tune—"That'll Be the Day"—playing over the store's sound system, when she turned a corner and bumped baskets with Reverend Silas Locke.

"Hi there." Diane smiled at the pastor when he noticed he'd actually collided with someone. He'd seemed preoccupied, and the frown he wore when he looked at her made Diane think she'd intruded on something very important, something he'd been cogitating on for a long time. He pushed his glasses up on his nose. "Good afternoon, Diane." He shot a quick glance at the assortment of goodies, mixed with the healthy stuff, in Diane's shopping basket and grinned. "You aren't stocking up to go out on another treasure hunt, are you?"

Diane shook her head, laughing. "My sister-in-law Jeanette is coming for a short visit. She's the one who introduced Beverly and me to the archivist—Dr. Standish— at Portland College."

"Ah, yes, I remember."

"I should have called you before now," she offered, leaving out the part that she'd forgotten, considering everything else she had on her mind. "Dr. Standish has found some documents that might possibly clear Reverend Thorpe's name, and Jeanette's bringing me copies."

Reverend Locke raised his eyebrows. "A diary? Letters?"

"I'm not exactly sure, but when Beverly and I were at the college, Dr. Standish told us he recalled seeing a newspaper article referring to Reverend Thorpe as the Bandit Preacher. He couldn't find the document at the time, but it appears that might be what he's sending along with Jeanette. There might also be some documentation that refutes what was in that newspaper article."

Reverend Locke removed his glasses and pinched the bridge of his nose, as if trying to staunch a headache. "I'll look forward to seeing them. That vicious moniker has plagued my family and tainted my ancestor's name for over two hundred years." He put his glasses back on slowly. "God knows my sister and I have nearly exhausted all our energy trying to learn the truth. I can only pray these new documents can restore Reverend Thorpe's good name."

"I hope so too," Diane said. "And with any luck, there might also be some revelations in the documents about the treasure."

His smile returned. "If it weren't for the fact that finding a treasure could possibly put a new roof on Old First and maybe do some restoration, I'd consider clearing Reverend Thorpe's name enough of a prize."

Reverend Locke looked at his watch. "I must be going, Diane. I'm sorry to say I'm heading out of town for a Christian counseling seminar this weekend. I hope when I return you'll let me know right away what you've found out."

"Of course." Suddenly Diane remembered that Jeanette had hoped to see the inside of Old First. "Is there anyone who could take my sister-in-law and me on a tour of Old First while you're gone? She'd really like to see the interior, especially the tower."

He shook his head. "You know that isn't possible, Diane. Until the damage from the fire has been repaired—God willing—the city won't allow anyone inside, especially the sanctuary, and as much as it pains me to say this, I won't let anyone in either. As it is, I only duck inside when it's absolutely necessary, and I don't stay long."

"You must miss holding your services there."

He nodded. "I like to think I can share the message of God's love and hope anywhere I am, and I'm very grateful to Marble Cove Community Church for opening its doors to us. But I must admit, there's a part of me that feels a little lost when my congregation and I are worshiping in another church in town."

Diane smiled warmly. "Then we'd better find that treasure fast so we can restore Old First."

"The work on the roof is starting up, and I'm hopeful one day we can get the building properly restored. In fact, I was talking with Dennis Calder earlier today—you know him, don't you?" When Diane nodded, he continued. "Mr. Calder has told me that should he be elected mayor in this November's election, he might be able to get a grant from the town—or some other source, possibly—to help finance a restoration, especially since the church is one of Marble Cove's most important historical landmarks."

Diane was skeptical. The town of Marble Cove had just enough money to keep necessities in service without doling out money to Old First, an allocation that could raise the ire of a few townspeople. It sounded to Diane like a ploy to get Reverend Locke and his flock to vote for him. How dare he, when Beverly was a member of Old First?

"Did Evelyn Waters ever approach you about the possibility of a grant?"

He shook his head. "No, but I did approach her, and even though she agreed it would be wonderful if the town could help out, she said it was an impossibility."

"Then how do you suppose Dennis Calder plans to do it?"

Reverend Locke opened his mouth to speak, then closed it for a moment. "I suppose you're right, Diane." He looked disappointed. "I just have to keep the faith that we'll be able to restore that wonderful old building."

"It's a faith that my friends and I share. And who knows—maybe some remnant of the treasure is still out there for us to find."

The two said their good-byes, and Diane headed once again for the checkout stand. She put her items up on the conveyor belt and took out her checkbook, thinking as she did so that she couldn't wait to see the expression on Beverly's face when she told her about Dennis Calder's supposed plan to get a grant for Old First. If Dennis Calder could feed such a crazy line to Reverend Silas Locke, there was no telling what kinds of promises he was making to other people in town.

And Beverly needed to meet his challenges head-on.

Chapter Nine

Beverly tried to ignore the knock on the front door, knowing her father was in his library and would get it himself. She concentrated instead on her computer screen and the layout for her campaign signs. At long last the knocking ceased and Beverly leaned back in her desk chair and stared out the window, thinking about her slogan, about Dennis Calder, and about Jeff, wishing she was with him now, wishing the hours until she saw him again would race by.

Again she heard the knock, and Beverly scooted down the stairs to see Diane standing in the doorway, her knuckles poised just inches away from the doorjamb. "Mind if I come in?"

Beverly smiled, always happy to see her friend. "Not at all." Beverly stretched, throwing back her shoulders, which had stiffened under the last few hours of work.

Diane, dressed in sky-blue capris, a sleeveless white eyelet blouse, and flip-flops, plopped down in one of the two living room chairs. She leaned toward Beverly with an eager expression. "You'll never guess what I heard straight from Reverend Locke's mouth."

Smiling, Beverly leaned in too, as if sharing a secret. "Don't tell me he's found the treasure?"

"I wish." Diane sat back, arms folded across her knees. "Dennis Calder has as much as promised Reverend Locke that if he becomes mayor, he'll have the town grant money to Old First to repair the roof and make other necessary renovations."

Beverly frowned. "What? It would be lovely if he could, but Evelyn Waters already shot down that idea, based pretty much on separation of church and state, even though Old First is a historical landmark."

"I'm sure Dennis knows that, Beverly, and I'm sure he hasn't one iota of a notion to actually try to get a grant—*if* he becomes mayor. It's just a ploy to get more votes."

Beverly sighed heavily. "I keep telling myself I should trust Dennis, that maybe I harbor too many unfair feelings against him, and then he does something like this. Of course, maybe he does know a way to get a grant."

"If there was a way, Mayor Waters would have seen that it was done, or she would have told Lee about it and suggested he have a talk with Reverend Locke so he could gain the reverend's vote and the votes of the parishioners. It's a good campaign ploy."

"It's not one I would ever use. Why get people's hopes up?" Beverly stood. "Can you come upstairs for a moment? I want to get your feedback on my campaign signs."

Diane rose and trudged up the stairs behind Beverly. Beverly set in her office chair and turned to her computer,

where she pulled the graphic up on the screen, showing off
the bright colors—not red, white, and blue, which most
people used in their campaigns, but gold and deep pink on
an aquamarine background, with her slogan, Embracing
Marble Cove's Heritage, right below her name, which was
printed in bold block letters.

"Unless you see something terribly wrong with this,"
Beverly said, "I'm ordering them tomorrow."

"It's wonderful." Diane's eyes had brightened. "I hope
you'll let me be the first to put a sign in my yard."

Beverly laughed. "I hope everyone on Newport Avenue,
plus all the business owners in town, will want to put one
up. But you'll be first."

She turned back to look at the bright colors on the screen
and sighed. "I need to make a bold statement. To save
Marble Cove, I have to beat Dennis Calder."

★ ★ ★

Margaret glanced up at the clock in her classroom,
wishing she and Adelaide had come at least half an hour
earlier than they had to set up. Her students should begin
arriving at any minute, and they still had easels to set up,
watercolor paper to attach to the easels, paints to put on
the palettes—all things Margaret wanted to have done in
advance so they didn't have to waste any time before class
started.

If Adelaide hadn't come with her, she'd be pulling her hair
out by now, and she couldn't help but smile at her daughter

as she bustled from one part of the room to another, carefully completing every task Margaret gave her.

They were still far from ready when Danny Wharburton and his mother arrived much, much too early. Margaret said a quick hello and introduced Adelaide. Danny tugged his mom's hand, taking her across the room to look at the kaleidoscope he'd painted last night. Margaret went about her work, but she kept half an eye on the exchange between Danny and his mother, whose face radiated displeasure. Margaret thought Danny might have a gift for painting; his creativity was far out of the box, very abstract, showing that he was imaginative and inventive. She'd liked him immediately, but considering the look on Mrs. Wharburton's face, Danny's mom wasn't quite as pleased with his work.

"Do you have a moment?" Mrs. Wharburton asked in a stage whisper, taking Margaret's arm and leading her to a far corner of the room. Before Margaret could say a word, Mrs. Wharburton said softly, "Danny has a mind of his own, always going in his own direction rather than sticking with the norm. I'm sure you mean no harm in teaching creativity, but I was under the impression this class would be all about technique, about how to paint...correctly."

Margaret was at a loss for words. She had been told to stick with the class plan, but children needed to flex their creative side, to expand their minds, their horizons. Mrs. Wharburton continued to glare at Margaret, her arms across her chest in a brook-no-argument fashion.

"I will be teaching technique, Mrs. Wharburton, but—"

"I hope it will begin tonight, otherwise I'll have to withdraw Danny from the class and request a refund of my money."

Margaret offered her a placating smile. She couldn't argue with Mrs. Wharburton, who was, after all, entitled to say what she had. Margaret was told to stick to the plan and hadn't. Now she had to switch gears—immediately—even though she felt ten- to twelve-year-olds were too young to think about technique.

Where to begin? she wondered as the classroom filled with students. Fortunately, she hadn't lost any. They'd all returned tonight, so she must have done something right.

"Last night we had a little fun," Margaret said after the parents dispersed.

"You mean we aren't going to have fun tonight?" Jake Morris asked, doing another handstand and getting applause from the rest of the kids. "I thought this class was all about fun."

"I love to paint," Adelaide said, standing close to Margaret, as if in solidarity.

Margaret smiled and then continued, embellishing Adelaide's statement. "It's especially fun when you know what you're doing. It's like driving a car, in a stretch-of-the-imagination way. If you got in a car and drove off when you didn't have a clue what you were doing, you could easily run off the road or run into someone else, and that could lead to all sorts of dire circumstances. But if you learn how to drive first, you can have fun—not by speeding, of course, but by taking Sunday drives and seeing places you've never seen before. Learning how to drive can open up new worlds to you."

"I don't think you could hurt someone by picking up a paintbrush and slashing cerulean blue across the canvas," Charlemayne countered. "And you definitely don't need instructions to do that."

"She's right," Jake Morris said from his upside-down position. "Comparing driving with painting is like comparing apples with oranges."

Margaret brushed a hand through her short gray hair. "Yes, I suppose you're right. Still, I hope you'll believe me when I tell you that you'll have a new appreciation for painting once you learn technique and know all the ins and outs of painting."

Jake righted himself. He scowled at Adelaide, then at Margaret. He scratched his head. "We have to learn all day in school."

"Once you learn technique and it becomes second nature, you'll be better equipped to explore your creativity. If you don't learn technique, like how to mix colors, how to splatter, how to blend, dry brush, wet brush, and all the other forms of painting—and I'm speaking of watercolor here, which is the medium we're going to use tonight—you won't have all the tools you need to be your most creative."

Jake did another handstand; Felicity busied herself drawing on her hand; Danny yawned. Some of the children looked at her blankly. Was she getting through?

These children had already spent a good six hours in the classroom today. Was it really fair to subject them to more instruction? Not in Margaret's mind, but that wasn't her call. She was here to teach an assigned curriculum, and she got right down to it. Even if the kids didn't seem very happy about it.

With Adelaide's assistance, she distributed paper, paint, and brushes. Then Margaret stood at her easel and demonstrated the dry-brush technique. Once she'd finished, she had them do the same thing on their own paper.

She walked around the room, from one student to another, her hands clasped behind her back, watching their work, correcting anyone who was having trouble with the simple technique.

Adelaide too walked around the room, asking the children if they needed more paper, a bigger brush, or anything else to help them. Margaret's heart swelled as she watched her daughter. The smile on her face, the beaming sense of purpose and pride, told Margaret that Adelaide was in her element.

The pounding in her head told Margaret she wasn't faring nearly as well. While the students seemed to have settled down to work on their assignments, Margaret felt drained.

When the students finished the simple assignment, Margaret said, "I want you to use your pen to write 'dry brush' next to what you've just painted. We're going to make a chart of many of the different styles tonight, and then we'll apply a few of those styles in the second half of our class time."

A few students grumbled. One girl rolled her eyes. A paper airplane sailed across the room. Teaching kids wasn't nearly as easy as she'd imagined.

★ ★ ★

A few moments later, signed release slips in hand, Margaret saw Beverly slip into her classroom. Beverly stood in the corner, snapping digital photos of Margaret moving about the room, watching as they mixed and applied many hues of cobalt-blue paint to their watercolor paper, creating a graded watercolor wash just as Margaret had shown them.

"You can use this technique to create quite a lot of different things," Margaret said, going back to her easel and applying the many shades of cobalt blue she'd mixed earlier. "I know you'd like to do your own thing right now, but why don't you follow what I'm doing and see if you can figure out what we're creating?"

Beverly moved about the room, snapping photos of Adelaide bending over to help one of the students who'd spilled his paint, then several shots of Margaret.

When she'd completed her demonstration, and the students had copied her painting, Margaret said, "Before the night's over, you'll have the beginning of a picture. Any idea what you're creating right now?"

"A mess," Jake Morris said, as Beverly zoomed in to snap a photo of his paint-splattered hands.

Margaret massaged the back of her neck, looking more than a little flustered, but she continued on. "I'm sure some of you have a better idea than that. Use your imagination. Think outside the box."

"Is it crinkled velvet?" Felicity asked. "My mom has an old prom dress that looks like this."

"Your painting won't end up being a prom dress," Margaret said, as Beverly snapped her picture for the umpteenth time, "but that's letting your imagination go, and it's definitely thinking outside the box."

"How about blueberry jam mixed with cream cheese?" Charlemayne asked, swirling different mixtures of cobalt blue around the paper.

"That's a good guess, Charlemayne," Margaret said, "and I suppose it does look something like that. But look again. Remember, think outside the box.

"Come on, everyone," Margaret continued, egging on her students. "Take a good, long look at what you've painted; look at what I've painted. It doesn't have to be a still-life painting like blue velvet or blueberries and cream cheese. Think of those blue swirls you've painted as something active, always in motion, sometimes tumultuous, oftentimes calm."

"Oh, duh." Danny smacked his palm against his forehead. "It's the ocean. I can't believe I didn't see that."

"Wouldn't the ocean have more green in it?" Felicity asked.

"It could," Margaret told her. "Would you like more green in yours?"

Felicity nodded. "Can I do that at this point? Won't it mess up the colors that are already there?"

"Not at all, provided you use the correct technique and don't go crazy with your color choices." Margaret walked back to her easel. "Let me show you on my painting how you can effectively add a color like green to this painting. By the way, green is a perfect color to add."

"Green is made from blue and yellow," Adelaide said, smiling at the students. She picked up a bottle of blue paint and another of yellow. "My mom taught me that when I was little." Wearing an artist's smock splattered with cat footprints, she was as proud of herself as Margaret was proud of her. Allan was going to be so delighted to hear how Adelaide had helped her out. It was the bright spot of Margaret's evening.

Picking up her brush, still bearing the cobalt blue paint she had last used on her picture, Margaret dipped the bristles into yellow, explaining to her students exactly what she was doing, and dabbed her new greenish color into an icy-blue area of the painting. "See how simple that one little technique can be?" she asked, stepping aside to show them how she'd enhanced the wave. "Why don't you give it a try on your paintings? Just remember to use a light hand, not too much paint to start out with."

While Adelaide distributed yellow paint to each student, Margaret walked around, relieved to see how carefully everyone had listened. Well—not everyone. She sighed. Jake Morris fidgeted behind his easel. He plunged his brush into winsor orange, which he must have snatched from the table full of paint near her easel. Margaret was afraid he was going to slash it across his painting and swept to his side. She was just about to grab his wrist when he stabbed the bright orange onto his painting, already a rather creative mess, and streaked it across the paper.

"My painting doesn't look much like waves," he said quietly, giving Margaret a mischievous smile. "Looks more like a scaly blue dragon, and this," he said, adding another streak of orange, "is fire. All dragons breathe fire, don't they?"

He had a point, she supposed, but he'd left her shaking as she walked around the room, looking at what the other students were doing to enhance their paintings, and thank heaven, all but Jake had listened and followed directions. A part of Margaret hoped that Jake would drop out of class; on the other hand, he did liven things up. She only hoped she could survive his antics.

Half an hour later, Margaret and Adelaide, with Beverly's help, were cleaning up the classroom, moving easels and paintings to one side, where they'd be out of the way for other classes until her students met again next Monday.

"You've got one tough cookie in your class," Beverly said, standing at the sink washing out brushes.

Margaret laughed. "My guess is he'd rather be outside riding his skateboard than spending the evening learning how to paint."

A few minutes later, when the three women left the community center and stepped out into the last of the evening light, Margaret smiled at her surroundings and at her friend Beverly, then tucked her arm through Adelaide's. She breathed in the fresh evening air and felt some of her earlier tension slip away. Despite the challenges Jake and some of the other students had given her, it had been a beautiful day, and she glanced up at the heavens and offered a silent prayer of thanks.

★ ★ ★

Moonlight shone down on the water, casting streaks of white across the deep blue ocean, just like in one of Margaret's paintings, Beverly thought, as she walked along the shore, her bare feet leaving prints in the sand. She hadn't been out walking this late at night—just past midnight—in a long time. Tonight, though, she had a lot on her mind—her campaign and Jeff: one energizing her, the other leaving her in a bit of a quandary.

Jeff was back in the States. Yesterday morning she imagined he'd rush to Marble Cove to see her after spending time overseas in Russia. The last time she'd seen him he'd said he hated the thought of being away from her, yet it seemed that had changed. Somehow.

She didn't like the thought of feeling needy or desperate, but she'd missed him. In a matter of months she'd gone from merely enjoying his company to wanting to be near him and sharing the events of her day. She wanted to talk about her campaign with him, ask his advice, listen to any helpful tips he might have.

But he hadn't rushed to see her. He hadn't returned any of her calls or text messages today. Right now, she felt more alone than she had in years. Falling in love could oftentimes be such an awful thing.

She kicked at a wave that rolled over her feet, then jogged along the beach, scaring off the shorebirds who'd been keeping her company. She looked toward the lighthouse, hoping to see its mysterious and miraculous light, but nothing shined through the glass at the top of the tower, only the moonlight illuminating the windows and the bright white paint on its centuries-old walls. She listened for the bells from Old First, the real ones and even the mysterious one that seemed to come in a time of need, but they were silent.

Sweeping up a piece of driftwood, she tossed it out into the waves, then tucked her hands into her pants pockets, realizing that it was actually starting to grow quite cool out. Summer was rapidly coming to an end. Was her relationship with Jeff coming to an end too?

Over the clang of the bell from a boat whose lights she could just barely see in the distance, she heard the chime from her phone announcing a text message. She wrapped her fingers around the phone, pulled it from her pocket, and finally saw Jeff's name. Her heart beat heavily as she read his message.

Long, hard day. Sorry I've been absent and absentminded. Will be later than planned tomorrow. Please change reservation at Spinella's to 8:00 PM and meet me there. Sorry.

Jeff had never been a man of so few words. What had changed?

Chapter Ten

Diane and Rocky raced through the front door and down the path to the picket fence the moment Diane heard Jeanette's pristine red vintage Volkswagen Beetle clattering up in front of the cottage. She paused at the gate, took a deep breath, and willfully pushed nagging thoughts of the dreaded doctor's appointment to the back of her mind. She even ignored the writing she needed to do. Now it was time for her to enjoy Jeanette's visit.

"Hi there!" Diane swung the gate open and, followed by Rocky, met Jeanette at the driver's side door. After giving her a welcoming hug, she helped Jeanette get her two small suitcases out of the tiny trunk at the front of the car. "This is Rocky," she said, introducing the friendly pet, who'd sat down directly in front of Jeanette, one paw held up to shake.

Jeanette reached out to give Rocky a tentative pat on the head. "You must have told me you had a dog, but I'd completely forgotten."

Diane had forgotten that Jeanette had cats and wasn't all that crazy about the canine population. "We adopted each other right about this time last year. He was a stray, I was lonely, and we clicked right off the bat. You'll like him, I'm sure. He's usually quite well mannered."

Jeanette looked doubtful but resolute.

"You didn't have any trouble finding the cottage, did you?"

"I may still have the first car I ever bought, but even I have a GPS these days. Works wonders." Jeanette smiled.

Diane ushered Jeanette through the gate and up the walk, with Rocky running around in circles, finding a bright yellow ball among the flowers and carrying it to Jeanette, thinking she might want to play. Jeanette didn't seem to notice, but she did stop along the way to smell some of the roses and to admire the lush, deep-blue hydrangeas. "It's beautiful here. Eric would have loved it."

Diane leaned against one of the front step's banisters, looking out across the garden she lovingly tended, then on to the Atlantic, so peaceful and calm today, the sky a perfect blue, with a few puffy white clouds scattered about for show.

Jeanette too looked out at the ocean, her light-brown hair ruffling in the breeze. Like Eric, she was tall and slender, and right now she wore the same type of faraway smile that quite often appeared on Eric's face when he dreamed about the future.

A year ago, even a couple of months ago, it had been difficult to think of Eric without an immense longing. That feeling still came on occasion, just not as often. He'd always be in her heart, of course, but she had to move on.

"Come on in and let me show you around the cottage." Diane practically skipped up the steps, happy to have company, delighted to spend time with Jeanette.

She took Jeanette's suitcases into the small guest bedroom, where she had set a crystal vase of English roses in shades of pink and yellow atop the round bedside table.

"There's an extra pillow and blanket on the shelf in the closet," Diane said, slipping out of the room to show Jeanette the rest of her home—the small office where she worked night and day, not bothering to keep any particular hours, her own bedroom, with a window that was wide open, letting in the sea breeze that fluttered the curtains, and the living room, dining area, and kitchen.

"Eric and I would have bumped into each other constantly in this place. I know it's tiny, but it's perfect just for me."

"I'm surprised you have room in here for all the furniture and other belongings you and Eric had," Jeanette said, looking through the glass in a corner display cabinet at the few knickknacks Diane had kept.

"I couldn't possibly have kept everything Eric and I owned. Getting rid of most of the things we'd shared was difficult, so I gave a number of things to Justin and Jessica, although I don't always think that kids these days appreciate antiques and sentimental items as much as our generation does."

"I see you still have my grandmother's teapot."

"That's one of the pieces I couldn't possibly have parted with. In fact, tucked away inside is the wedding card she gave us, telling us how much the teapot had meant to her."

"Did she give you any other belongings?"

"Not that I remember. If she'd given Eric something special, I'm sure he would have told me and, of course, I would have treasured it. If I remember correctly, her dementia was getting worse, and she was giving things away right and left right about then."

Jeanette laughed. "I don't know why, but I never really pictured you as the sentimental type, especially when you were so quick to clean out Eric's closets and get rid of his clothes and books."

Jeanette's words felt like a slap in the face, although Diane was sure Jeanette hadn't meant them that way. "I didn't need to keep those things to remind me of Eric. And besides, the homeless shelter is always in need of clothing, especially for men, and the college was more than happy to take almost all of Eric's books to add to their library." Diane sighed. "I'm sorry, Jeanette. I probably should have asked you if you wanted the books. Everything happened so suddenly, so out of the blue, that I wasn't always thinking clearly. You didn't ask for anything, and, well"—she paused—"I didn't think to ask you if there was anything you wanted."

Jeanette pulled a tissue from her pants pocket and wiped her eyes. "I didn't mean to bring all of that up. I guess I still have trouble believing he's gone." She waved off her emotions. "Do you have something cold to drink? Lemonade, maybe?"

"Freshly squeezed," Diane said, taking a couple of tall glasses down from a cabinet and filling them with ice.

She took a crystal pitcher from the fridge. "I've made my lemonade the same way for over thirty years. In fact, it's your grandmother's recipe."

Jeanette laughed. "In that case, would you mind if I add a little sugar to mine? If I remember correctly, Grandma could be a little sour at times, and so could her lemonade."

Diane filled the two glasses, let Jeanette stir some sugar into hers, then led her out to the front porch, where they sat side by side on Shaker rockers.

Diane took a sip of lemonade. "I'm so glad you came to visit."

"It was probably the wrong time to take a trip, considering that school's starting the middle of next week, but I felt the need to get away."

"Were you able to take any time off at all this summer?"

Jeanette shook her head. "Not after becoming head of the English department. I must have worked sixty to seventy hours a week all through July and August. I'd planned a trip to London, hoping to spend an entire month in the museums studying paintings by the Old Masters, and especially some of the books at the Bodleian Library in Oxford. Eric would have enjoyed a trip like that. You probably would have too."

"We talked about it, but something else always interfered."

Jeanette took another sip of her lemonade. "I recently read a series of documents, mostly letters, written by Winston Churchill and his family, his mother Jennie, his aunts Leonie and Clara, and a few of his cousins. Not that I was surprised at the sheer poetry in their words, but it is interesting that as you look back in time, people documented everyday life in a prose that's essentially nonexistent today."

"That's sad," Diane admitted. "I know I take a lot of shortcuts with my writing. I don't even write letters any longer—I just send text messages to Jessica and Justin, abbreviating every other word."

"We're going to forget how to write if we keep it up, and someday, future generations will be left wondering what happened to their ancestors, because there's no written record—nothing intelligible, that is."

Jeanette frowned, deep in thought. "Speaking of ancestors, let me get that paperwork Dr. Standish found." Jeanette rose from her rocker and went into the house with Rocky on her heels, and Diane found her heart had begun to beat rapidly, anxious to see if there was anything at all about a treasure, or anything that could clear Reverend Thorpe's name.

"I still haven't had a chance to look at any of this," Jeanette said, once she was on the porch again. She sat down easily in the rocker and pulled a sheaf of papers from a large manila envelope. "I hope there's something in here that's of benefit to you."

Diane thought her hands might shake right off her wrists as she took the papers from Jeanette. "At this stage of the game, we don't have much of anything that's beneficial, so whatever's in here definitely couldn't hurt."

Diane scanned the papers quickly. She wanted desperately to peruse each page slowly and deliberately, but Jeanette was here to visit; she couldn't ignore her.

"You know," Jeanette said, "if you want to fill me in on a few details about this mystery of yours, I could help you read through these papers and maybe spot something of interest."

"You're sure you wouldn't be bored?"

"I've been processing administrative paperwork for the past two months. Reading the ingredients in a box of oatmeal would be more interesting."

Diane smiled, leaned back in her chair, and rocked gently. "It would take hours to tell you everything, but I can probably relate the condensed version in five minutes or less."

Jeanette rocked in her chair too, her eyes closed. "Then hit me with it."

"This mystery—and trust me, there've been others since I moved to Marble Cove—began seven or eight months ago when Beverly, Margaret, Shelley, and I discovered a packet of centuries-old letters in the bell tower at Old First Church."

Diane continued, telling Jeanette that the letters had been written by Reverend Jeremiah Thorpe to his wife, who'd remained in England when he came to the America. "They were nearly impossible to read," Diane went on, "and it took us quite some time to decipher them, but in the end we discovered that Reverend Thorpe had acquired a treasure—"

"Was it given to him?" Jeanette asked, her eyes still closed. "Or did he steal it?"

"We'd like to believe he found it, but, unfortunately, Reverend Thorpe was given a nickname: the Bandit Preacher. Whether that's fitting or not, we haven't found out."

"And you're hoping the truth might be in these papers Dr. Standish has found?"

"I think we're hoping against hope. When Beverly and I met your Dr. Standish, he told us he remembered a newspaper article that claimed Reverend Thorpe wasn't quite the man of God he claimed to be. He'd been accused of stealing from the church, according to the document, and it basically accused him of being in cahoots with a notorious pirate. Thus the name the Bandit Preacher."

"Pretty serious charges."

"Charges that have never been refuted, and that moniker 'the Bandit Preacher' haunts two of his descendants even today. One of those descendants is Silas Locke, the pastor at Old First Church, which was founded by Reverend Thorpe."

Jeanette's eyes widened. "Dr. Standish did say there might be documentation here that gets to the truth."

"That's what I'm praying for," Diane said. "We're also hoping that there's information here that will tell us where the treasure is hidden, or at least what became of it."

"Which is the most important? Clearing Reverend Thorpe's name, or finding the treasure?"

"I'd say they're both equally important." Diane leaned forward, folding her arms across her knees. "If Reverend Thorpe was truly a good man, it's only right that his name be cleared. As for the treasure...Old First's roof was severely damaged in a fire a couple of months ago."

"And you need the treasure to repair it."

"You catch on fast." Diane smiled. "We haven't found it for lack of trying. We found clues that led us to an old cemetery here in Marble Cove, and searched the graveyard with metal detectors, but found nothing. We dug around the cliffs north of town, and found little more than a rusty lock and hinges." She leaned forward with a conspiratorial smile. "Well, that and the remains of a wooden box and one gold coin."

"I think I have a pretty clear idea of what you're looking for," Jeanette said, plucking half the papers off Diane's lap. "Let me scan this stack, and let's see what we can find."

"You've come here for a relaxing weekend. I can't possibly put you to work."

"Have you already forgotten? I'm the one who vacations inside Oxford's Bodleian Library." Jeanette grinned. "Looking through these papers will be absolute heaven."

★ ★ ★

An hour later Diane sent a text message to Beverly, Margaret, and Shelley. *Found some great stuff in the documents Jeanette brought with her. Can you drop by at eight? I'm dying to show them to you.*

Can't, Beverly texted back. *Having dinner with Jeff, but anxious to learn more. Spending tomorrow morning with him too.*

Margaret replied: *In bed with massive headache. I'm definitely not teacher material!*

Dan's home! At last! Shelley wrote. *Can't bear to be away from him this weekend, but dying to hear what you've found.*

"They say there's never a bad time to receive good news," Diane quipped to Jeanette, who was stretched out on the sofa. "Apparently that's not always true."

"Why's that?" Jeanette asked.

"We find some of the best information yet about Reverend Thorpe and there's not a soul around for me to tell."

"You could just text them the information."

Diane looked at her in mock disbelief. "Not on your life. They'll have to see this to believe it. Somehow or other, I'll get all of us together this weekend, and won't they be surprised to hear the news!"

CHAPTER ELEVEN

Beverly sat at a window table inside Spinella's, staring at the flickering candle, the same shade of red as the checkered tablecloth, then out the glass at the seagulls soaring over the beach, at a dark cloud moving in, at the moon rising on the horizon, its light shimmering on the water. Unfortunately she wasn't able to look at the face of her handsome date.

Jeff was late.

She forced herself not to look at her watch. If she did, she was sure that what had seemed like an hour since she'd last looked would have been only one minute, and then she'd have to force herself not to look again. It would become a vicious cycle.

Dennis Calder came in, accompanied by Charlotte Vincent, chairwoman of the chamber of commerce. They were probably here to talk about Dennis' campaign and what he could do to advance business in Marble Cove.

Dennis waved as she scanned the menu for what seemed like the hundredth time, and she waved back halfheartedly, embarrassed that he'd seen her sitting here all alone. Dennis had clearly been interested in her a few months back. The fact that she'd chosen Jeff over him had irritated him to no end. Seeing her like this—all alone—would probably make him gloat, so she smiled, picked up the menu again, and tried to think about what she'd eat if and when Jeff ever arrived.

She felt a light kiss on her cheek, a warm and familiar hand on her shoulder. "Sorry I'm late. There was an accident on the highway. A head-on, from the looks of it, and a dozen or more emergency vehicles were blocking all the lanes. It was chaos, and I couldn't get a signal on my cell phone to call you."

Jeff's chair scraped against the floor as he pulled it out from the table and sat down, taking a deep breath. "Have you ordered yet?"

Beverly shook her head. She laughed, refusing to make a big deal out of Jeff being late. She hadn't seen him in nearly two weeks, and she'd missed him terribly. Right this minute, she was just glad he'd actually arrived all in one piece, especially when it could have been him in that accident.

Jeff reached across the table and took hold of her hand, squeezing it gently. "I've missed you."

For a moment she thought her voice was stuck in her throat, along with a lump of emotion and the threat of tears. Her smile was soft, filled with longing. "Me too," she whispered.

Before they could say anything else, their waiter appeared to take their orders—Jeff had his usual lasagna, and Beverly ordered a Caesar salad with shrimp.

"Tell me about your trip." Beverly took a sip of ice water. She smiled, resting her forearms on the table, needing to be closer to him. "I loved the photos you sent, but your one-line text messages left a lot to be desired. I couldn't quite tell if you enjoyed the tour—"

"It was all and more than I expected." He pulled a packet of photos from the inside pocket of the sports coat he was wearing with a white polo shirt and jeans. "I had these printed yesterday. They're some of the best images I was able to capture."

He flipped through his photos, pulling out one depicting a regal room, all gold gilt, with black-and-white tile floors, and fabulous murals painted around the walls. "That's the Hunting Room inside the Yusupov Palace, and that's Ivan the Terrible." Jeff pointed out a princely figure in one of the paintings. "It's said that Ivan used to relax in this palace after his hunting trips, feasting luxuriously before slipping back to the Kremlin by underground tunnel. It's also said that the tunnel was discovered when renovation on the palace was done—in the early twentieth century, I believe—and that all along the corridor were skeletons chained to the walls, thanks to Ivan."

Beverly shivered. "Rather gruesome, which means the magazine probably loved that part of the story."

"It makes good copy to go along with the photos. That's what the travel magazine that sent me on this trip wanted."

"You did take photos of more tranquil settings, I hope."

He had, of course, and while they ate, he showed her photos of the blue-and-white Smolny Cathedral, its Italian baroque architecture stunning; the Ural Mountains with their sparkling silver-and-green forests of birch trees; and the incredibly beautiful Lake Baikal, the oldest, Jeff told her, and possibly clearest lake in the world.

"It's all so beautiful," she told him. "I never thought I'd ever want to travel to Russia, but looking at your photos has changed my mind."

"Then I've succeeded at my job." He grinned. "That's what they're meant to do—sell travel!"

"You're good at selling. Maybe you could find a way to get people to vote for me rather than Dennis Calder or Lee Waters."

"It's not all that difficult, Beverly. Just be yourself."

"Fortunately, I've never put on airs or claimed to be something I'm not. I'm a what-you-see-is-what-you-get kind of person. On the other hand, I've had a number of people tell me lately that I don't stand a chance against two born-and-bred Marble Cove citizens. One person told me I'd spread myself too thin if I became mayor, what with my business and taking care of my father."

Jeff smiled, his dark brown eyes radiating warmth. "Do you think you're spread too thin?"

"I've multitasked most of my life, and I've done quite well at everything."

"You've succeeded at all of that, and you've still found time to lend support to your friends, and then there's the treasure hunting and holding fund-raisers to help restore Old First." He reached across the table and took her hand again. "Not once have I ever heard you complain about all you had to do."

"You know, neither one of us is the type to take on something we can't handle. There are a lot of strong people in this world, but you and I might just be two of the toughest."

"As we say in Maine: Ayuh!" Jeff grinned. "We were blessed with a persistence gene."

"We accomplish our goals out of sheer doggedness. That's why we're so good at what we do, and that's not bragging. It's the simple truth."

Jeff laughed. "Now that we've pumped up each other's egos, let's get out of here and walk along the beach."

Beverly nodded, and minutes later they were walking along the sand, shoes discarded at the bottom of the stairs leading from the restaurant's parking lot down to the beach. Jeff had rolled up his pants legs and doffed his jacket. He held her hand as they strolled along, and she at last felt comforted. Still, she could sense a certain amount of tension in his body and had the distinct impression that something heavy weighed on his mind.

"Penny for your thoughts."

"I'm heading out on another trip tomorrow."

Beverly stopped. She pulled her hand from his and walked out into the surf until the gentle waves lapped around her ankles. "Why so soon?"

"I got an offer from the same travel magazine that sent me to Russia. They liked my work and asked if I'd go over to Jordan for a week. They want pictures of Petra, some of the

Roman ruins, and—" He shrugged. "I know it's sudden, and I know you'd hoped I'd stick close to home for a while—"

"I thought you wanted to stick around home for a while too. I thought—Oh, it doesn't matter what I thought."

Jeff waded into the water. He took hold of her shoulders. "I'm not trying to stay away from you, if that's what you're thinking."

She chuckled cynically, the sound breezing away on a sudden gust of wind. "You're doing an awfully good job of staying away. You knew I was expecting you yesterday, but you changed plans without an explanation. You were supposed to pick me up at six tonight. You could have said hello to my father, you could have shown both of us your pictures, we could have had a relaxing hour or so before going out to dinner, but again you changed plans without an explanation."

"I had to make preparations for the Jordan trip and it was taking longer than I expected. And...I didn't want to tell you I was heading to the Middle East in a text message. I wanted to tell you in person."

"I left you phone messages that you didn't return. Have you forgotten that you can do more than send a text message on a cell phone?"

He cradled her face in his hands, and she looked into his eyes. Oh, how she wished she could read what was going on behind them. Had he fallen out of love with her? If he had, then why had he come tonight?

"I'm sorry," he whispered at last, his words nearly drowned out by the surf. "I don't have to leave town until noon tomorrow. We can spend the morning together. Come out here and play on the beach. Take your dad out to breakfast. Whatever you want."

"What do *you* want?" she asked him flatly. "Right now, I can't tell if you want to be with me or not. You've become a complete enigma in the past few days."

"I do want to be with you," he answered, but she knew down deep that there was something more that he was leaving unsaid.

Somehow she found the energy to smile. She wasn't about to stay upset and ruin their chance to spend a few hours together. She wanted him; she was going to fight to keep him.

"How would you like to take some pictures of me tomorrow morning?"

One of his dark brows rose. "You want your picture taken? That's a new one."

"For my campaign, silly! I don't want anything fancy or too formal. A couple of shots taken in front of Father's house would work."

He shook his head. "I've seen way too many stuffy campaign photos in my lifetime. Why don't you put on a pair of white pants—"

"It's after Labor Day. A woman never wears white after Labor Day."

He rolled his eyes. "Okay, wear something breezy. That yellow sundress that I like. A pair of flip-flops."

"I don't wear flip-flops." She grinned. "You should know by now that I'm not a flip-flop kind of girl."

He winked. "Sandals, then."

She smiled slowly, happy that their banter was back to normal. "I've got a lot of sandals, but I know just the perfect pair."

He kissed the top of her head, her forehead, then her lips. "I've missed you," he whispered.

"Me too."

A strong wave hit their legs, knocking both of them off balance and into the surf, soaking them through and through. At last they were both able to laugh, and the laughter, along with being caught in his embrace, was just what Beverly had needed.

Chapter Twelve

It's Saturday morning, Dan. Couldn't you put your books away for just one day and go down to the beach to play with me and the kids?"

Dan looked up from the technical manual open wide on the kitchen table. His eyes were bloodshot from staring so much at one electrical diagram after another, all of which looked to Shelley like Emma's scribbles.

"You've been at that since five this morning, and you're looking a little downtrodden." Shelley kissed her husband's cheek. "Come on, honey, let's go out and play. One morning away from the books won't hurt."

Dan sighed heavily, downed the last of his coffee, and pushed up out of his chair. "Two hours and not a minute more," he said with a crooked smile, "and then I've got to hit the books again."

She'd complain, but becoming an electrician and apprenticing for Wayne Stover, learning a craft that was fulfilling and would put bread on the table, had put a new spring in Dan's step. He loved the work, and bringing home a good and steady paycheck had made him happier than he'd been in the last couple of years. For the first time since they married, there were a few extra dollars left over each week for the occasional splurge.

"I'll slather Aiden and Emma up good with sunscreen and get them into their swimsuits," Dan said, grabbing one of Shelley's freshly made cookies and taking a whopping bite. "Do you want to pack some sodas?"

Shelley smiled. "Already done. There's fried chicken and watermelon too."

"And just how long have you been planning this beach excursion?"

"Since you left for Bangor at the beginning of the week." She gave him another peck on the cheek. "I've missed you."

★ ★ ★

Shelley stretched out on her beach towel, lying on her stomach reading a magazine.

When she looked up she saw Dan and the kids playing in the sand and smiled contentedly. Rolling over on her towel, she reached into her tote bag for her camera, but grabbed her cell phone instead when she heard the ring telling her she had a text message.

BBQ on the beach tonight at six. Come meet my sister-in-law. Kids, spouses, and friends welcome. Afterward I'll tell you what we discovered in the documents. Diane.

It seemed ages since they'd all gotten together for a beach bash, especially an impromptu one. She'd have to run to the store for marshmallows, big fat ones to be roasted for s'mores. The kids would want hot dogs, of course. So would Dan. She'd have to put Aiden and Emma down for nice long naps this afternoon so they wouldn't fall asleep in the middle of the party.

And now she wondered what news Diane had to tell them about the treasure.

Shelley quickly texted Diane back, asking if there was anything she could bring. The answer came immediately.

Your appetites. This one's on me!

Just as she started to put the phone down and grab her camera, it rang again. This time it was an actual phone call, and Susannah's name appeared on the screen. That was twice in just a few days, and once again, Shelley wondered what was going on.

"Hey there!" She kept her voice bright, giving her sister the benefit of the doubt, hoping that Susannah wanted nothing more than to become close again.

"I hear giggling in the background," Susannah said. "Did I interrupt something?"

"No, not at all. We're down at the beach—"

"All of you? Dan too?" Susannah sounded surprised.

"It's been ages since we had a completely free day," Shelley said. "No work. No company coming. Nothing."

"Remember when we were little and Mom and Dad took us camping?"

She remembered it well. "Acadia National Park, and if I remember correctly, it was the one and only time."

"Mom didn't like the insects buzzing around."

"Dad had trouble putting up the tent." Shelley laughed, remembering those days. "I don't think you liked sleeping in the tent either."

The whole camping trip had concluded on a sour note, one of many family outings that had ended in the same way, Shelley remembered sadly. She looked up to see Dan holding Emma in one arm and Aiden in the other, running into the surf and letting them splash around. She'd worked hard to keep her own family from ending up a mess.

Susannah was quiet, the long silence stretching out until it grew uncomfortable.

"Are you okay, Suze?" Shelley's worry came back full force.

"Yeah. Fine."

Those words were said with so little energy and even less joy that Shelley knew something was wrong. "You can tell me, Suze. I don't know if I can help, but I can pray. That's what I do whenever I'm in trouble or hurting or even when good things are happening in my life."

"Well," Susannah said. She was silent, and Shelley could hear her breathing. "Do you remember the pact we made one of those times when Mom and Dad were arguing? We said if something happened to either of us, the other would step in and take care of the other sister's child or children?"

"Are you sick?" It was the first thing that came to Shelley's mind.

"No, I'm not sick. I'm simply asking a question. You know. For future reference."

A chill ran up Shelley's spine despite the sun and warm air. "I kind of remember the pact," Shelley said, and then the reason for coming up with the pact came back to her, as did the night they'd come up with it. It was the night of *the* big fight, the one that split their parents up for good, even though it was the culmination of an entire marriage full of turbulence that caused the divorce. "We were hiding under the covers in our bedroom. We had the radio on, listening to one of those boy bands—"

"Which was weird because you always liked country music." A touch of laughter had actually sounded in Susannah's voice. Maybe there wasn't anything really going on. Maybe Susannah just needed confirmation that Shelley would be there for her if she needed help.

"Yeah, I did, still do, and you never really liked boy bands that much either—"

"My tastes were a little...louder than that. So why in the world were we listening to that stuff?" They both laughed, and then reminisced about some of the good times in their lives. The conversation had turned away from "the pact," and Shelley hoped to keep it that way. She imagined she could take care of Hailey, if needed, but never in her wildest dreams could she imagine Susannah taking care of Emma and Aiden. In her teens, Susannah had turned into such wild child.

"So you do remember the pact?" Susannah asked, bringing Shelley back from her thoughts.

"I remember."

"Well, look, I don't want to interrupt your fun with Dan and the kids, and I've got to get going. I promised Hailey I'd take her to the show, although I'm not sure what we'll see. I'm not crazy about cartoons, but I suppose I'll have to give in."

They talked a few moments longer, at last ending the conversation with Susannah saying she hoped they could keep in touch. "I've really enjoyed talking to you, Shelley. We shouldn't have let so much time get between us."

A lot of time and different lives, Shelley thought, and completely different ways of thinking.

"Who was that?" Dan asked, plopping down on a towel beside her while Aiden and Emma continued to play in the sand.

"Susannah."

"You sounded pretty chummy."

"We don't have much in common," Shelley admitted. "In fact, except for looking like twins—"

"Shel, she looks much older than you."

"Hard living will do that to a person, I'm afraid. Even when we were teenagers we headed down different paths. I don't really know what path she's been on for the past ten years, but I'm afraid it hasn't been the best one she could have chosen."

"If you're worried about her influence spreading into our family, I don't think you need to worry. She doesn't live at all close and, from what your dad and Maggie told us, she has a lot of friends."

"A lot of the wrong friends, from what I've heard."

"If you're thinking you can change that, I don't know if that's possible, unless she wants to change."

"But I think there's something else going on. Something that might end up affecting us, just when we're getting our own lives where we'd like them to be."

Dan frowned. "Oh?"

Shelley told Dan about the conversation, leaving nothing out, including her worry that Susannah might be ill. She also told him about the pact. "What if she wants us to take care of Hailey?"

"She didn't come straight out and ask you to, did she?"

"No, but this is the second time she's called in only a few days, and both times she's sounded strange, as if there's something dreadful she wants to tell me."

"Are you sure your imagination isn't running wild?"

"It could be." Shelley finally took her camera from her tote bag and took pictures of Emma and Aiden, their bodies dotted with wet sand. "But what if it isn't? How would we deal with another child around the house, especially a young girl? I remember what I was like at nine and ten. I wanted so much to be grown up, or at least a teenager. I'm sure I wasn't always the easiest kid to live with."

Dan slung his arm around her shoulder and pulled her against him. "I remember my folks taking in a shirttail relative, a boy who was right about my age—eleven or twelve, I think—and it turned out to be pretty cool."

"You already had a lot of brothers and sisters. What was one more?"

"Something like that, I guess."

"Maybe I am overreacting about Susannah." She snapped a few more photos of her little ones, then drew in a deep breath.

"Let's just cross that bridge when we come to it," Dan said.

She smiled at Dan and kissed his cheek. "I love you. You know that, don't you?"

He grinned. "Yeah, I'm a pretty good guy to have around."

She couldn't agree more.

CHAPTER THIRTEEN

Whatever you do, don't take two giant steps backward, or you'll fall over the cliff."

Beverly stood on the rocky precipice of Orlean Point, holding her big straw hat on her head and smiling at Jeff, who aimed his camera in her direction, snapping one photo after another. "I'm not about to move, especially backward, but there's nothing that says the wind that's kicking up won't drag me over the edge right along with it."

"I might win a Pulitzer if I was able to snap a shot like that," Jeff teased.

"I'd rather you win it taking photos of something wonderful in Jordan. Just make sure you don't snap anything dangerous, anything that could get you in trouble."

"Jordan might be in the Middle East, but it's safe there. The crime rate's extremely low. If you're worried—"

"I'm not." She was far more worried that he might not come back at all—to her, that is. But she wasn't about to tell him that. Today—this morning, the last couple of hours they had together before he boarded another plane and flew half a world away—she wanted to believe that all was normal, that he wanted to be with her as much as he always had.

"Come here," Jeff said, walking toward her and taking her hand. "Let's get some pictures with the lighthouse in the background."

"Everyone takes pictures with the lighthouse. I thought you wanted to do something different."

"Trust me, Beverly, mine will be different. Who knows? The mysterious lights might return and I'll capture them shining down on you."

She laughed. "And everyone in town will say they were doctored up or computer enhanced, and the last thing I want is for people to think I'm a fake."

"That's not going to happen. The people who know you— and love you—admire you because you're open and honest. They know you won't steer them wrong on anything."

Jeff snapped his fingers. "I've got an idea. The perfect place to take your photo."

Beverly looked at her watch. "It's almost noon. Not that I want you to run off, but you said you had to leave by twelve in order to catch your plane. I don't want you to be late, not for something as fabulous as a trip to Jordan."

"This photo and the caption you're going to put under it is going to be incredible."

Jeff captured her hand and tore off. It was all she could do to keep up with him. She was a runner, but she was wearing a dress and sandals right now, not spandex and running shoes, yet somehow she raced down the steps right behind him, headed for his Subaru Forester. He opened the door for her to climb in.

"Are you going to tell me where you're taking me?"

Jeff shook his head. "It's a surprise."

This was the Jeff she was used to, the Jeff she'd fallen in love with, a man who did things on the spur of the moment, who'd dragged her—almost kicking and screaming—out of her straitlaced and orderly ways. Well, dragged her a little bit out. She couldn't possibly change completely.

They raced through town, Jeff taking some of the turns a little too fast. "Do you mind slowing down? I want to be sure we get to this secret place all in one piece."

"We're almost there."

The moment they hit the dirt road she knew exactly where they were going, to a beautiful plot of land surrounded by lush forests that overlooked the ocean. "This is where Dennis Calder wanted to build his resort."

"Exactly."

Jeff pulled the SUV to a sudden halt, hopped out of the car with his camera gear, and met her on the other side.

"This is what you need to put on your Web site. This is what you need to put in your campaign brochures. Photos of you and this glorious landscape that would have all been destroyed if you hadn't stopped its development."

Jeff used his light meter to check the lighting, positioned Beverly exactly where he thought he could find the perfect shot, then started snapping pictures, having her pose with one arm hanging down at her side and the straw hat dangling from her fingertips. "Shade your eyes with your hand and look all about, from the trees to the ocean, to that crane flying overhead."

He snapped and snapped.

"You won't need to mention any names—*ahem*, Dennis Calder, for instance—along with these photos. You just need to tout what *you* did, not what a big developer wanted to do to this pristine forest. You'll need a headline, something along the lines of 'She's a Fighter—and She'll Fight for You.' It'll be perfect. Absolutely perfect."

She believed him—how could she not? His enthusiasm was like a jolt of adrenaline. She'd wanted him working at her side during the campaign, but sadly that wasn't going to happen, not at this time anyway. Maybe later, when—*if*—he came back to her after his trip to Jordan.

He had to come back. She would definitely fight for him.

★ ★ ★

"This is Old First," Diane said, standing beneath a giant maple that cast its shade on the two-hundred-plus-year-old Gothic church.

"If only it could talk. Imagine the stories it could tell," Jeanette said.

It does talk, in its own way. Diane couldn't help but think of the bell the friends had heard ring out the night of the fire and on several other occasions.

Jeanette snapped photos of the church with a tiny digital camera. "As much fun as shopping has been, it's architecture like this and the history of the building that excites me most when I'm vacationing."

"I wish I could take you inside, but Reverend Locke was adamant about keeping everyone out for safety's sake."

"What fun it would be if we could explore the interior." Jeanette's smile bore a touch of impishness that reminded Diane of Eric. "I know you and your friends have searched the tower, but there could be a secret crypt far beneath its floor or rooms hidden behind bookcases in the pastor's office, you know, where escaped slaves were given sanctuary as part of the underground railroad. Perhaps your Jeremiah Thorpe played a role in fighting slavery."

"I wouldn't be surprised." Diane chuckled. "If only we'd found something like that in the documentation. However, if there were secret rooms and passageways, I'm sure Reverend Locke would have found them by now. And trust me, my friends and I have examined everything possible looking for Reverend Locke's treasure, but we've found nothing—only clues that have led us nowhere."

"Maybe you're too desperate to find the treasure. Someday, when you least expect it, it might pop into your hands."

"That would be lovely. Until then"—Diane laughed— "maybe we should get back home and start preparing for tonight's barbecue."

It wasn't long before they were back at the cottage, and Jeanette and Diane were bringing in groceries. "I'm going to get started on the potato and fruit salads," Diane said, "but you're my guest, so—"

"Don't you dare relegate me to another part of the house or out on the porch to sit in a rocker and watch the world go by. Give me something to do or I'll go stir-crazy."

"Feel like carving the watermelon?"

"Just give me a knife. Unless you're set on putting the whole thing in a bowl, I can whip up a pretty decent watermelon basket in no time at all."

"I'd forgotten all about your culinary skills," Diane said, envying Jeanette's ability to turn a box of macaroni and cheese plus a few additional items from the pantry into a gourmet dish. Her kids had always loved eating at Auntie Jeanette's.

"It helps when you go on sabbatical to places like France and Italy and take cooking classes while you're there."

"And here I thought you locked yourself away in libraries all day."

"Not on your life, although I do more than my fair share of that." Jeanette put the extralarge watermelon into the sink and washed the outside. "I sometimes wonder why I didn't become an art historian instead of an English professor. I could have done both, I suppose, especially after I spent so many years filling my head with details about the Old Masters, the Realists, Pre-Raphaelites, and all the others."

"You'll enjoy talking with my friend Margaret," Diane said.

"I'll look forward to that. But when it was all said and done, in spite of my love for art, it is the English language that intrigues me the most."

"You and Eric both." Diane sighed.

Jeanette dried off the watermelon and expertly cut into it. "Yes, you could tell we were related. But tell me more about your movie deal."

"It's just an option."

"Not *just*." Jeanette shook her head. "It very well might be made into a movie, and whether it is or not, there aren't that many people who can say they've had a book published *and* had it optioned by a Hollywood studio."

"Well if the movie gets made it could help pay off Jessica's student loans and maybe, just maybe, help put a new roof on Old First."

"You really are fascinated by the place, aren't you?"

"It kind of grows on you."

It wasn't long before Jeanette had cut the watermelon into a beautiful basket with scalloped edges. She'd made melon balls from honeydew, cantaloupe, and what was left of the watermelon that she and Diane hadn't eaten while they worked. She tossed in blackberries, blueberries, and bananas, and the fruit salad was suddenly a feast for the eyes.

"Need help with the potato salad?" Jeanette asked. "Want me to pack things up to take down to the beach?"

"All under control," Diane said, standing at the sink peeling the potatoes. "Why don't you kick back and relax. You're going to need a little downtime before school starts, and you definitely haven't had any yet."

"Don't mind if I do."

But Jeanette didn't sit down. She walked about the living room, opening the cabinet where Diane kept the old teapot that was a Spencer family heirloom. From the corner of her eye, Diane could see Jeanette looking deep inside the cabinet, as if she might be looking for something else, then taking the teapot out of the case, holding it gingerly—almost lovingly. "This teapot is stunning," Jeanette said, carefully holding the lid in place while turning it upside down to look at the marker's mark. "It's Meissen, you know."

"Actually, I didn't." Diane chuckled. "China doesn't exactly fall in my areas of expertise." But it was apparent that Jeanette knew quite a lot.

"Probably from the mideighteenth century." Jeanette turned it upright again. She looked at Diane and smiled. "Your Reverend Thorpe might have brought something similar with him when he came to America."

Diane stayed put at the kitchen counter, mixing up a batch of cookies, but watched the gentle way Jeanette traced the dark red roses painted on the pot. She couldn't remember ever doing something like that. She usually gave it a quick dust and put it back in the display cabinet.

"Will you be giving the teapot to Jessica someday?" Jeanette asked.

What, Diane wondered, was Jeanette's fascination with the teapot? It was old and chipped. Did it hold some sentimental connection between Jeanette and her grandmother? She hadn't said so. Of course, maybe she just wanted to make conversation.

"I'd give it to her now if she had more time in her life to devote to antiques and collectibles," Diane answered. "Until she has a china cabinet where she can keep the teapot, I'm hanging on to it."

Jeanette looked thoughtful as she put the teapot back into the cabinet and closed the door.

Chapter Fourteen

The sun was sinking fast in the west and the moon was slowly on the rise. The women—and it was always the women, Margaret mused, except for her dear Allan, who could always be counted on to help—had cleaned up, throwing away paper plates that had held a bounty of potato salad, fruit, and hot dogs. Dan and Allan and even Beverly's aging dad, Mr. Wheeland, had grilled dozens of hot dogs to feed the hungry crowd. It had been such a beautiful evening, even though Diane had refused to divulge even the slightest tidbit about what she and Jeanette had discovered in the papers until the barbecue was over.

Adelaide grabbed Margaret's hand only seconds after she tied up a heavy black trash bag. "Come on, Mom. We have to sing songs with Aiden and Emma."

"Why don't we see if we can get everyone to sing?" Margaret looked a short way down the beach and spotted Shelley playing Frisbee with Dan, Diane, her sister-in-law Jeanette, and even Allan, who would definitely complain of sore knees and shoulders tomorrow morning.

"Find a comfy place for you and the little ones around the fire," Margaret told Adelaide. "Just make sure Aiden and

Emma stay right by your side and don't get too close to the fire. I'll round up everyone else so we can get the singing going."

"I'll help with the kiddies," Mrs. Peabody said. She'd been so quiet most of the night—something quite unusual—that Margaret had almost forgotten that her Newport Avenue neighbor had come out to spend the evening with the crowd.

"Listen up, everyone," Margaret called out, and it only took a good thirty seconds or so for the Frisbee crowd to actually stop what they were doing to listen to what she had to say. "Before we roast marshmallows for the s'mores, we're going to have a sing-along." She heard her husband groan first. "I don't want to hear complaints out of any of you. Now come gather around the fire. Adelaide's going to kick things off."

"Well done." Beverly brushed up against Margaret and smiled. "Spoken like a drill sergeant. Maybe you should be running for mayor instead of me."

Margaret let out a halfhearted chuckle. "You're going to nail the election in a landslide. Besides, most everyone in Marble Cove knows I'm a pushover. I just put on a good show every once in a while."

"So what are we going to sing?" Dan asked Adelaide, pulling Aiden up and into his lap when he sat down beside her on a beach chair.

"I got a list of kid songs from my teacher at college. We can sing some of them, to give me practice for when I start working."

"Perfect idea." Allan smiled his encouragement to his daughter. "But let's put a limit on the number we sing. Does three sound good? Your mom won't let me eat s'mores all that often, and I'm dying to have something sweet."

"Okay. Three. My teacher—Miss Stewart—says it's not good to sing too long because little kids get bored. They need a...a variety"—she sounded out the four syllables slowly—"of activities."

"Okay, three it is." Shelley sat on the other side of Adelaide, bouncing Emma on her lap, and everyone else sat around the fire. "What's first?"

Adelaide thought hard for a moment or two. "How 'bout 'She'll Be Comin' 'Round the Mountain.' Do you know that song?"

"I haven't sung it in a good fifty or sixty years," Mrs. Peabody said, "but I'm willing. Just don't anyone laugh at my voice. This night air isn't kind to it."

"All right," Adelaide said, holding her hands up, index fingers extended, as if she were about to lead a band. "I'll start." She cleared her throat. "She'll be comin' 'round the mountain when she comes."

"When she comes," Allan and Mr. Wheeland echoed in tandem baritone voices.

"She'll be comin' 'round the mountain when she comes." Everyone gathered around the fire sang, and again Allan and Mr. Wheeland followed up with, "When she comes," now joined by Dan.

"She'll be drivin' six white horses when she comes."

"When she comes!"

Margaret had tears of laughter streaking down her face by the time they finished the song, most everyone forgetting what lyrics came after "We'll kill the old red rooster when she comes," but that was okay with Adelaide and Aiden. They were ready to move on to the next song, and Adelaide chose something softer, a song Margaret remembered from her Girl Scout days, when she went to camp with her friends. "Michael, row the boat ashore, hallelujah!" they sang. Beverly and Diane had linked arms and everyone was swaying, even the little ones.

They ended with "Row, row, row your boat, gently down the stream." Adelaide had even assigned groups to sing each round. All in all, it was a rousing success, and Adelaide would get even more extra credit for what she had done tonight.

Margaret, Beverly, Diane, Shelley, and Jeanette jumped up to get the marshmallows on the sticks, and the men started toasting away.

"Make sure they're a nice golden color," Mrs. Peabody said flatly. "I don't like mine burned."

Mr. Wheeland held the marshmallow he'd been toasting out in front of Mrs. Peabody. "How's this look?"

She smiled, the thin, wrinkled skin on her face crinkling even more around her eyes.

It was nice to get Mrs. P. out and about, socializing with most everyone else on Newport Avenue. It was probably an evening she wouldn't soon forget. Margaret knew she wouldn't.

The moon was rising quickly in the sky when Dan, a fast-asleep child in each arm, headed for home to put the little ones to bed. "I've got to hit the books for an hour or two," he told Shelley, "so stay out here and have fun for a while."

Allan gave Margaret a kiss and told her to do the same, then he and Adelaide, their arms tucked through Mr. Wheeland's and Mrs. Peabody's, helped them across the beach, planning to escort both of them home. That's the way things were done on Newport Avenue, and Margaret wouldn't have it any other way.

"Anyone care for another s'more?" Diane asked, holding up the still half-full bag of marshmallows.

"Quit stalling, Diane." Beverly laughed. "You know we're dying to learn what you and Jeanette discovered in the paperwork Dr. Standish sent."

"It's late, and I'm tired," Margaret said, but quickly added, "but not too tired to talk mystery!"

"Why don't we pack up everything and head back to your place, Diane?" Shelley suggested. "We can toast marshmallows over the stove, if you're insistent on having more s'mores, but I really think we want to see those papers."

Diane grinned. "All right. I suppose I've kept you in suspense long enough."

Fifteen minutes later, with the countertops in Diane's kitchen covered with leftovers, the five women gathered around Diane's dining table, all eyes focusing on the paperwork Diane and Jeanette had spread out.

"Remember the document Dr. Standish told us about?" Diane asked, looking at Beverly. "The one that tagged Reverend Locke with the moniker 'the Bandit Preacher'?"

"The one that said he was in league with pirates?" Beverly asked.

Diane nodded. "Dr. Standish actually found it." Diane lifted a sheet of pure white copy paper and waved it in the air. "Here it is. It's actually a newspaper article."

"You're having fun with this, aren't you, Diane?" Margaret shook her head, but Diane couldn't miss the grin on her friend's face. "Why don't you read it to us so we all know what it says?"

Diane tried not to laugh as she set her reading glasses on the end of her nose. She knew her friends were getting impatient. At last she began to read. "One week ago, May 20, one Robert Gilbert, parishioner of First Church, publicly confronted the Reverend Jeremiah Thorpe before a crowd of his peers, accusing him of absconding with funds from church coffers. While no proof has been offered, it is well known amongst the gentlemen of Marble Cove, according to Robert Gilbert, that the reverend and the once notorious pirate, Booth Adair, deceased, had been in business together."

"I guess it wasn't *Old* First way back then," Shelley noted.

Diane looked up, then continued. "While Reverend Thorpe does not acknowledge the truth of Robert Gilbert's accusation, neither does he refute it. In the words of Reverend Thorpe, 'I adhere to the principle that all men should be allowed freedom of speech, whether that speech is right, wrong, or blasphemous. Our Lord and Savior knows the truth, and it is only our Lord and Savior to whom I will answer.'"

Beverly shook her head. "Our Reverend Thorpe obviously practiced what he preached, but that stubbornness didn't do anything for his reputation. He ruined it."

"With the help of a newspaper that printed the accusations without having any proof," Shelley said.

"Unfortunately, the news media does the same thing today," Margaret added. "I've nearly stopped listening to and reading any news reports. It's all so depressing, and I never know what's right or wrong."

"The press at the time was known for printing scurrilous information," Jeanette stated, then chuckled. "What was it George Washington once said?" She wrinkled her brow for a moment. "Oh yes. Something along the lines of 'I'm tired of being buffeted in the public prints by a set of infamous scribblers.'"

"There is more, a little further down in the article," Diane said, squinting at the awkward print in the newspaper article. "Robert Gilbert, according to one Henry Fellowes, proprietor of the local candle factory, raised his fist in the air and shouted, 'You're nothing but a Bandit Preacher' at Reverend Thorpe. As of this writing, six parishioners have called for the resignation of Reverend Thorpe and another nine have left First Church to seek spiritual comfort elsewhere."

"So that's where that vicious nickname came from." Beverly shook her head in disgust. "Robert Gilbert could very well have been nothing more than a disgruntled parishioner."

"Very true," Margaret added. "Reverend Thorpe could have discovered Robert Gilbert lying about something, or spreading malicious gossip, or who knows what, and confronted him."

"I bet this Robert Gilbert wanted to tarnish the name of Reverend Thorpe," Shelley said, "so no one would believe him should the truth about Mr. Gilbert's discretions come out."

"Unfortunately," Beverly said, "this article doesn't shed any light whatsoever on the truth. Unless we find something to disprove Mr. Gilbert's story, the Bandit Preacher moniker could stick with Reverend Thorpe for another couple of centuries—or longer."

"Yes—it could," Diane said, "except Dr. Standish found some other documents too. Nothing that sheds any light on the treasure, but"—Diane smiled—"internal church memos detailing an investigation that was undertaken by the church council following Robert Gilbert's diatribe."

"Have you read them all?" Beverly asked.

Diane shook her head. "I wish. Thankfully Jeanette has been able to help translate some of the writing. The old flowery cursive can be such a challenge to read. We've only gotten through a portion of them, but it does appear that Robert Gilbert was indeed disgruntled, and the accusations should never have been leveled at Reverend Thorpe."

"But did they say he was innocent of all the charges?" Beverly asked.

"No, but I'm sure we'll find that once we're able to read more of the documents," Diane stated.

"At least there's some good news," Beverly exclaimed. "If only Reverend Locke were in town so we could call him and let him know."

"If only there was something in those papers about the treasure." Shelley laughed. "I know, I have a one-track mind. I mean, it's wonderful to learn the truth about Reverend Thorpe, but that doesn't help much with Old First's restoration." Her face turned serious. "Promise me you won't say anything, but Dan's mother told me that Reverend Locke is refusing to take a salary until after the roof repairs are finished."

The others looked at her in surprise. "Well, I always knew he was an honorable man," Margaret said, but then chuckled. "Even if we did suspect him a bit there for a while."

"It would be wonderful if we could find something definite in the papers Dr. Standish sent us," Shelley added. "I'd love to help Reverend Locke start collecting his paycheck again."

"I have to head home early tomorrow morning, but I could take the papers with me and try to find time to decipher them," Jeanette offered.

"We'd hate to put you to all that trouble," Diane said, but she knew she herself didn't have any more time than anyone else to read through everything, not with her doctor's appointment coming up and a book that desperately needed to be worked on.

"You forget, Diane. Reading old documents is one of my passions."

"But school starts—"

"I'll find the time." Jeanette smiled. "And I'll come back next Friday night, if that's okay with you."

"It's more than okay," Diane said, thrilled at the thought of having Jeanette with her for another couple of days.

"If only we could get back inside Old First," Jeanette said. "I'm just sure there's something you've missed while looking around."

"Reverend Locke will never let us back inside," Beverly said. "But...I'll ask again. He knows our motives are good, and we've all pooled our information now."

Jeanette frowned, her face filled with puzzlement, then glanced at her watch. "Did you hear that?"

Diane looked from Beverly, to Margaret, to Shelley, each of them wearing a knowing smile. Jeanette shook her head. "I thought I heard a church bell, but it's seven minutes after ten. Church bells never ring at such an odd time."

CHAPTER FIFTEEN

Beverly sat beside her father inside Marble Cove Community Church's spacious auditorium. The seats were plush and comfortable, different from the hard wood they sat on in Old First. Still, she shifted uncomfortably in her seat as she looked around. Only thirty or so members of their congregation had come to the services Reverend Locke held on Sunday afternoons, two hours after Marble Cove Community's parishioners finished their fellowship, cleaned up, and went home. It felt hollow inside, and Reverend Locke's voice echoed as if they were in a cavern.

Beverly had been surprised to see him standing at the pulpit this afternoon. Hadn't he told Diane that he would be at a seminar this weekend? *What had happened?* she wondered.

"Why does he insist on using the microphone?" Mr. Wheeland asked, leaning close to Beverly to whisper loudly in her ear. "If he'd just ask us all to move a little closer to the front, we could hear him quite well without use of that electronic gadget he has clipped to his collar."

Like so many others, he wanted to be back in his own church. The roof wasn't finished yet, and even those repairs threatened to deplete the church's resources. Beverly had even looked through the town charter and through all the legal documents on file in the mayor's office to see if it was possible for the town council to give Old First a grant to restore it to its former glory. But that was an impossibility. Grants of that kind weren't allowed—period—in spite of what Dennis Calder had told Reverend Locke.

Dear God, she prayed silently, *help us find a way to restore our place of worship.*

Reverend Locke looked tired when they filed out of the church, yet he smiled at all his parishioners, many of those in attendance were long-time residents of Marble Cove. "Lovely service," Beverly said, taking Reverend Locke's extended hand. "It's a shame the entire sanctuary wasn't filled to capacity to hear your message."

"It's God's message. I'm just the messenger."

"Well then, His messenger did a rather nice job delivering it, and I'm so glad it was you doing the delivering." Beverly smiled. "I'd heard you'd be away this weekend and was expecting a substitute pastor this morning."

He nodded. "I left the seminar yesterday afternoon. Being here with all of you seemed far more important. The congregation has already had to deal with too much sudden change, and there are many people who don't feel as comfortable worshiping here as they do at Old First. I couldn't very well spring a substitute pastor on everyone too."

"Well, I for one am thankful you were here with us this morning."

He patted her hand gently before letting it go. "How was your party on the beach last night? You and your friends looked like you were having a great time. I particularly liked the way everyone was singing 'Michael, Row the Boat Ashore.' It's an old favorite of mine."

"You should have joined us."

"Thank you, but it was one of those beautiful nights when I needed a quiet walk on the beach. I also didn't know yet what message God wanted me to deliver today, so I was out there talking with Him about it."

Beverly laughed. She wanted to ask Reverend Locke if he'd have a few minutes later in the afternoon to talk about Old First, about the new documents that had been discovered, but there were still a few others behind her waiting to wish the reverend a good afternoon and to thank him for his words, so she moved on, holding her father's arm as they walked out to the grass and stopped in the shade of a trio of fir trees. Her father always liked to stop after church, hoping to chat with old friends.

"Not many people here today," he said. "I suppose there isn't much reason to hang around, except that it's good for your run for mayor. Gives you a little extra exposure."

"I'm sure most of the people in the congregation are getting tired of me these days. After all, I've asked them to buy fund-raiser tickets and for rummage sale donations, baked goods donations, and plain old monetary donations, anything extra they can spare to put in the repair-the-church coffers. It's tough to keep asking the same people over and over, especially when they're on fixed incomes or struggling from a sluggish economy."

"On the other hand, they're more than likely happy that you're the one doing the asking, so they don't have to do it. Someone's got to stand up and fight for the church, and I've begun to think that a lot of our congregation has just grown too tired to fight. Not that they wouldn't do it if they could."

"I just wish all my begging would do some good."

"Have faith, Beverly."

The pastor turned his attention to some other parishioners and Beverly and her father spoke to a few other couples, long-time friends of Mr. Wheeland's and Ralph and Frances Bauer.

It was nearly half an hour later, when most of the congregation had departed, that Beverly caught sight of Reverend Locke strolling across the parklike property surrounding Marble Cove Community Church. His hands were tucked into his pants pockets; his head was down. He could be praying as he walked, or he could be downcast, completely disheartened by the near loss of his church.

"Would you mind driving yourself home?" Beverly asked her father. "I'd like to talk with Reverend Locke, and it's such a pretty day that I won't mind the long walk home."

"You're sure? I could wait here for you."

"No, please. I'll be fine."

Beverly took her car keys from her purse and handed them to her father. "Don't speed."

He gave her a swift salute and sauntered slowly toward his big Buick, the lone vehicle left in the parking lot. Once she saw that he was in the car with the seat belt on, Beverly struck out across the churchyard. She had a feeling that Reverend Locke was headed for Old First, and she hoped she could catch him before he went inside, something she imagined he did quite often, even though the inspectors had said it wasn't safe.

He was leaning against the trunk of an ancient maple, one reputedly planted by Jeremiah Thorpe, staring at the stone exterior of the eighteenth-century church. "We should build a circular bench to surround this tree when we get around to doing restorations," he said, as if he'd heard her footsteps or knew that she'd followed him to the church.

"Something tells me you've been visiting the sanctuary and your office and any number of places inside, even though you've been warned to stay out."

His sudden grin was infectious. "I've been told I have a hard head. If something falls, it might knock me out for a minute or two, but I'm sure I'll rise again. It's hard to keep me down."

"I wouldn't mind going back inside."

He shook his head. "No."

"If it's safe enough for you, why shouldn't it be safe enough for me?"

Reverend Locke sighed, "Beverly, I can't put my parishoners in danger, you know that."

Trying to change the subject, he went on, "Your friend Diane told me last week that her sister-in-law was bringing some archival documents to her over the weekend that might clear Reverend Thorpe's name."

"Yes, in fact, if we'd known you were here last night, we would have invited you to join us at Diane's to look at them."

One of Reverend Locke's eyebrows rose. "Did you uncover anything interesting?"

Beverly smiled brightly as she nodded. "We discovered that it was a disgruntled parishioner who tagged him with that dreadful moniker."

"Then he wasn't a bandit?" Reverend Locked smiled, but he seemed to sense Beverly hadn't told him everything.

"Most of what we've just been given are internal church memos. Heaven only knows how they left Old First's possession and ended up at Portland College, but they did, and they've obviously been hidden for decades."

"And what did they tell you?"

"We haven't been able to read them all. Diane's sister-in-law has taken them back to the college with her and she's going to decipher them for us. The handwriting is difficult for most of us to read, and she's an expert."

"Please, Beverly, I know you want to fill me in on all the details, but could you tell me what you were able to find?"

"I'm sorry." She smiled, realizing she was still caught up in the excitement of what they'd learned. "The church council investigated the allegations against Reverend Thorpe—that he'd siphoned church funds and was working with a pirate named Adair. We haven't found details of the actual outcome, but I'm sure Jeanette will. We did, however, find that the council launched an investigation into the man who leveled the scurrilous charges against Reverend Thorpe. Apparently the man was upset with the reverend and got back at him by claiming that he was a thief—a Bandit Preacher! The name, unfortunately, has stuck around all these years."

"It doesn't appear that the church council made much effort to see that the slur was expunged from Reverend Thorpe's reputation."

"Sadly, no, but that doesn't mean that we can't do that, once we know the whole truth."

"I don't know if we'll ever know the whole truth, after all these years, but it seems you've found at least some important parts of it."

Reverend Locke seemed to relax, and he offered Beverly a genuine smile. "I'm certainly glad I've gotten to know you and your friends, Beverly. The whole Bandit Preacher nonsense has haunted me since before I went to the seminary. Who would have believed that the hunt for buried treasure could lead to the restoration of a man's good name?"

"That hasn't quite happened yet, but it will. I'm sure of it."

"By the way," Reverend Locke said, "there were a few moments last week when I believed we might not need that treasure after all."

Beverly frowned. "Really?"

"Really. Dennis Calder tells me that if he's elected mayor, he'll have the town council issue a grant to repair the roof. It seemed like such a generous offer when he first approached me about it, but after a couple of sleepless nights, thinking how far off the election is and how long it might take to get a grant approved, I realized that the town could no more issue a grant for Old First than they could for any of the other churches. They couldn't set a precedent. Besides, the town coffers are almost always just shy of empty."

"I did check into the feasibility of a grant, and you're right. It can't be done."

"Do you have any ideas you can pull out of a hat?"

"More fund-raisers."

"And a ten-year wait." He chuckled. "We need more than bake and rummage sales, and the hopes of finding gold doubloons to save the day."

"Let me go back into the church." Beverly said the words softly. One of these times he'd get tired of saying no.

"There's nothing more in the church. There are no secret passages. No hidden rooms. I ought to know—I've looked. We could sell off the stained-glass windows to cover the cost of a new roof, but those windows are part of the heart and soul of our sanctuary. I could no more give those up than—" He took a deep breath. "I'm sorry. My frustration continues to get the better of me."

"We may have missed something the last time we were in the tower. The key to finding the treasure has to be there. There's nowhere else to look."

"I don't know why you're so insistent on thinking there's a treasure. There might have been one two centuries ago, but whatever that treasure consisted of—more doubloons, maybe—it's probably long gone. We have to face reality, Beverly."

"Just one more trip up into the tower. Please. If we could go up there next Saturday—"

"*We?*"

Beverly nodded. "Diane, Margaret, Shelley, me, and Diane's sister-in-law."

"I already told Diane no."

"You're being too stubborn. Think about it. *Please.* Diane's sister-in-law has a fresh pair of eyes. She's a college professor, with expertise in art history and English. She might see something we've overlooked."

"Impossible."

"I disagree. All things are possible with God. Isn't that what you said in one of your messages recently?"

Locke smiled again. "Thanks for that reminder."

"So please, let us go into the tower next Saturday when Jeanette's back in town. The five of us, plus you, *plus* God, will climb the stairs together. Who knows? We just might experience another miracle."

"You're awfully persistent."

Beverly laughed. "Just wait until I'm mayor of Marble Cove. There's no telling what I can do once I set my mind to it."

★ ★ ★

The moon slid behind a cloud and she was surrounded by deep darkness, as if someone had dumped jet black ink over the sky and everything around her. Somewhere in the distance—from the cliffs near the ocean—she heard the plaintive ringing of a lone church bell. Suddenly a dark figure emerged from the thick fog, and a scream split the air around her. It was her own voice...

Rocky gave Diane what she felt sure was a skeptical look. "What's wrong, Rocky? I thought it sounded pretty good. I'm just not certain what should happen next. Should someone grab our heroine by the throat? Should she run toward the figure in the fog?"

Rocky's tail stopped thumping. He growled.

"Okay, I know, running toward him is maybe somewhat risky for a woman who's all by herself in the middle of the night when she can't see a thing and she doesn't have a flashlight."

Diane plopped down in her office chair, swiveled around and faced the computer screen, now filled with her words, including her comments to Rocky. "It appears I shouldn't talk to you while I'm writing," she said, watching the words appear on the screen. Rocky dropped his head on her knee and she scratched right between his eyebrows, one of his favorite spots, as she read back through her prose.

She'd thought it would be difficult getting back into her routine after Jeanette left at the crack of dawn. At first the cottage seemed empty, but all was normal again after she returned from church. She picked up her teacup and took the last remaining sip, staring at the computer screen and the words she'd written over the last hour. Setting the cup down again, she deleted a few words, added some others, and quickly typed out a short action scene.

A speck of moonlight peeked out from behind the cloud and again she heard the howl. But that's not what frightened her. It was the figure streaking through the trees. At one moment only a shadow; the next, a man—

Diane laughed. *A man doing what?* She was grasping a bit with this plot, but she was determined to just keep pushing and see where the story led.

She leaned back in her chair. Beside her she could hear the squish, squish sound of Rocky gnawing on his favorite soft rubber ball. She chewed on the end of a pencil, deep in thought, then let her gaze drift toward the calendar on the wall. *Don't go there*, she told herself, but she didn't listen. The words penciled in on Wednesday—DOCTOR'S APPOINTMENT: 11 AM—glared back at her.

Suddenly her train of thought was gone. Whatever she might have added to the scene next disappeared in an instant.

Pushing up from her chair, she walked across her office, through the living room, and out to the front porch. She sat in one of the Shaker rockers with her eyes closed and even in the warmth of the sun, she shivered. She didn't want to visit the oncologist. Not this Wednesday. Not the next. Not ever.

Why couldn't the doctor just call and tell her that the cancer was gone? Forever. Never to return, ever again. She thought that's what remission meant. That she was free and clear. But the doctor insisted on routine checkups. The first four had been perfect. Everything looked great. She'd skipped the last two appointments, but she was sure they would have turned out fine.

This one would too.

"Hey there."

Beverly walked up the brick path, looking impeccably put together—a perfect candidate for mayor. "Mind if I join you?" she asked, and as soon as Diane smiled, Beverly sat gracefully in the rocker beside her, leaning back, a soft smile on her face.

"Just get home from church?" It was a pretty good guess, Diane thought, considering that Beverly was carrying her leather-bound Bible and a small fuchsia-colored purse with an extralong strap slung over her shoulder.

Beverly nodded. "I had a long talk with Reverend Locke afterward."

Diane sat up straight. "Did you tell him what we've found in the documents Dr. Standish located for us?"

"I told him everything. Of course, just like us, he's anxious to hear more. And once we find the truth, you'll have to put your old news reporter hat back on and write an exposé, telling the truth about Reverend Thorpe."

"Gladly." Diane smiled.

"I also talked to him about letting us go up into the tower again."

"Don't keep me in suspense. What did he say?"

"After a few very firm no's, he had a change of heart. We're on for noon next Saturday."

"This calls for a celebration. Do you have time for a glass of ice-cold lemonade?"

Diane bustled into the house when Beverly said yes and a few minutes later came out with two tall frosty glasses, a slice of thinly cut lemon wedged onto the rim, and a couple of flowery linen napkins edged with lace.

"Everything okay?" Beverly asked, and only then did Diane realize she'd been staring out at the ocean.

Diane took a sip of lemonade and offered Beverly a weak smile. "I have an appointment with the oncologist on Wednesday and, for the first time in five years, I'm scared to see him. I don't want to go through the blood work or get poked and prodded. I just want to stay home."

Beverly set her glass down on the small table between their chairs and took Diane's hand. "You can't hibernate."

"I can. Quite easily."

"And you'll spend every day wondering if you're still cancer free or if it's returned. I know you, Diane. You'll walk around like a zombie. You won't be able to write. You won't enjoy working in your garden. You'll sit in a daze when you're with your friends, not that we wouldn't understand, but—"

"Oh, I know. I have to go, but I'm frightened this time. I feel like I've been blessed with five good years, years the doctors told me I'd never have, and maybe I wasn't destined to have those good years. Maybe I was supposed to have died before Eric."

"Nonsense. God gave you those five good years. I know He brought us and Shelley and Margaret together for a reason."

"I know He has a plan for all of us; He doesn't dish out more than we can handle. But—"

"Is anyone going with you?" Beverly asked, interrupting Diane, keeping her from drowning in her worries.

Diane shook her head. "I'll be fine."

"I'm sure you will." Beverly squeezed her hand. "But I'm going to take you, all the same."

CHAPTER SIXTEEN

I don't want to go to school. I hate it!" Aiden pulled the covers over his head and Shelley tugged them back.

"You loved school last week," she said gently, sitting on the edge of the bed. "Did something happen to make you change your mind?"

Aiden's lower lip quivered. A fat tear slid from his eye and down his cheek. "I miss you. I miss Emma. I don't want to go."

"If you don't, you'll miss out on story time and you won't see your new friends."

"I don't have any new friends. They all hate me."

"That's not what your teacher told me. She said everyone loves you. That you take turns on the swings and the slides and that you share your crayons."

"If you make me go, I won't share. Never!"

If only Dan hadn't left for Bangor late last night. Here it was Monday morning and she already missed him. Aiden's whining was not making life any easier.

Down the hallway she heard Emma whimper. She'd fussed with her ears last night. *Please, dear Lord, don't let her have an ear infection.*

Shelley kissed Aiden's forehead. It was cool, which meant no fever, so she didn't have a good excuse for letting him stay home. As much as she wanted to coddle him, insisting he go to school was the right thing to do.

"I have to get Emma up, so please, Aiden, be a big boy and get out of bed."

He shook his head.

Shelley felt the muscles in her neck tightening and a hint of a headache forming. "Going to school or not isn't your choice, honey. You have to get up and go. If you don't, there's no telling what you'll miss out on. And really, Aiden, you're so good at so many things, like art and science and reading, that going to school will make you even better at all those things you love. You'd like that, wouldn't you?"

Aiden shrugged, but he didn't utter another "No." It seemed to be a fairly good sign, so Shelley ruffled his hair and stood. "I'm off to get Emma now. I thought I'd make waffles for breakfast."

"Fancy waffles? With chocolate chips in them?"

"How about blueberries instead of chocolate chips? And a big glass of chocolate milk on the side."

"And orange juice?"

"And orange juice." Shelley smiled as she walked toward the bedroom door, hearing Emma just beginning to cry. "Let's see who can get dressed and into the kitchen first—you or Emma."

Aiden bolted out of bed and raced for the bathroom. He was going to win the race, of course, but Shelley didn't mind. For her there was no competition when it came to her kids.

A little over an hour later, with Aiden happily playing with one of his newfound preschool friends, Shelley and Emma slipped out of the preschool door. She'd just started to push the stroller down the street when her cell phone rang. It was Susannah again, and she couldn't help but sigh. Each call seemed to lead closer and closer to some dramatic event.

Shelley put on a happy face and a voice to go with it. "Hi, Suze. How you doing this morning?"

"Good. Busy. I've got a lot on my plate today, but just wanted to say hi."

Shelley couldn't bring herself to ask if everything was okay. Not yet. Susannah would tell her, she was sure. Instead she asked about her niece.

"Is Hailey enjoying school? Does she like her teacher?"

"Yes to both questions, but we might be moving, and if we do, she'll be going to a new school. I haven't told her yet, but I know she won't be happy."

It was such a bad time to pull up a child's roots, but there had to be a reason for the move, another thing Shelley was afraid to ask about. Susannah had moved a lot of times, mostly because she couldn't pay the rent or *hadn't* paid the rent. There was always an excuse.

"She probably won't be happy," Shelley said softly, "but kids are amazingly flexible. She'll adjust in time."

"You think so?"

"Of course she will. She's a good kid. Smart. Sweet. She'll do fine." At least Shelley hoped she would.

"If she has a hard time with it, maybe you could talk to her. You're so good with Aiden and Emma."

"Sure, I could talk to her. Anytime."

"I suppose you could say that's all a part of our pact, you know, about taking care of each other's children if something happened."

There it was again, hanging between them like a thick fog. What was going on? Shelley shook her head, took a deep breath. "Pact or no pact, Suze, I'll always be there for you and for Hailey."

★ ★ ★

Margaret fussed with her feather duster, pretending she was busy getting rid of nearly nonexistent specks of this and that in the gallery's front window. In reality, she was watching Adelaide walk up Main Street and at last stand at the bus stop. Her little girl—no, Margaret reminded herself, she was really a grown woman—waited patiently, tugging at the straps of her backpack, while her gaze remained fixed on the road, waiting for her ride to the college.

Would she ever get used to this occurrence? This seemingly impossible miracle? She and Allan had never believed that Adelaide would have a life beyond their home or Marble Cove's community center, but she'd proved them wrong. One day she might even work in a day care center, spending time with children—which she loved—assisting the teachers.

Margaret smiled softly, yet when the bus arrived, the muscles in Margaret's shoulders were taut and her head ached.

Give me the strength to let her go, Lord. She's happy and I'm happy for her. Still, I'm frightened.

She drew in a deep breath, turned away from the window, and only then realized that she wasn't really afraid for Adelaide's safety at all; she was afraid she was losing her. Taking the bus on her own, going to college on her own . . . what was next? A boyfriend? An engagement? Marriage?

Margaret shook her head, trying to clear away the images. One step at a time, she told herself. And she prayed they'd be baby steps.

Putting the feather duster away, she went to her desk and flipped the calendar over to Monday. She'd almost forgotten that she had an out-of-town client coming in at 1:00, a very proper Englishman with a strong accent who'd bought a few of her Seal Island puffin paintings for his wife last Christmas. She looked forward to seeing Mr. Cabot again, and went into the back room to find some paintings that would suit his tastes. It was awfully nice to have customers with ready cash, especially ones who loved art.

She was carrying a trio of smaller, unframed canvases out into the gallery, ready to set them up for display, possibly with a few pieces of locally handcrafted jewelry that she hoped she could tempt him with, when the chimes at the front door rang, and a woman walked in. It took a moment or two of racking her brain for Margaret to remember the face. Danny Wharburton's mother. He was the inquisitive and out-of-the-box thinker from her art class. She was the one who wanted her son to be Rembrandt, not Picasso or Dali.

"Good morning, Mrs. Wharburton." Margaret held out her hand to the thirty-something woman with sleek, highlighted blonde hair and big diamonds in her ears.

"Good morning, Mrs. Hoskins." Mrs. Wharburton smiled and shook Margaret's hand warmly, something she hadn't done on their first meeting. She looked around at the paintings on display, the glass cases filled with jewelry and other trinkets, not to mention the gorgeous pottery and glasswork made by local artisans. "Your gallery is beautiful. I can't believe I haven't been in here before."

Margaret thanked her. "Is there something special I can show you?"

"Actually, I wanted to apologize for being so abrupt the other night."

"That's not necessary. You were concerned about your son, and I can understand that."

"He insisted over the weekend that his father and I take him to that big art store in Bramford to buy him his own watercolors and a set of brushes, plus a few canvases." She laughed. "I really wanted to tell him to wait until he'd had a few more classes, to make sure his interest wasn't just a passing fancy, but he was adamant. In fact, he talked about technique all weekend long. Even spent half a day on the Internet reading all he could find."

"I imagine he'll be full of questions tonight, and raring to go." And she'd better spend some time this afternoon preparing her lesson plan. She should have done it before now, but time had gotten away from her.

"I have to say, Danny's constant chatter and that trip to the art store sparked an old interest I had in painting."

"So you painted at one time? Oils? Watercolors?"

"Watercolor. I wasn't much older than Danny. I started out doing paint-by-number." She laughed. "Goodness, who does paint-by-number anymore! The next thing you know, I spent my babysitting money buying cheap watercolors and I painted on everything."

"What did you like to paint?"

"Flowers." She shook her head. "But they were ghastly."

"In your mind, maybe, but in all likelihood they were probably very good, as long as they expressed your emotion."

"My mother did the same thing to me that I've tried to do to Danny. She wanted to cramp my style. We went to the Museum of Fine Arts in Boston and she insisted I study neoclassicism—her favorite art movement, while I found myself attracted to Van Gogh. 'He was such a rogue!' my mother always said."

"A talented rogue, for sure."

"I adored his work, but then...I found myself interested in boys, and gone was my love of painting."

"It happens to the best of us, I'm afraid."

Margaret ignored the phone that rang in her office, letting it roll over to voice mail. She was intrigued by Mrs. Wharburton, surprised by all that she was divulging.

"Anyway, having Danny take your class was my idea. I wanted to see if he had the same affinity for it that I had had, but only because there weren't any classes here in town for people my age. And when he spent most of the weekend talking about your technique and how easy you made it all look, I wanted to start painting again, doing it right this time, and...and I was wondering if you might give me a few—or maybe quite a few—private lessons."

Margaret certainly hadn't expected that question. It was flattering, but when would she find the time? And did she really want to do it? A week ago today she'd thought about the free time she was going to have now that summer was over. She'd thought of closing the gallery a couple of days a week and going out to the islands to paint or sitting on the wharf with acrylics or oils and bringing the Marble Cove Harbor scenes to life on canvas.

Margaret smiled weakly, not wanting to say yes, not sure she wanted to say no. Instead she said, "I'd love to, Mrs. Wharburton, but—"

"Nicole, please, call me Nicole."

"And call me Margaret. My schedule's been very busy, Nicole, at least for the rest of this month, what with the art class I'm teaching."

Mrs. Wharburton opened her purse and took out her card, which Margaret took. Nicole Wharburton, Attorney at Law, it read.

"Would you give it some thought?" Mrs. Wharburton asked. "Perhaps we could start next month?"

The front door opened and Mr. Cabot, the handsome Englishman, strolled in. *Saved by the bell*, Margaret thought.

Margaret fingered Nicole's business card. She smiled and shook Nicole's hand. "I have to help this customer. We have an appointment," she said hesitantly, "but I'll think about the classes."

"That's all I can ask. Thank you." Nicole smiled, and as she walked out the door, she added, "See you tonight."

Margaret waved good-bye, and when Nicole was gone and she walked toward Mr. Cabot, who'd spotted the Seal Island puffin paintings she'd set out, she tucked Nicole's business card into her pocket. She'd been flattered, but in all honesty, she didn't want to think about teaching any other classes. Especially not tonight.

★ ★ ★

Beverly climbed out of her car and strolled toward Marble Cove's one and only print shop. Her jaw tightened when she saw a big Prosperity and Progress—Dennis Calder for Mayor sign in the front window. His handsome face with the deceptive smile dared her to enter. Of course, she wasn't about to go out of town to get her campaign material printed. Marble Cove needed the business; so did Ace Printing.

The big man behind the counter had bulging muscles and every inch of his arms was tattooed. His name badge read Hi! I'm Sarge, and although he was nothing but friendly at first, he looked a little sheepish when Beverly opened her folder and began to give him complete details about her order.

"You're running for mayor?"

Beverly nodded.

"Then we've got a problem."

Now Beverly frowned. "Why's that?"

"The boss—Ace—is a friend of Dennis Calder's. Says *'He's the man.'* Told me I'd be a fool to vote for anyone else." Sarge scratched his forehead. "I'm not too sure he'll want us printing your promo stuff."

"The business is doing so well that Ace can turn away customers?" Beverly asked.

"Now, now, Sarge, is that any way to talk to a prospective customer?" Ace—more than apparent from the badge he wore—walked out of a back room carrying a case of paper, which he dropped on the floor at Sarge's feet. "Why don't you put that away, and I'll take care of the lady."

Beverly wanted to tell Ace that the lady had a name, but she didn't want to go out of town to get her printing done. Somehow she had to win Ace over, but the short fellow with the bushy black mustache and slicked-back black hair didn't look like a man who gave in easily to anything.

"How can I help you?" Ace asked, his elbows resting on the gray Formica countertop. "Actually, that's a ridiculous question. I know who you are. Beverly Wheeland." He nodded, a grin on his face. "Are you sure you want to spend your hard-earned money getting campaign materials produced? From what I hear, Dennis Calder already has the election sewn up."

"I hadn't heard that." Beverly remained nonchalant. She wouldn't let Ace—*or* Dennis—get the better of her. "Was there an announcement in the newspaper? Maybe on TV?"

Ace shrugged. "Dennis has a lot of friends in town. Has something to do with the fact that he grew up here. So did Lee Waters, for that matter. You've only been in town what? A year?"

"That's all that's required to run for the office. One year's residence."

Her cell phone, buried deep in her shoulder bag, rang out its text message tone, which jolted her out of the sparring match she had been on the verge of getting into with Ace. She ignored the ring, but didn't ignore Ace. She smiled politely. "I'm guessing you don't want my business."

"Not when your business has to do with your campaign. That wouldn't be fair to Calder."

"No, I suppose it wouldn't." Beverly closed her portfolio and smiled. "Thanks anyway, Ace."

By the time she reached her car, her jaw hurt from clenching it so tight. She tossed her portfolio onto the passenger seat, climbed inside, put on her seat belt, and started the engine. The knock on the window nearly scared the living daylights out of her. She was tenser than she thought.

She jerked around to see Sarge staring through the window, holding a business card between his thumb and index finger. She rolled down her window. "A friend of mine in Bramford does great print work, but business has been slow. I'm sure he could use the work. I can give you references if you'd like."

"Is this his card?" Beverly asked.

Sarge nodded. "His and mine, really. I'm working here to make ends meet." He looked at his watch. "If you're interested, I could meet you at your place in fifteen minutes or so, as soon as I take my lunch break, and I can do the work for you tonight. That's a faster turnaround than you'd get most anywhere else. I can bring it back to you tomorrow."

Beverly took the card and studied the embossed green lettering. She didn't know Sarge from Adam, but she liked him. He might look like a renegade from a motorcycle gang, but there was something about his demeanor that invited trust.

She gave him her address and directions, although most everyone in town knew how to find Newport Avenue. "I'll see you there in fifteen minutes," Beverly said, offering him a quick handshake, "and if you're a little late, don't worry."

Her father was asleep in his library when she walked into the house. She tried tiptoeing around quietly, not wanting to wake him up. The party on the beach Saturday night had worn him out. It hadn't helped that his blood sugar had skyrocketed from eating too many s'mores and too much potato salad. She'd have to make sure she and Mrs. Peabody could keep him on a straight and narrow diet for the next month to make up for the one slipup.

"I wasn't expecting you back so soon," her father said, sitting up straight in his favorite chair. He rubbed his eyes. "I mixed up some tuna fish with lots of relish and a hard-boiled egg. Could I interest you in a sandwich?"

"I'll make one later, but thanks. A guy named Sarge is dropping by in a few minutes." She told her father about the encounter at Ace Printing as she spread her materials out on the dining room table.

"How do you know this guy's any good? What makes you think he isn't coming here to case the place?"

"I don't, but I've got to put my trust somewhere, and I wasn't about to put it in Ace. If he'd done the work, he probably would have added horns to the top of my head, two black eyes, and a mustache."

Her father laughed. He got up from his chair and stretched. "Heard from Jeff yet?"

All of a sudden Beverly remembered the text message ring tone she'd heard while sparring with Ace. "I'm not sure." Grabbing her purse, she dug the cell phone from the very bottom, where it was hidden beneath her checkbook, keys, and an empty business card case, one she hoped she'd be filling tomorrow with the stunning cards she'd designed.

"He's landed in Jordan," Beverly said, when she saw the first words of Jeff's message.

"Tell him to stay safe."

Beverly quickly read the rest of the message detailing his first impressions of Jordan.

Beverly's father rested a hand on her shoulder. "You're smiling."

"Jeff's in his element," Beverly told her father, who casually looked down at the text on her phone. "He loves to travel, and something tells me he'll never settle down."

"Has he talked to you about settling down?"

Beverly shook her head and sighed. "No. It seems like whenever I think he'll be sticking around for a while, another chance to travel comes up. I can't blame him for taking advantage of all these trips. I imagine I'd do the same thing if I were in his shoes."

"And if you didn't have to take care of me."

Beverly winked at her father. "You're a piece of cake."

The knock at the door startled her, even though she'd anticipated Sarge's arrival. After inviting him in, she introduced him to her father, who hung around like a vulture, watching Sarge's every move while Beverly explained what she wanted. She had everything detailed on paper, but they talked about the project to make sure there were no misunderstandings.

"Could I suggest a slight change in colors?" Sarge picked up one of the flyers Beverly had printed out on plain white paper.

"Please don't say red, white, and blue. It's not that I'm not patriotic, it's just that everyone uses those colors. I want to stand out from the crowd."

"Your colors are fine. But they need more saturation if they're going to pop. Would you trust me to make that happen for you?"

Beverly thought about it for a moment, then looked at her father, who nodded twice. His seal of approval meant a lot to her. "I trust you."

They spent another half hour talking, not just about work but about Beverly's campaign, and when he said he had to get back to the shop, Beverly walked him to the door. "I'm glad I met you, Sarge."

"Me too, ma'am." He marched out to his truck, then turned. "I'll have everything back to you at noon tomorrow. And if you need campaign volunteers, you can count me in."

"But you live in Bramford."

"My business is there, my home's here. Me, my wife, and three kids. I've run into too many Dennis Calders in my life and know that I don't want him for mayor. You have my vote."

★ ★ ★

It was well past midnight when Beverly turned off the computer in her office and headed downstairs. She'd spent the evening adding some of the photos Jeff had taken of her to her Web site, creating upbeat captions to go with each one. Now all she had to do was get people to come to the site and learn all about her and what she would do for Marble Cove if she was elected.

It was quiet in the house, everything still. She tried not to make any noise walking barefoot into the kitchen to make herself a cup of tea, something decaffeinated that wouldn't keep her from falling asleep when she finally decided to call it a night.

She stepped out onto the back porch with teacup in hand and sat in her father's favorite old patio chair. Its brown wicker was sorely in need of a paint job, not to mention new covers for the cushions. Last spring when she'd taken the winter covers off the furniture on the porch, she'd given serious thought to refurbishing the chair. She'd gone so far as to look at fabric on a few different Web sites, thinking she'd have better luck finding what she wanted online than trying to find it in one of the few fabric shops in the area. Then she'd gotten busy and forgotten all about it. Maybe next year. Of course, then she might be too busy in her new job as mayor, along with her business and watching over her father.

She took a sip of tea, listening to the soft lap of the waves. It had been so easy to fall in love with Marble Cove. She really did want to be its mayor, although she imagined a lot of people thought she was running for office on a whim. Not at all. She was already working on her first-day-in-office to-do list. She wished she could include getting a grant to repair the roof on Old First, but no. She wouldn't go there. Dennis might, but it would be wrong. She wouldn't make false promises in an attempt to win friends and influence people.

Over the screech of a few seagulls flying overhead, looking for a very late-night snack, she heard the ring of her cell phone and grabbed it out of her pants pocket. As she'd hoped, it was yet another text message from Jeff.

I didn't wake you, did I?

Beverly responded quickly, her fingers nimbly tapping out the text.

Drinking a cup of hot tea out on Father's back porch. It's a lovely night. Wish you were here.

Jeff's message came back in an instant.

Had a campaign thought this afternoon. Wanna hear about it?

Hmm, he hadn't reacted to her "Wish you were here" comment. She tried to tell herself that he was understandably preoccupied, that he had more important things on his mind than trying to make small talk with his girlfriend—if he still considered her that. His mood, where she was concerned, had been wishy-washy. Still, she answered back:

Of course! You can be my campaign manager in absentia.

It took a moment for Jeff's response to come through.

You need to organize a debate. You, Dennis, and Lee on a stage answering questions from, oh, I don't know who, but I'm sure you can think of a couple of people. The owner of the newspaper, maybe. Journalists are supposed to be impartial. How about one of the pastors in town?

Beverly typed out her response.

Do you think I stand a chance debating Calder? He can be charming. A lot of people fall for that.

She'd never been big on text-messaging, but it was certainly better than nothing.

Charm's fine and dandy for a beauty pageant, but not a political campaign. Be yourself, and you can win over the world, or at least Marble Cove.

Beverly smiled.

Thanks…How's everything there?

She imagined Jeff smiling from what seemed a million miles away.

Great. I think you'd love it here.

Possibly. Then, again...

I doubt I'll ever visit Jordan.

Jeff's response came back in an instant.

Maybe I'll

His message stopped in midstream. Had they lost the connection? Had he been interrupted by someone?

Suddenly there was another message from him.

Gotta go. Sweet dreams.

She didn't know if he was still looking at his phone or not. Still, she sent one more text:

Do you have to leave so soon?

She waited. And waited. But no answer came.

CHAPTER SEVENTEEN

L ook, Emma, it's a piece of sea glass."

Shelley let go of Emma's hand and let her daughter wander close to the tide pool where she'd spotted one of the rarest finds of all. Emma stuck her little hand into the frothy water and oohed and aahed when she grasped hold of the stunning piece of oblong red glass, its edges tumbled by who knows how many years of washing around in the ocean.

"Isn't it pretty?"

"Pretty." Emma held it up to her mom, smiling brightly, her lovely blue eyes squinting in the early afternoon sunshine.

Shelley opened up the small tote bag she was carrying, which was filling up fast with other treasures Emma had found in the past hour. "Drop it inside, sweetie, and we'll take it home later and put it in the bowl with the rest of the sea glass you've been collecting."

Emma grinned and held on tight. "No!"

It would have been so easy to roll her eyes at the utterance of one of Emma's newfound favorite words, or to insist she give up the piece of sea glass for now, but Shelley forced herself not to, and just let Emma hang on to the stunning piece of glass. She'd already had one tug-of-war today with Aiden. Just like

Monday morning, this morning had been nightmarish. For the second day in a row he hadn't wanted to go to school, and getting him there had been a definite struggle.

It was such a pretty day, the first that she'd really had to spend strictly playing with Emma, devoting all of her time to her little girl. This was what she'd longed for when she and Dan decided to enroll Aiden in pre-K. As much as she missed her four-year-old scamp, school was good for him; it would be good for her too, once she got over the feeling that she'd abandoned him.

Emma struggled in Shelley's arms. "Shell," she repeated, and Shelley set her down on the beach, letting her toddle about looking for shells or pretty rocks. In a few more years she wouldn't be able to hold on to Emma. She was getting more and more independent all the time. Children grew up way too fast.

The cell phone she'd tucked away in the pocket of her shorts rang, and keeping a keen eye on every one of Emma's moves, she answered it. Aiden's teacher was on the other end. From the sound of her voice, she was exasperated about something, and Miss Davidson had been sweet as pie and nothing but calm every time they'd met last week. Even earlier today.

Obviously something was wrong.

What on earth had Aiden done?

"I'm sorry, Mrs. Bauer, but Aiden's been acting out in class ever since you dropped him off. I told him if he didn't behave, I'd have to call you and he'd have to go home."

Oh dear. More than likely, that's exactly what he wanted.

"Are you sure I can't pick him up at the regular time? That's just an hour from now."

She could almost see Miss Davidson shaking her head no. "I have to stick to my word on the punishment, Mrs. Bauer. It's the only way the children will learn that there are consequences for their actions."

Shelley held back her sigh. "I'm down on the beach with Emma, but I'll be there as soon as possible."

Emma screamed, scaring off the seagulls and at least half a dozen sandpipers who skittered to and fro probing the sand for food.

"Sorry, baby, but we have to go to Aiden's school and bring him home."

Emma scowled. "No!"

"I'm afraid you have to say yes this time around. It can't be helped."

Emma struggled in Shelley's arms while she jogged up the beach. Five minutes later she had a not-too-happy Emma strapped into her car seat for the drive to school. She much preferred walking, but this incident obviously didn't qualify for a leisurely stroll through town.

Miss Davidson met Shelley and Emma just inside the door of Aiden's pre-K class. A heartbeat later Shelley spotted her son, looking blue. Literally. "Oh dear."

"He was a pig half an hour ago, crawling around on all fours, oinking and squealing." Miss Davidson grinned. Shelley, on the other hand, didn't find it all that funny.

"What about the paint?"

"He did that during the time-out I had to give him. It appears that while my back was turned, he got into the poster paint. He said he wanted to know what he'd look like with blue hair and skin."

Shelley sighed. "I'm so sorry, Miss Davidson. I'll take him home right now and we'll have a nice long talk before I bring him back tomorrow."

She set Emma on the floor, told her to stay put, and went after Aiden, catching him only after he climbed up on a few more chairs and tabletops, jumped down on the floor, and ran around the room. At long last Shelley captured the blue boy. Once he was tight in her arms, he clapped his blue hands to her cheeks and smiled. "You came. I knew it! I knew it!"

Shelley frowned. "What do you mean, you knew it?"

Aiden grinned. "Noah got in trouble yesterday and his mom came to get him."

"Let me guess. You figured if it worked for him, it would work for you?"

Aiden nodded up and down, over and over, a big smile on his face, proud of his accomplishment.

"Well, young man, don't go thinking you can get away with this again. We're going to have a good long talk after I get you home and give you a bath."

"Will you read me a story then?"

"After our talk." Somehow or other she had to make him understand that acting out in class might have gotten him what he wanted today, but not again.

★ ★ ★

Shelley and Aiden sat on the back porch steps and watched Prize chasing birds and butterflies and anything that moved in the backyard. A mild breeze had picked up since she'd brought Aiden home from school, given him a bath, and put Emma down for a nap. It wouldn't be long before Prize would be chasing autumn leaves. She wished the changing weather and seasons was all she had on her mind right this moment, but Aiden's commotion in class had to be dealt with, whether she wanted to do it or not.

She wished Dan was home to help her with this.

"So, young man, are you ready to talk?"

Aiden looked up into his mother's face. He smiled his biggest and brightest smile, thinking that would get him out of trouble. But not this time. "What do you want to talk about?" he asked innocently.

"I think you know. Why don't you tell me why you painted your face and hair at school today?"

Aiden picked at a scab on his knee. He scratched his shoulder. He looked everywhere but at his mom. Finally he said, "I saw Emma's red sea glass. If you'd taken me to the beach, I would have found it, and it would have been mine."

"You already have a lot of sea glass and sand dollars and seashells, sweetheart."

"But I won't get any more, because you won't take me to the beach no more."

"Anymore," Shelley corrected him, then went on. "Aiden, honey, we live right next to the beach. We go there all the time."

"Not just you and me."

Had she been ignoring him? She didn't think so, but there was no telling what went on in his little boy's mind.

Aiden nodded. "I heard you and Dad talkin' about you havin' Mom-and-Emma time when I'm in school. When does she go to school so I can have Mom-and-Aiden time?"

Shelley tried not to laugh, but she couldn't help but smile. "Emma's not ready yet for school. She won't be going to school until she's as grown up as you are now. Until then, she has to stay home with me, just like you stayed home with me for four whole years."

"I want to stay home too."

"If you did, you'd miss out on an awful lot."

"Yeah, but if I didn't, I could go to the beach with you."

Hmm, this conversation was going in circles. Shelley struggled for words that would make him understand that life couldn't always remain the same.

"You know, honey, Emma and I won't be going to the beach every day. Some days I have to work, and Emma will have to play by herself. And then you'll think you're the lucky one because you got to go to school and play with your friends. You'll get to paint—not your hair and face, of course—"

Aiden giggled. After a moment of trying to hold a straight face, Shelley joined him. "Aiden, we should not be laughing at that. What you did was not okay. Do you understand?"

Aiden sighed. "Okay, Mama—Mom."

Shelley ruffled his hair. "Now, which would you prefer? Going to school like a big boy and having Miss Davidson read you stories and being with the other kids, or staying at home watching Emma, making sure she doesn't get into something she shouldn't, while I'm in the kitchen baking cookies that somebody else—not you—will get to eat?"

Aiden shrugged. "I guess I'd rather listen to Miss Davidson read stories."

"I had the feeling you'd say that." Shelley slipped his little hand into hers. "You know, you're growing up awfully fast."

"I'm a big boy now."

"Yes, you are. And big boys are good in school."

Aiden shook his head. "If I'm good at school the whole rest of the week, can we have some Mom-and-Aiden time, just you and me?"

"Most definitely." It was a promise she'd look forward to keeping.

CHAPTER EIGHTEEN

How would you like to make a few campaign stops with me this afternoon?" Beverly asked Diane, holding the phone between her ear and her shoulder as she gathered up some of the campaign materials Sarge just delivered—Tuesday at noon, as promised. "Nothing formal or fancy or anything like that. I've just gotten my campaign materials from the printer—they look fabulous, by the way—and I want to drop a few pieces by Margaret's, then stop in to see Lee Waters. Maybe go to the chamber of commerce after that."

"Why on earth do you want me to go along?"

To take Diane's mind off tomorrow's doctor's appointment, that was the biggest reason, but that's not what she told Diane. "I also hope to see Dennis Calder, and I'd like a little company when and if I do. Are you game?"

Beverly could hear Diane chuckle on the other end of the phone. "When?"

"Right now."

"I'm wearing jeans and a T-shirt. My hair's a mess."

"Put on that apricot-and-white checkered blouse of yours, pull your hair back into a ponytail, and if you're wearing slippers, substitute them with flip-flops."

"Are you my personal stylist now?"

"I'm your friend, and I love your look, especially that apricot blouse. And it just so happens I have the perfect necklace and bracelet to go with it."

"I'll need five or ten minutes."

"Great. I'll meet you out by my car, and take a look at the campaign sign at the edge of the driveway when you come over. It's terrific!"

Beverly jogged upstairs to her bedroom, found the chunky apricot-and-white beaded choker in her jewelry chest, slipped into a pair of turquoise heels and examined herself in the cheval mirror. Even if she did say so herself, she thought she looked like a pretty good mayoral candidate, her heels perfectly matching the turquoise linen blazer she wore over a black tank and slim black slacks.

She poked her head into her father's library, where he was sitting in his favorite chair, reading the latest book he'd sent for, one about Abraham Lincoln. "I'm heading out," she said. "Wish me luck."

"You might meet some resistance on the debate idea." She'd told him all about it over breakfast this morning, and he'd given her two thumbs up.

"You're probably right. I can't see Lee Waters standing in front of a crowd and answering questions."

"The chamber of commerce might not go for the idea either. You know a lot of the chamber board members are all about growth."

"Then I'll just have to convince them to come around to my way of thinking."

Her father smiled. "Don't forget to put on one of your campaign buttons. And take a bunch with you to hand out to everyone you meet—even the Dennis Calder fans."

"Got it!"

Diane was standing out front studying the campaign sign Sarge had pounded into the ground right after dropping off the materials he'd printed late last night. "It's perfect," Diane said. "Kind of chic—like you, and eye catching, just because it's different. And I love the colors."

"They're brighter than I'd originally planned, but I couldn't be happier."

Beverly reached into the turquoise-and-black handbag slung over her shoulder and first pulled out the necklace for Diane. "What do you think?" she asked, holding it up for Diane to see.

"It's not me. I'm your typical New Englander in jeans, fleece vests, and hiking boots."

"It is you. Trust me!"

Diane rolled her eyes and turned around, standing still while Beverly latched the necklace at the back of her neck. "Let me see."

Slowly Diane faced Beverly, a sardonic smile on her face.

"It's gorgeous! So are you. Now for the pièce de résistance!"

"Please don't tell me you have ruby-red lipstick inside your purse, plus blush, eye shadow, and all that other stuff."

"Not quite." Beverly dug into her bag again. "So, who are you going to vote for for mayor?"

"I believe I have every right to keep that a secret, but if you must know...you."

"Good. So how about wearing a campaign button?"

Diane grinned. "All right, give it here." She held out her hand, graciously accepted the button that read Embracing Our Heritage—Vote Beverly, and pinned it on her shirt. "It's a nice addition to the attire, don't you think?"

"Perfect. Now, let's go! We have a lot of ground to cover."

★ ★ ★

Margaret was just wrapping up a painting in brown craft paper, getting it ready to send off to a customer, when Beverly and Diane walked into the gallery. "You two look lovely," Margaret said, smiling from behind her worktable. "Like you're trying to make a fashion statement here in Marble Cove, a place not particularly known for glamour."

"Just don't make the mistake of thinking I'm out to change things," Beverly said, laying one of her posters in front of Margaret. "What do you think?"

Margaret perused it for less than five seconds. "That we should hang it in the front window immediately. Well, as soon as I get this painting wrapped." She looked at her watch. "UPS will be here in five minutes, so I've got to hurry."

Margaret slipped the wrapped painting into a box that looked as if it had been made for that particular sized frame, and wrapped generous amounts of tape around it before affixing the mailing label. "There, all done. Now—" Grabbing a small roll of adhesive tape, she picked up the poster and walked to the front of the store. "What do you think? Should I put it at eye level, or in a corner?"

"Eye level sounds great," Beverly said, "but you're running a business. You don't need to block the view of all that you have on display."

"All right, the corner it is." Margaret positioned the poster carefully and began to tape the corners, just as Beverly's nemesis, Dennis Calder, walked into the gallery, his own posters in hand.

"Good afternoon, ladies." He grinned as he looked first at Diane, offered Beverly a quick glance, then shifted his gaze to Margaret. "Looks like I should have gotten here a little earlier. I was thinking that was the perfect place for one of my posters." His smile widened, although that seemed almost impossible. "I hope, Margaret, that you'll consider putting mine up somewhere else in your gallery."

"Sorry, Dennis, but I'm a one-candidate kind of gal. In fact, I even turned down Lee Waters' request earlier today."

He shrugged. "I suppose I can't fault you for that, especially knowing that you and Beverly are close friends. Although…" He frowned. "I'd think a business owner like yourself would be all for prosperity and progress."

"If you'd come in a time or two, you would have noticed that the Shearwater Gallery has done nothing but grow *and* prosper since we opened a little over a year ago."

Beverly tried to hide her grin. *Touché!*

"Also, like Beverly and Diane, I believe in embracing our heritage"—she tapped the campaign button she was wearing—"not tearing it down. So Beverly's nailed my vote as well as my support."

"Since you're here, Dennis," Beverly said, before he could leave in a controlled huff over having been rebuked, "I'd like to have a debate with you and Lee. In fact, I'm heading to the chamber of commerce in a little while to talk with them about supporting it and possibly taking care of the logistics."

Dennis' brows nearly knit together. "That would be a complete waste of time."

"Oh? Why's that?" Beverly asked, as Diane and Margaret formed a line of defense on either side of her.

"Because come November, I'm going to win the election."

"How odd. I ran into a friend of yours yesterday—the owner of Ace Printing—who also told me you would win. It must be nice to have a crystal ball that helps you see into the future."

"You've lived in Marble Cove just a short time, Beverly. Not everyone here likes newcomers showing up and trying to run the place. That's going to be held against you."

She knew that already, but she wasn't daunted. "I'm not worried about that, Dennis."

He chuckled as he walked toward the door. "You should be." With those parting words, Dennis Calder was gone.

"I shouldn't have been so rude." Beverly sighed. "It's just that he raises my ire."

"It's bound to get worse before the election," Diane said. "Are you sure you're up to it?"

Beverly smiled. "More than ever."

After saying their good-byes, Beverly and Diane walked up Main, rounded the corner at Water Street, and entered the Pet Place, owned by Lee Waters. The tall, gangly owner of the store was in the back sprinkling fish food into one of the many aquariums.

"Hello, Beverly. Diane." He pushed up his glasses and smiled first at Beverly, then at Diane. "How's Rocky? You haven't been in with him for a while."

"As rambunctious as ever and trying to eat me out of house and home." Diane smiled. "He loves that bright yellow squishy toy you recommended."

"I've sold quite a few of those since I got them in. Don't know what it is about them that dogs like so much, but they do." He shook food into the next tank. "Is there something I can help the two of you with?"

"We've come to talk about the mayoral race."

Lee nearly dropped the container of fish food when Beverly mentioned the campaign.

"I hope this isn't too inconvenient a time," Beverly said.

"It won't take long," Diane added.

Lee didn't say a word. He lifted the lid on the next tank, one containing only a single fish—a red-tailed shark, it said on the aquarium. At last he spoke, staring into the tank. "I have to keep this guy all by himself. He doesn't tolerate most of his own species."

Beverly wondered if the shark's name was Dennis, but she didn't ask.

"You *are* still running for mayor, aren't you?" Beverly asked Lee, and finally he put down the fish food and turned around. She was probably imagining it, but it seemed as though most of the color had drained from his face.

"Yes, I'm still running," he said at long last. "Don't mind me, but I have to feed the ferrets."

"So what is it you want to talk about?" he asked, lifting one of the ferrets from a four-sided glass case. He cradled it in the crook of one arm and rubbed the top of its head with the index and middle finger of his other hand.

"I think it would be a good idea for all candidates—you, Dennis, and me—to have a debate. I've already talked with Dennis—"

Lee had a distinct deer-in-the-headlights look. "We've never had a debate in Marble Cove, not for mayor, at least."

"Lee's right." Evelyn Waters seemed to materialize from nowhere. "There's never been a need for a mayoral debate and I don't see the need for one now. To be honest, the last thing we want is to set a precedent."

"It's one of the best ways for the citizens to get to know the candidates," Beverly countered, trying her best not to look or sound argumentative.

"This isn't a presidential election, Beverly. Besides, most everyone in town already knows Lee. Dennis too."

"Not everyone knows me."

Evelyn smiled. "I understand your problem and I do sympathize with you. It's difficult for a newcomer in town to go up against lifelong citizens."

"What do you think, Lee?" Diane asked, smiling gently. "Wouldn't you enjoy the chance to talk with the people in town—face to face—about your ideas for Marble Cove?"

He looked uncomfortably toward his mother, then back at Diane. "It does sound like a rather good idea—for you. But between my mother and grandfather, someone in our family has been in the mayoral position for all but four of the past fifty years, and everyone in town knows that I'm a strong proponent of my mother's views when it comes to Marble Cove. The town has run quite well since Mother took office twenty years ago. I don't see a need for me to make any changes when I take over the position."

"I see." Beverly nodded. She saw everything quite clearly. Lee would be a direct extension of his mother. More than likely she'd continue to run things while Lee became nothing more than a figurehead. You could almost sense that he wanted nothing at all to do with the job; he wanted to be in his pet shop with his fish and ferrets. It would do no good for her to try to convince Lee to enter into a debate, especially now, with Mother watching over him.

"I wish you'd change your mind about the debate," Beverly said.

"That goes double for me," Diane added. "Of course, you'll always have my vote when it comes to best pet consultant."

Lee laughed. "I appreciate the vote of confidence."

"Well, I guess there's nothing more to say about the debate," Beverly noted. She smiled, and a few minutes later she and Diane were out the door.

"That went over like a lead balloon." Diane grinned. "First Dennis Calder pooh-poohs the idea, now Evelyn. Of course, there's no way of knowing what Lee really thinks."

"No, and I doubt we ever will know. My guess is it's his mother who's convinced him to run. He doesn't seem particularly keen on the idea himself."

"Not only not keen," Diane said, "but scared."

"Public speaking isn't for everyone."

"Especially a man whose mother has been doing most of his speaking for a good portion of his life." Diane shook her head. "I like Lee. He's a nice guy—a great guy. But mayor? No, I'm pretty sure running for office wasn't his idea at all."

Beverly looked at her watch. "You know, I think I'd like to skip talking to the chamber board, at least for now. In order to make the debate a reality, I think I need to talk to someone with a lot more clout in this town."

"Any idea who?"

Beverly nodded. "If I'm not mistaken, Reverend Locke has a prayer meeting with several other ministers in town on Tuesday afternoons. Why don't we head down to Captain Calhoun's and see if we can squeeze in on their meeting?"

★ ★ ★

"Are you sure you want to have a debate?" Reverend Locke stirred a heaping spoonful of sugar into the mug of coffee the waitress had just refilled. "Finding an impartial moderator or two in a small town like Marble Cove could be difficult."

"Couldn't one or two of you moderate?" Diane asked, looking from Reverend Locke to Pastor Carl, from her own church, Marble Cove Community, and lastly at Pastor Tim, who was young and energetic and led the equally young and energetic congregation at Light the Way Chapel. "Surely each and every one of you could be impartial."

"I'm afraid I'd have to bow out," Reverend Locke said. He took a sip of coffee. "It wouldn't look impartial at all if I were one of the moderators, not when Beverly is one of my parishioners. But I do have a thought."

"I'd love to hear it," Beverly said, "as long as you're not about to recommend that I abandon the idea."

"Not abandon, but I believe you should rethink it."

"In what way?" Diane asked.

"Have a town hall meeting instead. I'd be happy to provide introductions for each candidate and keep the meeting under control, but by using a town hall format, the attendees will ask the questions, not a couple of men or women who might not have the same concerns as the people in the audience."

"Wonderful idea," Pastor Carl said. "In fact, I'd be happy to organize it and invite the candidates, the citizens of Marble Cove, and, of course, the *Marble Cove Courier*. I'll have to get our church board's approval, but I imagine there would be no problem holding the town hall at Marble Cove Community. We have the stage. We have a good sound system. What do you think?"

"Sounds like a plan," Pastor Tim agreed.

It sounded like a plan to Beverly too, only now she'd have to prepare. That meant a lot of studying, researching, digging into a part of Marble Cove history that she hadn't dug into already, and learning all there was to know about the original charter, the town's founders, and its politics. She couldn't leave any stone unturned, not if she wanted to do a good job. And she did.

She wanted to be mayor of Marble Cove.

★ ★ ★

Later that night, curled up in one of her office's white wicker chairs, with an afghan pulled over her silk pajamas to ward off the surprising chill of the evening, Beverly pored through historical records of Marble Cove. The state of Maine had a wealth of information online, and she'd printed out page after page, determined to learn all she could about her newfound home.

She rubbed her eyes. They were blurry from reading tiny print and handwritten documents from as far back as the seventeenth century. She'd been particularly intrigued by a 1607 account of the cove's discovery by English seamen that read, *"We could discern no sign or token that any Christian had been to this inlet before. As such, we erected our cross on a point overlooking the rocky coast and the ocean beyond, and the chaplain said a prayer, giving thanks to our God for this land, for our lives."*

She yawned, wishing so much that she could find the original town charter. For that, she imagined, she'd have to go to the town hall and dig into their archives. But as she'd learned on the state of Maine's Web site, many documents from those early years had been destroyed by fire and turbulent years.

Fire had destroyed so many things. Just a couple of months ago it had almost destroyed Old First. She sighed, once again wishing they could find the treasure and repair the roof.

On a whim, she went to her computer and searched a name she hadn't even considered looking up before. Booth Adair, the notorious pirate Reverend Thorpe had supposedly been in cahoots with.

She'd expected to find numerous entries to sort through when she searched on the name, but the first to pop up was a reference to him contained in a book titled *Pirates!* Fortunately it was available in e-book format, and she downloaded it instantly, ignoring the fact that it was $19.99. If she found good news, the book would be worth every penny.

Scanning the index, she found several references to Booth Adair, and quickly went to the referenced pages.

A colorful character, she read, *Booth Adair was a pirate/ buccaneer who plundered and stole large amounts of booty from Atlantic- and Mediterranean-going ships. No seagoing vessel, no matter how well armed, was beyond his self-avowed superiority when it came to battle. Adair plowed the seas for nearly half a century, longer than any other pirate of renown. Yet by the middle of the eighteenth century, the notorious pirate was an old man, and his days were numbered.*

Traveling to America, he contracted what is now believed to have been scarlet fever. The ship's doctor, a German named Johannes Grüner, wrote about Adair in his diaries:

The old man was mad with fever, begging for a priest to hear his confession. A foul wind was blowing and the storm was tossing the ship. With none onboard, a youthful minister, whose name I've long since forgotten, kept vigil at Adair's bedside, listening to the old man's perhaps delusional tales of adventure. In turn, the young man spoke of his wife—Evangeline, a beautiful name I've never been able to forget—and children, how he'd left them behind in England while he ventured to the new world to form a church and win souls there.

"I too wish to start over in America," the old man said, as the young minister and I bathed his forehead and body with cool water and attempted to give him broth for sustenance. He would not live through the night. I knew that with certainty, but the minister encouraged Adair to fight for his life, while at the same time striving to help the old pirate make peace with his Maker.

When the old man sensed his time had come, he ordered me to leave, wanting to talk to the minister only, yet I kept my ear to the door, which I hadn't tightly closed, and could hear the rattle of his voice, although it was little more than a whisper. "Take my only earthly possession, I beg of you."

"It should go to your family," the young man told Adair, but Adair's tone became insistent.

"It's little more than a leather valise, but it contains enough to build your church and possibly more. Please, I beg of you. Help me to atone for my terrible transgressions."

If I were an immoral man, I would have taken the valise myself. In truth, I did contemplate the thought of having gold beyond my wildest dreams, but then I heard Adair's last whispered words.

"Beware! A man named Vickers has been chasing me. He will hunt you now."

With that, he was gone. I looked at the young minister as he claimed the valise and said a prayer for his soul.

Booth Adair was the connection they'd somehow missed in all their research! The young minister whose wife was named Evangeline could only be Reverend Thorpe. And if that was his only association with a pirate, it was only pride in him that people should have, not abhorrence. She wondered, too, about this man named Vickers. She and her friends had always puzzled about what drove Jeremiah Thorpe to use such cryptic and cloak-and-dagger means to write about the treasure. If Vickers was trying to get his hands on the money, as Grüner implied, that could easily explain his secrecy.

Beverly wished she could copy the pages and send them to her friends and Reverend Locke, but she couldn't do that with an e-book. Instead she typed up a summary, sending it to everyone and asking Diane to forward it on to Jeanette. Then she texted each of them, telling them to check their e-mail as soon as possible.

It was well past midnight when she finished, long past time when she should have gone to bed, especially when she had to be up early in the morning to take Diane into Augusta for her doctor's appointment. Diane was still frightened; Beverly realized that she was also afraid for her friend. But she wouldn't let on. Diane needed Beverly's strength to see her through.

Setting her cell phone aside, Beverly stretched, yawning. She was just about to get up when her cell phone rang. Was one of her friends already responding to her note?

She smiled when she saw that it was a text message from Jeff and, amazingly, she noticed she'd somehow missed several of his messages.

Maybe things were getting back to normal. Maybe whatever was troubling him—their relationship, perhaps?— he'd come to terms with it. She hoped.

Traveled to Petra today. Petra is far more than the iconic photo you normally see of pink sandstone cathedral carved into the cliffs. So much more than what was filmed in the Indiana Jones movie. Its beauty is immeasurable. Sending photo of Ad Deir— the Monastery—although pictures cannot do it justice. Long climb to see it worth every sore muscle. Would do it again in a heartbeat. You would love it here.

The picture Jeff sent of the architectural marvel carved into the mountainside of rose-pink stone was extraordinary.

She could well imagine the wonder and awe in Jeff's face. She knew if she stood beside him, that his heart would be beating hard, that his hand would squeeze hers tightly, and he wouldn't be able to settle down until he'd explored every inch and photographically captured every sight from every angle. Travel and photography were his passion. He would never settle down. Could never stay in one place for long.

With each of the messages she read, she realized the truth of those thoughts. Maybe Jeff had realized it too, and was slowly, gently, trying to cut the strings of their relationship, because he knew in his heart that Beverly would never leave Marble Cove, that it had become her home, and she loved it.

CHAPTER NINETEEN

The sun refused to come out from behind the clouds on Wednesday morning, and the clouds let loose the rain.

"I'm not one to believe in omens, but this is an ominous beginning to our trip to see the doctor." Diane attempted to smile, but she knew it looked like a halfhearted grin. "The rain's coming down in sheets," she said to Beverly when they were no more than five miles away from Marble Cove. "Why don't I call the doctor's office and reschedule?"

Beverly chuckled. "Good try, my friend, but you're going to see Dr. Crowley and that's all there is to it. Besides, I've driven this road more times than I can count, and all too often it was covered with ice and snow. I'm not going to let something like a little rain make me turn tail and run back home."

"You're far braver than I."

"Ha! If it hadn't been for you, I might have pulled out of the mayor's race last week. I know exactly what it's like to be a chicken; I just try not to show it, while you usually show your emotions on your sleeve."

"I'm a writer. We know emotions and make good use of all of them."

They spent most of the long drive discussing what Beverly had found on the Internet the night before about Booth Adair and his connection to Jeremiah Thorpe, wishing they could have seen their friends' faces, and especially Reverend Locke's, when they read Beverly's note. Along the way they stopped for breakfast, but Diane felt her fear building the moment they drove into the city. Beverly, who knew the streets like the back of her hand, maneuvered through the downtown area like an expert, pulling into the parking lot of Augusta Oncology Group without missing a beat.

"I think I should have had something more substantial for breakfast this morning," Diane admitted. "I think my blood sugar's out of whack."

"Feeling dizzy?" Beverly asked, concern written all over her face as she pulled into a parking space and shut off the engine.

"A little. More queasy than anything else."

Beverly squeezed Diane's hand. "Do you think it's more nerves than low blood sugar?"

"Could be."

"Want to say a little prayer?"

"I've been talking to God for most of the trip." She grinned weakly. "Couldn't you see my lips moving?"

"I was too busy watching the road. But if I had to guess what God had to say, it was something along the lines of 'Buck up, Diane.'"

"Using my own words against me, eh?" Diane teased.

Beverly tucked her keys into her purse and pulled the hood of her raincoat over her head. "Now let's go in and see the doctor. The sooner you get this over with, the better."

It was a good thing Beverly had accompanied her today, Diane thought as they walked across the parking lot, trying to avoid puddles and hoping the wind and rain wouldn't change direction and pelt them directly in the face. If she'd come by herself, she would have turned right around and driven to the mall for a little therapeutic shopping instead.

There wasn't a familiar face in sight when they entered the doctor's office and hung up their coats alongside several others. Beverly remained at her side while they checked in, and she sat next to her in the only two seats that weren't occupied.

Diane tried to concentrate on the women's magazine that Beverly had found among a pile of sports and news magazines, but nothing held her interest. She tried to keep her eyes on the articles she'd been staring at—and not reading—but it was difficult not to look at the women who wore scarves around their heads. Some looked gaunt; some bloated; others worn out. She didn't want to look the same way.

As if Beverly sensed her worry, she again took her hand. She squeezed it tightly. "Want me to go in with you when you see the doctor?"

Did she? She shook her head. "I can do it."

The door leading to the examining rooms opened, and Diane could swear the nurse stared right at her, but then she called another name. It opened again and again, and each time, Diane tensed.

The door opened one more time. "Diane Spencer."

She drew in a deep breath, then turned to Beverly and smiled. "I'm okay."

She tried not to feel like she was walking into the lion's den as she followed the nurse. She hadn't weighed herself in a long time, but when she got on the scale, realized she'd lost eight pounds. She hadn't even realized that her clothes were a little looser. Then again, she'd never been Miss Fashion Plate, her clothes fitting snug in all the right places.

It seemed to take forever for the nurse to take her temperature and blood pressure, and to ask at least a million questions—the same questions, as a matter of fact, that she'd already answered on the paperwork she'd given to the receptionist when she checked in. Maybe they liked to double-check your answers, to make sure you hadn't made a mistake.

And then she was alone, sitting in one of two chairs, staring at the walls, at the posters of the male and female anatomy, a big pink ribbon, and photographs of Dr. Crowley running in a lot of different races, all of them cancer related. His smile was big and infectious, and she found herself smiling when the knock sounded on the door and he stepped in.

"So nice to see you again, Diane."

She couldn't quite agree that it was nice to see him again, but he was a charming man and a good doctor, and his palm and fingers were warm when they shook hands.

"You're looking great," he said. "What's it been? Five years?"

Diane nodded. "Pretty close."

"I was sorry to hear about your husband. I always liked Eric."

She smiled softly. "Me too."

Dr. Crowley had a rust-colored crew cut, blue eyes, and that smile that lit up the room. He patted her knee gently. "I know you're scared, but you shouldn't be. You had such a miraculous cure the last time, and I want to make sure there's no recurrence of the cancer. It's just a precaution."

Like the nurse, he asked what felt like a million questions, several of which she'd already answered twice. She felt good. She didn't have any aches or pains. She hadn't felt any lumps.

"Would you mind me doing a physical exam?"

Diane shook her head and Dr. Crowley stepped out of the room while she changed into a gown. Several minutes later he came back in with his assistant. It was Rhonda, the woman who'd called her earlier.

Every muscle in her body tensed as he examined her. She couldn't relax. She just wanted it all to be over. When he finished, he didn't stand there talking to her about this and that, but went out of the room again to give her time to put on her clothes. Gave her a moment to breathe, and she needed that desperately.

Again the knock came, and Dr. Crowley came into the room. He sat on the low spinning stool that was a mainstay in most doctors' offices—Diane had seen her fair share of them—and looked her square in the eye. "Rhonda will be in in a few minutes to draw some blood." He scribbled a few things on a lab sheet. "I know you live a good hour from here, but if you have time before heading home, I'd like to have you go over to our radiology lab for a few more tests."

"Is that necessary?"

He smiled as he nodded. "I don't believe in taking chances with a patient's health."

She swallowed. "Did you find something during the exam? A lump? Something I might not have found during my own exams?"

He frowned slightly, and suddenly his words mixed together. All she heard was a conglomeration of mush, none of it making sense, except for the bottom line. There might be a recurrence of the cancer. "But," he said, with a strong emphasis on the *but,* "I'd like to see the lab and radiology reports. I can't make any determination without them, and I'm not going to give you an all clear or a negative response without them. Fair?"

That word *fair* stuck with her while she shook his hand and heard him say he'd call her hopefully by Friday. It rumbled around in her brain as Beverly drove her to the lab and she underwent an MRI and an ultrasound.

No, it was not fair. Not at all.

★ ★ ★

One day had never seemed so long, Beverly thought, sitting in the laboratory's waiting room all by herself. She'd scanned nearly every magazine, but it was impossible to concentrate, not when Diane's fear-stricken face continually came to mind.

Beverly took a deep breath and prayed silently for her friend.

Dear God, be with Diane and give her hope and courage. Please.

Beverly's cell phone rang, interrupting her prayer. She grabbed the phone quickly and glanced at the display. Jeff.

Last night's stars were surely a gift from heaven, his text message began. *Looking up at them from the darkness inside Petra's stone walls, it seemed as if I could reach out and touch them, they were that bright and appeared that close. I wish you could see them.*

She wished it too. Right this moment, she wished she could whisk Diane away from this laboratory, take her off to Petra with the magic blink of an eye, and take all her worries away. And just as much as she wished that, she wished Jeff was here beside her, holding her hand. Diane needed comfort, but Beverly needed strength to help Diane through this.

"Call your children," Beverly had told her in the car. "At least call Jessica. She can take off work and be with you."

Diane had shook her head. "No. They're both just getting over the death of their father. I'm not going to inject more worry into their lives."

Beverly had smiled at her friend. "I'd keep it hush-hush too."

"I'm glad I've got your shoulder to whine on," Diane had said. "Thanks for coming with me today. I wouldn't have been able to see well enough to drive, not while trying to look through my tears, not to mention the rain."

Beverly thought about what she wanted to say to Jeff, then typed the words slowly. *I'm in Augusta with Diane. She's undergoing tests; her cancer may have come back. Please make a wish upon one of those beautiful Petra stars tonight—a wish and a prayer for Diane's health. I know God will be listening.*

It wasn't more than a minute later when Jeff texted back. *I'll be praying for Diane.*

Another note came from Jeff before she could reply. *Since you're in Augusta, why don't you stop by to see Grandpa? I think it's Wednesday in your neck of the woods, which means lobster night. If you can, stop by Larry's Lobster, pick up a couple of big ones, and drop them in Grandpa's pot. He makes the best drawn butter and cheese biscuits. It'll be good for you and Grandpa to get together; even better for Diane. You know he can brighten a day.*

It was Jeff's grandfather who'd proved to be their miracle last Christmas. He'd saved her, Diane, Margaret, and Shelley when they'd almost been swept over Orlean Point in the storm of the decade. Maybe he could help to save Diane tonight, simply by giving her hope.

CHAPTER TWENTY

What had she gotten herself into?

Margaret wanted to pull her hair out during Wednesday evening's class. "Mind if I ask what's gotten into all of you tonight?"

"What are you talking about, Mrs. H.?" Jake Morris had stuck Margaret with that name during class number three and it seemed to have taken hold with the rest of her students. "I, for one, am my usual self."

"What I'm talking about, Mr. Morris, is the fact that I asked you to create a monster. What possessed you to think I was talking about something other than creating a monster on paper? Why, pray tell, did you decide to turn Danny Wharburton into a cross between a mummy and the Creature from the Black Lagoon?"

"It's actually pretty cool," Danny said, his words garbled since he was trying to speak through the papier-mâché covering a big portion of his body, including his head. She never should have gone outside for a quick walk, in an attempt to make her ever-present—of late—headache go away. She should have known the headache was a symptom of this class, and nothing more. What she hadn't known was that her kids could find a way to make her head hurt even more.

"I agree it's pretty cool," Margaret said, "but the ramifications of covering a human being—like Danny—are that, number one, his mother is going to have a fit; number two, that the papier-mâché will probably have to be cut off of him; number three...Oh, who cares about number three. Did you have to paint it so quickly? And in black, lavender, and neon green?"

"Do you have a problem with the colors, Mrs. H.?" Felicity asked. "We thought they complemented each other quite well."

I give up. Margaret slumped down in her chair, but only for a moment. She had to put scissors to papier-mâché and cut Danny out of the slop that was covering him. She didn't hold out any hope of getting him cleaned up before his mom arrived.

Not that she'd really wanted to give Mrs. Wharburton private art classes, but if she had, that plan was now dead in the water.

If only Adelaide had come with her to class tonight! But she'd had homework, and she reminded her mom and dad that homework always comes before fun and games. If only Adelaide knew. Tonight's class hadn't been fun and games at all, at least for Margaret. Margaret had missed her daughter's calming presence in the classroom.

Fortunately, the month was half over. Margaret smiled as she took the pair of scissors to the papier-mâché. Only four more classes to go.

★ ★ ★

"This is crazy. We can't just barge in on Mr. Maker with a couple of lobsters and expect him to cook for us."

Beverly stood in front of the lobster tank staring at a couple of live ones that Larry, owner of Larry's Lobster, was fishing out for Beverly and Diane. "You don't know Mr. Maker as well as I do, and I can tell you right now, he'll love having us drop by."

"What if he has company? A lady friend, for instance."

Beverly rolled her eyes. "He's eighty-five. Maybe eighty-six. Do you really think he'd have a girlfriend?"

Diane shrugged. "You're trying awfully hard to make me laugh."

Beverly slung an arm around Diane's shoulders. "Better to laugh than cry."

It wasn't long before Beverly had paid for the lobster and they were standing at the door of Mr. Maker's century-old sage-green bungalow, with its garden that could easily rival Diane's.

Beverly knocked not once but twice.

"He must not be home," Diane said. "Why don't we get out of here, donate the lobster to a homeless shelter, and head for home?"

"He doesn't move all that fast, Diane. Besides, I hear music inside. I know he wouldn't be playing the stereo—or whatever—if he wasn't around to listen."

It seemed forever, but finally the door opened and Edward Maker appeared, looking sharp with his thick head of salt-and-pepper hair neatly combed, instead of mussed, as it usually was, and wearing a jacket and tie. Maybe they had made a mistake in coming tonight, Beverly thought. It certainly looked like he was ready to go out on the town.

"Hello, ladies." He had a smile as big as all of Maine on his face and smelled like Old Spice, the same aftershave her father always used. "Nice to see you. Come on in."

"Are you sure we aren't disturbing you?" Diane asked, hanging back, looking like she wanted to rush back to the car.

"Nope. Got a friend here, but she won't mind the company, not when she sees who it is."

"I had a text message from Jeff today," Beverly said, "and he reminded me it was lobster night."

"Ayuh. Been having lobster night as long as I can remember—well, been having it since I could afford to. I'm fixin' to drop a couple in the pot in the next half hour or so."

Beverly pulled out the bag she'd been holding behind her back. "Have room for another two? Fresh out of the drink."

"The more the merrier." Beverly had seen Mr. Maker in a good mood a time or two, but this time his cheerful words and twinkling blue eyes made him seem almost giddy.

"Come on in." He threw the door open wide and no sooner had they stepped into the living room than Celia Patterson, Coral Peabody's older sister, popped into view, her snowy white hair done up in soft curls and wearing a powder-blue pantsuit. She was a picture of perfection, her smile as bright as Mr. Maker's.

"You know Cece Patterson. Right?"

"Of course. Both Diane and I know her." Beverly handed the bag of lobsters to Mr. Maker and took Celia's—Cece's—hand. "It's nice to see you again."

Diane, not looking much less uncomfortable, said hello to Cece, then turned to Mr. Maker. "I'm so sorry we're intruding. Why don't we leave those two lobsters with you and Cece and—"

"Oh no, we wouldn't hear of you leaving," Cece said, as if this were her house and she was the hostess. "Edward and I get together every Wednesday. We usually watch a little *Jeopardy* or work on a jigsaw puzzle. It'll be nice to have a couple of young ladies to keep us company."

"We can't stay much past clean-up-after-dinnertime," Beverly said. "That storm's blowing back in again, and I'd rather not be caught in it when it's dark. Makes it nearly impossible to see the road."

"Well, let's get the pot a boiling and get the lobster cooked up," Mr. Maker said, heading to the kitchen, with everyone following. "Cece makes the best drawn butter."

"Coral gave me the recipe years and years ago."

"You don't just use unsalted butter?" Diane asked, easing up a little.

"Oh, I definitely use unsalted butter, but I add a touch of fresh-squeezed lemon juice, some finely chopped chives, and fresh ground pepper." Cece licked her lips. "It's amazing what a few extra touches can add to the flavor of something as simple as drawn butter."

"Well, let's stop lollygagging and get this show on the road." Edward filled a large lobster pot with water and set it on the stove, while Cece went to work on her drawn butter. "Why don't you set the table, Beverly? You know where everything is."

"What about me?" Diane asked. "I do a mean job of doctoring up French bread. Do you have any on hand?"

"Picked some up just this morning," Mr. Maker said. "And there's salted butter in the fridge."

"What about garlic?" Diane opened the refrigerator door. "Mind if I smash up a few of your garlic cloves?"

"Be my guest."

Sitting around the table forty-five minutes later, they were still laughing, even Diane, who had color in her cheeks, something that had been missing for nearly a week.

"I feel like my fingers are sticks of butter," Beverly said, trying to wipe her hands with a few flimsy napkins, then getting up from the table and going to the sink for good old soap and water. "But you know what? That has got to be the best lobster dinner I've ever had."

"That grandson of mine doesn't know what he's missed out on. Of course, he thinks borscht is good." Mr. Maker shook his head. "He even brought me home some Russian caviar after his Trans-Siberian Railway trip. Don't think I'll be eating that anytime soon."

"It's a delicacy," Cece said. "And expensive to boot. We should do Jeff the honor of at least giving it a try."

"One of these days. Next time he's home, maybe."

"Why don't you show Diane and Beverly the postcards Jeff sent you from his trip?"

Beverly looked from Cece to Mr. Maker. Postcards? She hadn't received any. Not one. No caviar either. She tried to put that out of her mind.

Mr. Maker got up from the table, went into the living room, and came back with a stack of postcards. "Must have cost him an arm and a leg to send these. They got here fast too, much to my surprise." He spread the postcards out on the table so Beverly and Diane could see, and started talking about all the places Jeff had seen. He always had pride in his eyes and in his voice when he talked about his grandson. Beverly couldn't blame him, of course. Jeff was a pretty great man.

But maybe they weren't meant for each other, not like they'd once thought.

By seven thirty Beverly and Diane were on the road again. The sky had cleared; the dark clouds that had been predicted were nowhere around. Even Diane's moodiness had scurried away, at least for now. Beverly, on the other hand, felt a little lost.

"You know," Diane said, "you've spent so much time the last several days cheering me up, that I hadn't realized until tonight just how little you'd talked about Jeff in the last couple of weeks. Is everything okay between the two of you?"

Beverly shrugged. "I don't know. Before he went to Russia, I thought things were great. I thought he might actually be in love, or close to it. Now he seems to be pulling away."

"What makes you say that?"

"A whole host of things." Beverly told Diane about Jeff's return from Russia, how he hadn't rushed to be with her, and how he'd left for Jordan just a couple of days later. And then there were his text messages, filled with beautiful prose, but no "I miss yous" or "Wish you were heres." "And now, I think the worst thing of all is that he didn't send me any postcards. I didn't even get caviar, and I love caviar."

Diane laughed.

"What are you laughing about? This is my love life, or lack thereof, that we're talking about."

"I think you're blowing things way out of proportion. If Jeff wanted to back away from you, he wouldn't send you text messages half a dozen times or more a day."

"It's more like three or four text messages a day."

"As for the postcards, Mr. Maker probably doesn't have e-mail and I seriously doubt that he has a cell phone or even a computer for sending text messages. If Jeff wants to communicate with his grandfather, he does it with postcards. With you, he sends you his immediate thoughts. He sends you pictures he's just snapped."

"Maybe you're right. Maybe I am overreacting."

"You are overreacting. There's no maybe about it. And you want to know the truth?"

"Why do I think you're going to tell me even if I say no?"

"Because you know me well. The truth, my dear, is that you're still a little scared of this relationship with Jeff. You're rationalizing everything, to make it seem like Jeff's the one with cold feet, when your feet are actually frozen."

"That's not true."

"It is. So"—Diane laughed—"in the words of two wonderfully strong women...buck up!"

CHAPTER TWENTY-ONE

"Why on earth the two of you went to Augusta in that storm yesterday is beyond me."

Margaret took a bite out of the cinnamon roll she'd ordered at the Cove and chewed slowly, shaking her head at Diane and Beverly. They had to be out of their minds to go shopping in such a gale.

"If it had been me," Shelley said, bouncing Emma on her knee, "I would have turned around and come home. It was tough enough just driving Aiden to school in that wind and rain."

"You mean he didn't want to stay home?" Diane asked. "I thought he'd been begging to stay with you."

"It's a miracle." Shelley grinned. "He woke up Wednesday morning a changed little boy. He was eager to go, but he's been talking a lot about his new friend Bethany. It's Bethany this and Bethany that. He even asked if I could make a special cookie that he could give to Bethany."

"What did you say?" Beverly asked, stirring sweetener into her coffee.

"I told him that I'd be happy to bake special cookies for the whole class, but it wouldn't be right to single out one person. We talked about hurting people's feelings."

"Do you think he understood?" Margaret asked, remembering Adelaide's first crush.

"Miss Davidson, his teacher, says next week he'll probably have another best friend. That it's certainly nothing to worry about, not that I would ever worry."

Shelley laughed, as did all of the friends sitting around the table on Thursday afternoon. The gallery had been quiet for three days, so Margaret had decided to take the day off, keeping the Closed sign up at Shearwater Gallery because she still was nursing a headache from last night's class. Shelley had an hour before leaving to pick Aiden up, and Beverly and Diane had both told Margaret they'd love to get together for coffee.

"How's the art class coming along?" Diane asked, then took a sip of hot tea.

"We created a monster last night. Literally." She held up her hands for all to see. "Notice the black and blue on my hands? Those aren't bruises. It's the stain from all the paint that I tried desperately to get off one of my students." She told them the whole awful story.

"How did Danny's mother react?" Beverly asked.

"She actually laughed, which took me completely by surprise." Margaret took another bite of cinnamon roll. "Did I tell you she's asked me to give her private art instruction?"

Her friends all shook their heads. "She did, but I haven't committed yet. I really want some free time this fall and winter."

"We've heard you say that before," Shelley reminded her. "Every time someone comes to you for help, you hem and haw because you never have any free time and you're desperate for some—but then you give in."

"But you never complain," Diane added, "except maybe about this art class."

Margaret waved away their compliments. "I'm not cut out to teach kids."

"What about Caleb?" Shelley asked. "You worked wonders with him."

"Caleb already knew how to paint. He just needed a grandmother figure to help him through a personal crisis, and I'm the one he found. But enough about me." Margaret tilted her head toward Beverly. "What's the news on the town hall meeting?"

"Haven't heard a word yet. I hope this doesn't mean that Pastor Carl was unable to convince Lee and Dennis to give it a go, or that he met too much opposition from people he talked to about it. After all, Evelyn Waters told me the people in Marble Cove would balk at the idea since it had never been done here before."

"Probably because Evelyn doesn't like to debate," Margaret said. "I've known her a big part of my life and she's a wonderful woman. She's done a good job steering this town, but she's not all that keen on change."

"But I don't want to change Marble Cove." Beverly was more than adamant. "I only want to have the opportunity to let everyone in town know who I am, what I can do versus what Dennis or Lee can do."

"People are already seeing your face all over town," Shelley said. "I've seen Beverly Wheeland: Embracing Our

Heritage signs up in shop windows and in front of people's homes all over town."

"That's good for starters." Beverly smiled. "But there's still a lot to do."

"Count me in for door-to-door contact," Margaret said, "but that'll have to be next month."

"Door to door isn't my thing," Diane said, "but I could make phone calls or stuff envelopes."

"I'll do whatever I can," Shelley added, "but—"

"You have two kids, a business, and a husband who's working and studying full time. I think you have enough on your plate," Beverly told Shelley.

"You've said a mouthful," Shelley agreed. "I don't know if I told you all this. My sister keeps bringing up a pact the two of us made when we were kids. You know, pretty much a blood oath concocted in a moment of despair."

"Mind telling us what this oath was?" Margaret asked, taking the last bite of her cinnamon roll. Along with the coffee, it was working wonders on her headache.

"If something happened to one of us"—Shelley paused— "the other would take care of the other's children."

"Sounds pretty natural," Diane said. "I think all of us would do that for a sibling or a close friend."

"It's not that I wouldn't do it or wouldn't want to do it," Shelley stated, looking uncomfortable with the fact that she'd even brought it up. "It's just that, well, Hailey, my sister's daughter, has had a sort of rough upbringing. Not that my sister isn't a good mom, but she—" Again she sighed. "I'm not crazy about the people she hangs out with. I don't know how much influence those people might have had on Hailey. And I don't want Emma and Aiden exposed to anything that might not be good for them."

Diane reached across the table and patted Shelley's hand. "You could look at it the opposite way. If, and I do mean if, Hailey were to come and live with you, she'll have the opportunity to be exposed to all the good things you and Dan have taught Aiden and Emma."

"I guess I hadn't thought about that."

"I think we all have a tendency to overlook the positive," Margaret said. "It's human nature."

"Speaking of positive." Diane leaned her arms on the table. "Jeanette's coming tomorrow evening and Saturday it's off to the bell tower."

"Has she been able to decipher the documents?" Margaret asked.

Diane shook her head. "I was afraid she'd be too busy, with school starting this week, and I was right."

"None of the rest of us would have had the time to make sense of them either," Beverly stated. "Still, it would have been nice to know if she'd found out anything of interest."

"Well you found out some interesting information about Booth Adair and our preacher, Beverly," Margaret said.

"Yes," Beverly agreed. "It seems that there's evidence to support the idea that Thorpe once had his hands on a significant amount of money. Whether any of that 'treasure' is still around is another question."

"I wonder what the story is with that Vickers fellow who was mentioned on Adair's death bed," Diane chimed in. "A bad guy looking for Adair's treasure would certainly explain why Thorpe was so secretive about where he kept the money over the years."

"Well, I'm hoping we find some more answers when we go up into the tower Saturday, but I'm not feeling that positive at the moment," Margaret said, massaging her temples.

"Bite your tongue." Shelley grinned. "I'm thinking nothing but positive thoughts. After all, Jeanette heard the bell last Saturday. That must mean that we're going to discover something."

★ ★ ★

Diane didn't leave the cottage at all Friday morning. She couldn't, not when Dr. Crowley had said he should have the results to her by today. She sat at her desk, unable to write, just barely able to function, and stared at the calendar. It was definitely Friday.

Jeanette would be here soon, and she didn't want to hear bad news and find that she had to tell Jeanette before she could tell Justin and Jessica, not to mention Beverly, and then her other friends. She owed all of them that.

At eleven thirty she picked up the phone and dialed Dr. Crowley's office and asked to speak to him or his assistant Rhonda.

"I'm sorry. Dr. Crowley's been called away on an emergency. We don't expect him back today. And this was a scheduled day off for his assistant. Is there someone else who can help you?"

Diane sighed heavily. "Dr. Crowley told me he should have results of my lab tests in today, and that he'd call me."

"Well, I can't tell you the results, but I can certainly tell you if we've received them. If we have, I could possibly have another doctor call you."

Diane shook her head. "No, I'd rather talk with Dr. Crowley. He's been my doctor for years."

"Do you want to know if the results are in? It's no trouble looking. They'll be on my computer."

Diane gripped the phone tightly. She fought back tears. "No, that's okay. Will Dr. Crowley be back on Monday?"

"Yes, although we never know when he might have to go into surgery. Like today, sometimes there's an emergency. But he always gets back to his patients as soon as he can."

"Would you leave him a message that I called?"

"I'd be happy to."

After she gave the receptionist her name and number and hung up, Diane broke down and cried. She had to get it out of her system now, then run into the bathroom and wash her face with cold water before Jeanette showed up. She couldn't let anyone see her cry.

★ ★ ★

"I certainly hope the date we've picked for the town hall meeting will work for you," Pastor Carl told Beverly Friday afternoon.

She'd been surprised to receive his call so soon. "You were able to set it up?"

"Absolutely. We—my wife and I—found a great deal of interest among the people we talked with. We've come up with what we believe is a very workable format for the audience to use when asking questions, and among Pastor Tim, Reverend Locke, and me, we've come up with a press release and an announcement for each of us to include in our church bulletins."

"You didn't meet any resistance from Dennis Calder or Lee Waters?"

In the silence that followed, she could easily imagine Pastor Carl shrugging. "None that couldn't be worked out."

"We will be able to use your church auditorium?"

"It's a go. We'll have the sound system ready, ushers to make sure people are seated properly, and all the logistics under control. All you need to concern yourself with is being there and being calm enough to answer the questions."

She'd given so many speeches in her life, she wasn't worried about standing up in public. She didn't want to argue with Dennis or Lee, but if it happened, she'd stay focused and in control.

"So when's the big day?"

"Saturday, September 29. Seven in the evening."

That was just over two weeks away, and she still had a lot of preparing to do, not to mention campaigning, plus her consulting work. So far she'd been able to take care of her clients without a hitch; she had to make sure it stayed that way.

She was breathing hard by the time she got off the phone with Pastor Carl. She wanted to shout to the world that she'd soon be doing her first town hall debate, but the world could wait. First off, she wanted to tell the man who was most on her mind.

She picked up her cell phone and texted Jeff.

Chapter Twenty-Two

Somehow, by the time Jeanette pulled up in her vintage Volkswagen late Friday afternoon, Diane had regained her composure. Her tears were washed away. She had a lavender-scented candle—for tranquility—burning in the living room, and she had a pitcher of fresh lemonade waiting in the fridge.

Diane took a deep breath before throwing open the front door and welcoming Jeanette in.

"Do you have a cold?" Jeanette asked. "Your nose is red and so are your eyes."

Diane smiled, determined not to tell her sister-in-law the truth. "Could be allergies."

"Well, I hope it isn't a cold. The ones you get in the summer are atrocious."

Diane slipped into the kitchen while Jeanette put her things in the guest room. She could have rushed into the bathroom to powder her nose and put eye drops in her eyes, but the allergy excuse had gone over well. It was best to leave well enough alone. In the end, she just poured two glasses of lemonade.

"Is there anything special you'd like to do this evening?" Diane asked Jeanette when she came out of the guest room. "Go shopping? Take a walk on the beach?"

"The beach sounds nice, but later, maybe." She sat on the sofa, kicked off her shoes, and tucked her feet up underneath her. "It's been a horrendous week. If I'd known that I'd be working fifty to sixty hours a week in this new job, I might have retired."

"But you love your job, don't you?"

"Too much, I think, although I miss the constant interaction with the students. I'm finding myself spending more and more time with college administrators and instructors now. We professors can be somewhat pompous at times." Jeanette grinned. "It's mighty hard to deal with people who know everything."

It was so nice to have Jeanette here. Diane hadn't realized how much her sister-in-law could make her laugh, merely by being herself.

"You know, Diane, I feel just awful not getting around to looking at the documents I took home with me."

"Don't. None of us would have had time either."

"Do you think your friends might be able to come over now? With five people looking them over, we might be able to get through all of them in just a couple of hours, and possibly have some news to share with Reverend Locke tomorrow."

"Let me see if I can get in touch with everyone."

Diane was at the phone in an instant, and as luck would have it, Margaret, Beverly, and Shelley were able to get away, although Shelley had to get home in an hour to help Dan tuck in their little ones.

It wasn't long before all five women were sitting around the table with iced tea, ice water, and lemonade, poring over the papers. Shelley had brought along a freshly baked blueberry cobbler for later, its scent wafting around the room as they worked.

Even though she was wearing her reading glasses, Diane felt the strain in her eyes from reading such awkward script, but she kept on going, taking a sip of hot tea here and there, wishing someone would hurry up and find something.

"Aha!" Margaret's index finger pressed hard against a spot on the page she'd been reading. She grinned at her friends. "Wait until you hear this."

Margaret leaned back in her chair and lifted the paper so it was just the right distance from her eyes. "This is one of those internal church memos," she said. "It appears the council spent hours on end interviewing Reverend Thorpe, hoping to get to the bottom of the theft accusation." Margaret scanned the paper again. "Listen to this. *'On the third day of discussions with Reverend Thorpe, we ascertained that he had diverted monies from his own funds, which he states he received from a wealthy benefactor—'*"

Margaret glanced up from her reading. "Booth Adair, no doubt."

"That would be my guess," Beverly said.

"Where did he divert the money to?" Shelley asked.

"This is good, something Reverend Locke will admire. To help Native Americans buy their long-term servitude back from colonists."

"Why would he want to keep that a secret?" Diane asked. "It was his money."

"It doesn't say," Margaret said, setting the paper down. "My guess is that interfering with what was considered to be ideological and legal in the colonies was frowned upon."

"Especially if that interference messed with a family's economics," Beverly added. "It was basically slavery, no different from what was going on in the South."

Margaret nodded. "In the end, this memo states, it was determined by the church council that there was no money missing from the church coffers, that Reverend Thorpe had done nothing illegal, and that Robert Gilbert had lied."

"Was he punished?" Diane asked.

Again Margaret nodded. "Banished from the church."

"Good riddance. Of course, it would have been nice if the newspaper that printed that horrid story about Reverend Thorpe being the Bandit Preacher had also printed a retraction." Shelley shook her head. "I suppose that would have been hoping for too much."

"We can print a retraction now," Diane said. "As soon as we sum up all the details we've learned."

"So does anyone think there's still some treasure left somewhere in Marble Cove?" Beverly asked. "It looks like, except for whatever was left in that old box we found on the cliff, he must have used it all up for good. What was that last line Jeremiah Thorpe wrote in one of his letters to Evangeline?" She frowned, giving it some thought, then paraphrased, "What could have been used for evil will ultimately be used for good."

"And it was. Just think about it: the lighthouse, the church. Helping to free people from...slavery, basically."

"I still think we should search the tower tomorrow," Shelley said. "I'm not buying the idea that there's nothing there."

"I'm with you, Shelley," Diane said. "I'm certain the bells are calling us there for a reason."

★ ★ ★

Beverly leaned against the ancient maple tree that Jeremiah Thorpe was said to have planted over two centuries ago and waited for Reverend Locke and her friends to arrive. She was excited at the prospect of climbing once again into Old First's bell tower, whether there was treasure there or not. It might be old and dusty and musty inside, but the moment a person stepped onto the wooden floors, surrounded by stone walls, she couldn't help but feel blessed.

She'd arrived early, but she felt comfortable here in the shade of the tree, looking at the church's stained glass windows, turrets, and tower. She just might tell Diane about this spot. It was a good place to stand and pray; she thought of Diane and realized it could even be a good place to sit with her laptop and write, especially if her creativity felt stifled.

The sudden ring of her cell phone startled her. It shouldn't have, of course. It had been ringing nearly constantly of late, with calls about the town hall meeting or her candidacy, with people wanting to donate funds to help get her elected or wanting to tell her off for having the nerve to run against good men like Dennis Calder and Lee Waters, especially when she was a newcomer in town. It was all part of the process. She had to get used to it. Because she would be mayor.

She found Jeff's new text message as comforting as the place she stood.

A couple of days along the Jordan River could never be enough. From the first moment I arrived, I thought of you and your friends singing 'Michael, Row the Boat Ashore' at your beach party. You should come here, Beverly.

If only she could. Someday, perhaps, but right now her life was here.

Before she could text him back, Diane and Jeanette clattered up in Jeanette's Beetle, with Margaret and Shelley arriving less than a minute later. Reverend Locke appeared just as her friends walked toward the ancient maple tree, as if they'd been summoned once more by the bell.

"Thank you so much for letting us see the inside of the bell tower," Diane said, holding her hand out to Reverend Locke. She introduced Jeanette, who also expressed her delight in getting to see the inside.

"It's all of you who deserve thanks." He smiled fondly, taking off his glasses and wiping off the lenses with his handkerchief. "I wish my sister Priscilla were here. The information you e-mailed to me this morning was the revelation I'd long hoped for. Whether the rest of the world ever learns the truth about Reverend Thorpe or not, my sister and I know it. I can rest easy now, knowing he was truly a man of God."

"We gave some thought to giving up our search for the treasure, given the information we found last night," Beverly said, "but Shelley and Jeanette still believe there's something in the tower that we need to find."

"I was hesitant about it myself last night, but I'm sure now that there's something up there," Margaret said. "I haven't always been a believer. Most of you know that. But God led me to Him, just as He's leading us to this tower."

Reverend Locke smiled. "I haven't always been a believer, either, Margaret. Not about your treasure, that is, but I've prayed about this all week and I believe you're right. God has led us to this time and place."

"If only we knew what to look for," Shelley said.

"Perhaps it's another gold doubloon or a precious coin or jewel wedged into one of the floorboards," Jeanette offered. "Something as simple as that could be worth enough to rebuild the roof."

Beverly shook her head. "Something tells me we just need to keep our eyes and hearts and imaginations open. The most amazing treasures are often the ones we overlook."

Chapter Twenty-Three

The bell tower was musty and the telltale scent of smoke still lingered, even though the fire had occurred nearly three months ago.

"You know," Shelley said, "I wonder if we should have worn hard hats, just in case a piece of roof decides to fall down on us."

"You're being overdramatic," Margaret said. "Still, I think we should be extra careful while we're here."

"We really shouldn't have come." Reverend Locke stood in the center of the tower, turning in circles, using his flashlight to illuminate one part of the room after another. "I feel responsible for each and every one of you, so please, let's try to get through this inspection as quickly as possible."

"Just make sure you don't leave any stone unturned," Diane added. "We're here; let's make the best of this."

Beverly smiled at Diane, wondering if she realized how fitting her words were, not only for what they were doing now, but for what she was going through in life.

"I should have suggested this before we came up here," Jeanette said, shining her flashlight through cobwebs, floating dust, and soot. "Let's do this in an organized fashion, each of us taking one part of the room and thoroughly searching it. It's not that big, but make sure you look through everything. As you already know, even an old piece of paper can be an invaluable find."

Beverly turned her section of the tower inside out, then went through it yet again, shining the beam of her flashlight along the cracks between the floorboards, and when she was finished, she ran her fingers through those same cracks, trying not to cry out when a sliver went into her index finger.

Sweat beaded on her forehead. She could feel it sliding down her back and at the base of her neck. As much as she'd wanted to inspect the tower again, she also wanted to get out quickly.

"This is getting us nowhere," Reverend Locke said. "We've been in here far too long, it's far too hot in this weather, and have any of you found anything at all?"

There was a chorus of no's.

"Then let's go."

They were on their way toward the exit when Jeanette called out, "Reverend Locke, do you know anything about these paintings? They were covered by a pile of old clothes and wrapped in quilts. They appear quite old."

Reverend Locke made his way to the far side of the room, to a niche nearly hidden by downed beams and support posts. He looked at the paintings she'd uncovered. "No, I'm afraid I don't. They could have been stored here years before I came to Old First."

"Then I strongly suggest we take them out of here so I can inspect each one. I believe we should take a careful look at the quilts too. They could easily be a couple of centuries old and quite valuable."

"Other than some portraits of the church's pastors, the church has never been the recipient of paintings," Reverend Locke said. "Our stained glass is basically the only adornment we have."

"They could have belonged to a former minister. Maybe they go as far back as Reverend Thorpe," Beverly suggested. "We do know that a lot of his things were stored here at one time."

"Maybe his picture of Evangeline is among them," Margaret said. "His second wife might well have asked him to store it away in here."

"Don't get my hopes up, ladies. No matter how strong my faith, another disappointment could do me in."

★ ★ ★

As gently as possible, the five women and Reverend Locke removed old quilts from each painting and laid them out on the worktables at the back of Margaret's gallery, while Allan and Adelaide stayed out front should any customers come in to browse.

A slip of paper fluttered out from among the quilts. Shelley stopped to retrieve the yellowed paper and gasped. She handed it to Beverly. "What's this?"

"I don't know. But I'm afraid it's very badly stained and torn," she said as she carefully laid it flat on the table.

"Can you read any of it?" Shelley asked, straining to see around the heads of the others as they gathered around the fragile paper.

Margaret adjusted the lighting over the table and scrounged through drawer below where she kept assorted instruments, coming up with a large magnifying glass. "Diane, you had the best luck deciphering our Jeremiah's handwriting before. Care to give it another try?"

The group held its collective breath as Diane squinted down at the faded ink and angled the paper slightly sideways. She sighed. "I think I can make out a few things here and there, but hardly any words together. Look: this clearly says 'portrait,' but the next word is torn off. Here are some recognizable numbers a few lines down near the end, but what do they mean?"

"May I see?" Beverly asked, edging closer to Diane as she handed her the magnifying glass. She studied the numbers carefully and nodded, as if to herself. "I see a *17* and a *15*. Is that what you see, Jeanette?"

Jeanette took her turn with the glass and affirmed Beverly's guess.

"And," Beverly added, excitement building in her voice, "the three letters before the 17 are a-l-m. Could it be 'Psalm'? Margaret, do you have a Bible here?"

Before Margaret could reply, Reverend Locke spoke up in a thoughtful voice. "I know that reference. Jeremiah Thorpe signed some of his letters with the words from that verse: 'I will behold thy face in righteousness: I shall be satisfied—'"

"'—when I wake, with thy likeness,'" Beverly finished triumphantly. "I remember that verse! It was printed in Reverend Thorpe's prayer book. It was the only one that was underlined."

There was a reverent pause before Margaret breathed, "So could this verse be connected to the portrait mentioned in the letter?"

"And do you think," Shelley added, wide-eyed, "that the portrait could be in this dusty collection?"

"We'll see," Jeanette said, as she resumed freeing the old paintings from their hiding places.

"I'm not an art historian," Margaret said, "but I might be able to tell the approximate age of each painting."

"You take half and I'll take half," Jeanette said. "I'm not an artist like you, but I've studied art history for a good long time. I would hope I have the eye to spot something of value."

"I'd settle for the painting of Evangeline," Reverend Locke said, but that one special picture didn't seem to be in the lot.

Margaret could almost feel Reverend Locke, Beverly, Diane, and Shelley breathing down her neck as she moved from mundane picture to even more mundane picture, their frames even less exciting. She wished she could deliver good news, but she couldn't see that happening. "I'm afraid there's nothing important here. They could easily have been purchased at a five-and-dime fifty or sixty years ago."

"What about yours, Jeanette?" Beverly asked. "Any luck?"

"The first two fit the same description as yours," Jeanette said. "Your basic slap-any-old-thing-on-the-wall artwork. But—"

"But what?" Shelley asked. "If you've found something, please don't keep us in suspense."

Jeanette's gaze didn't move from the landscape in front of her. To Margaret, its colors were drab, with little to no life. Still, a deep frown had formed on Jeanette's face as she inspected every inch. At long last, she looked at Margaret and said, "You might want to see if you agree with me, but I'm certain there's another picture beneath this landscape. A little of the top layer of paint is missing and what might be a portion of a signature."

Margaret moved in closer. She went to her desk and grabbed a magnifying glass, then went back to the painting. "You're absolutely right," she said to Jeanette. "Even with the bare eye I could see a variety of different strokes beneath the newer paint; with the magnifier, I can definitely see previous strokes."

"I won't go into all the technical aspects," Jeanette said to the others gathered around, "but many artists, even today, use old paintings when they run out of canvas. As Margaret could tell you, oil paint goes over old oil paint quite well."

"Is there a way of getting rid of the newer paint so we can see what's underneath?" Beverly asked.

"Most definitely," Margaret said. "I only wish I had the skills and I could work on it now."

"I took a restoration class eons ago when work was being done in the Sistine Chapel," Jeanette said, "just so I'd know how the work was being performed. I'm sure I could do a little of this myself, just to get a sense of what's beneath."

"Don't you need special tools for that?" Shelley asked.

"I brought tools with me, just in case."

"Can you do it now?" Diane asked, her excitement building.

"I'd rather not." Jeanette turned to Reverend Locke. "Would you mind greatly if I took this one painting back to Portland College with me? I'd planned to stay overnight, but I have an associate who's done a considerable amount of restoration work. On the off chance there's something valuable beneath, I'd feel far more comfortable having him do the work."

"By all means, take it."

"How long does it take?" Shelley asked. "A day or two?"

Jeanette and Margaret both chuckled. "If only that were possible. No, it takes quite some time to do it right, but we can also X-ray the painting. What I'm most interested in right now, though, is trying to find a signature."

"You wouldn't care to venture a guess as to who the artist is, would you?" Diane asked.

"I rarely venture guesses," Jeanette stated. "Although…if I'm seeing it correctly, it could be the work of Sir Joshua Reynolds, one of the greatest English portrait painters to ever live. On the other hand, I can't be sure. In truth, I think we'll all just have to wait and be surprised."

CHAPTER TWENTY-FOUR

Curled up in one of the comfy old patio chairs on the back porch, Beverly couldn't wait to text Jeff and tell him what they'd discovered earlier in the day.

Treasure found! Maybe. It could be wishful thinking, but the prospect is exciting.

She could almost hear Jeff's laughter as she read his answering text. *You can't hint at a discovered treasure and not tell me where and what.* His words sounded like those of the old Jeff, the one she'd fallen head over heels with.

She'd tease him, but it wasn't all that easy in a text message, so she quickly outlined the details. *We found an old portrait in the bell tower that could very well be a Joshua Reynolds. If true, there's no telling how much it could bring at auction. Museums might even want to bid on it. I'm trying not to get my hopes too high, but wishing and praying...and trying to concentrate on work, as well as an upcoming town hall meeting.*

Jeff's response came quickly. *Will add my wishes and prayers to yours.*

Beverly drew in a deep breath, not sure she wanted to ask Jeff the next question, but she chose to be brave: *Will you be back in time to attend town hall meeting Saturday, September 29?*

This time it took Jeff far too long to answer. *May be in Ephesus, Turkey, to take photos of the places where the apostle Paul lived, was imprisoned, and wrote 1 Corinthians.*

He was giving her an ancient history lesson when she'd wanted to hear "Will run across land and swim the seas to get there in time for your moment in the sun." She could think of little to say in return. She went for sarcasm, which wasn't her style, but seemed to fit the moment. *I'm so glad they love your work.*

His response too seemed glib. Is this what their relationship had come to? *Grateful for the steady work and having enough money to set some aside for the unexpected. Perhaps another trip back to Jordan.*

The way he went on and on about Jordan, he might as well move there full time. Getting upset with him only served to get herself upset. It was best to ignore his odd moods.

Must get back to work, she wrote, sent those few brief words, then turned off her cell phone.

She felt petulant and irritable. Right now, she didn't care if she ever heard from him again.

But of course that wasn't true. Not even remotely.

★ ★ ★

Jeanette left early Sunday morning, leaving Diane's house far too quiet. It was exactly what she needed for writing, but she was too keyed up from the discovery of the painting and now the waiting, waiting, and waiting for Monday to come, when she hoped she'd hear from the doctor.

Monday afternoon came and she sat in her favorite chair, bare feet up on the coffee table, eyes closed. As if Rocky knew his best friend was a little out of sorts, he scooched up to her side, dropped his head on her lap, and let her absently run her fingers through his fur. It was a comfort for both of them; it was the only comfort she wanted right now as she waited for the phone to ring.

Opening her eyes just a crack, she peered at her watch. It was already two twenty-seven. He must have the reports by now, and he must have had time to review them. Surely he wouldn't make her wait another day or two to know if she was cancer free, if more tests were needed, or whether or not she needed treatment. Chemo again. More radiation.

She rubbed her eyes, trying to put it out of her mind, clicked on her earpiece, and thought about her book. She had to write at least twenty-five hundred words today, though five thousand would be better, merely to catch up with what she'd missed during Jeanette's visits.

She took a deep breath, hoping that would give her the strength to push on with her story. One more deep breath, and then she began.

"*'Come back! Please!'*

"*If the shadow—a man; a beast—heard her, it refused to stop or even turn around. It was in a hurry to get back into the woods, to the cover of fir trees and dusky darkness.*"

The phone rang and every fiber in Diane's body panicked. Rocky jerked up, his eyes wide, and immediately jumped down from the couch, heading for Diane's office, no doubt to safety under her desk.

Diane grabbed for the phone. It slipped out of her shaky hands and fell on the tabletop, skittering around before she could pick it up again.

"Hello." She could barely get the word out, and then it sounded like a croak.

"Hi, Mrs. Spencer, it's Rhonda Howard from Dr. Crowley's office."

If his assistant was calling, that must mean good news. Dr. Crowley would call himself if there was something bad to say.

"I know this is short notice, but is there any possibility that you could come in to see Dr. Crowley tomorrow morning around eleven?"

No! she wanted to shout. I don't want to go into his office.

She took yet another deep breath, and uttered real words. "It's bad news, isn't it?"

"We do have your tests back, Mrs. Spencer, and the doctor would prefer speaking with you face to face rather than over the phone."

Miss Howard wasn't about to tell Diane anything. Nurses always sounded sweet when they called, even when they knew there was horrendous news to deliver. Dr. Crowley's nurse in Boston had sounded exactly the same the first time she'd been diagnosed with cancer.

At long last, even though her throat was tight and silent tears streaked her face, Diane managed to say, "Yes, I'll be there. Eleven tomorrow morning."

★ ★ ★

Margaret stretched out on the sofa in her living room, an hour after her Monday night class was over. "What I want to know," she asked Allan, who sat beside her, pulled her feet onto his lap, and began to massage them gently, "is why I can stand all day in the gallery, and my feet are perfectly fine, but I teach one class in the evening and I end up feeling like I've been not only walking on a bed of hot coals, but on a bed of nails to boot?"

"I could venture a guess," he said, "but you might not like what I have to say."

"Spill!"

"Because you love the gallery. You love being surrounded by artwork and talking about painting with people who genuinely enjoy looking at fine art. Being in the gallery makes you happy. On the other hand, you walk out of this house after dinner on Monday and Wednesday nights with your jaw nearly locked and your shoulder muscles standing at attention, as though you're prepared for a fight."

"Teaching...or trying to teach some of those children, one in particular, is a fight."

"This isn't exactly a professional medical evaluation, but I believe your feet are taking the brunt of your angst."

"Well, there's not too much I can do about it right now. I have three more classes to teach, so I'll just have to put up with the angst and the sore feet."

"Perhaps you'd better stop teaching…in the future, that is. Maybe the time's come to slow down."

Margaret stiffened. "Slow down and what? Sit in the house in my pajamas and watch TV all day?"

Allan rolled his eyes. "That's not what I mean, dear, so don't take your grumpiness out on me." He grinned, not that he needed to. Margaret knew he'd never scold her.

"You know, I always thought I was a good teacher, that I knew how to talk to students, to help them free their creativity and find their inspiration, but Adelaide is far better with this class of kids than I could ever be. And don't say it's because she's closer to their age!"

Allan grinned again. "She is closer to their age and she doesn't hold back her feelings, but when she expresses herself, she does it with pure gentleness. Something about her nature provides them with a calming influence. You don't find that in everyone. I think the kids respond to her."

"Are you saying I'm not gentle?"

"Goodness no, Margaret. You are a gentle creature…at times." He winked. "But you're also a good teacher."

"You wouldn't know it by the artwork I've seen most of these kids turn out."

"If you want my opinion—"

"I always do."

"The community center does a whole lot of things right, but not these art classes. The kids are tired enough when they get out of school each day. They have homework. A lot of them have sports and other extracurricular activities. And now they have a month's worth of art classes that they might not have wanted to take."

"In most cases, I'm sure it's the parents who thought the art classes were a good idea."

"I'm sure they're right. Their kids, however, might have been far more excited about the class if it was only one day a week. Or maybe if the class had been scheduled during the summer, rather than the very beginning of the school year."

"You're right, as usual."

"Of course I'm right." He chuckled. "So don't be so hard on yourself. You are a good teacher. But maybe working with kids is not your strong suit."

★ ★ ★

"Sleep, my child, and peace be with you, all through the night."

Shelley sat on the edge of Aiden's bed, smoothing his hair off his forehead, singing one of his favorite lullabies, which she hoped would help him fall asleep. He'd been wound up ever since the end of the school day, as if something was troubling his sweet and innocent mind, and Shelley hoped the song would take away his worries.

"Guardian angels God will send you, all through the night."

"Do you have a guardian angel?" Aiden asked.

Shelley nodded. "I think we all do."

"But I can't see mine."

"You can't see God, either, but you know He's with you."

"Billy—he's my new best friend at school—he said it was silly for boys to believe in angels or even Santa Claus. Is it silly?"

"Not at all! What fun would life be if we didn't believe in all those good things?"

"I told him that and he said his dad was Santa Claus, but I told him his dad was too skinny."

Shelley smiled. "What did Billy say then?"

"'Come on, let's go play on the swings.'" Aiden giggled. "Billy's strange sometimes. I'm not sure he'll be my best friend tomorrow."

Shelley couldn't help but wonder how many best friends Aiden would have before the end of the month. After all, he ditched Bethany after only four days, and somehow he'd squeezed Madyson in as his very best friend before Billy took her place.

"You know, sweetheart, if you don't get to sleep pretty soon, you're going to be too tired to play during school tomorrow."

"I could stay home and you could take me to the beach to collect shells."

"Do you really want to?"

Aiden shook his head. "No...I guess not."

"As much as I'd love for you to stay home, you have to go to school. Remember our talk last week? You're a big boy now, and big boys go to school every day—except Saturday and Sunday and special occasions."

Even in the near darkness, she could see a questioning look on her little boy's face. "Are you happy when I'm at school?"

Shelley kissed his brow, hoping that alone would take away some of his concern. "If you want to know if I miss you, the answer is a big ol' yes. But I know how good school is for you. I also know that you like your teacher and your friends and that you have fun learning new things. I would hate for you to miss out on any of the good stuff."

"Me too." Aiden yawned. His eyes fluttered closed then opened. "Does Emma have a guardian angel?"

"Yes, honey. In fact, her guardian angel is in her bedroom right now, watching over her."

"Will my guardian angel be here when you leave?"

"Your guardian angel's with you always. Just like God."

"Good." He yawned again, rolled onto his side, and tucked his hands under his head. "I told Billy you sing me bedtime songs and he said I must be a baby or a scaredy-cat, and I told him nuh-uh. I told him I let you sing to me because you sing real pretty, and that's the truth."

Shelley felt tears welling up behind her eyes. "I love singing you to sleep."

"I love it too. But don't tell Billy."

Shelley leaned over, planted a warm and loving kiss on Aidan's forehead, hoping her tears wouldn't drop right next to it. Her little boy was growing up too fast, and sadly, there was nothing she could do about it, other than to help him grow in all the right ways.

CHAPTER TWENTY-FIVE

Have you called Jessica or Justin?" Beverly asked Diane, not long after they'd driven out of Marble Cove, heading for Augusta and Diane's appointment with her oncologist. "What about Jeanette? Have you talked to her?"

Diane shook her head. "I'm not ready to tell the kids yet, not till after I've seen Dr. Crowley. And I'm not going to tell anyone else—other than you—until I know all the ins and outs. Besides, Jessica's in the middle of a big trial—"

"You can't keep making excuses, Diane. Both Jessica and Justin would want to know. They might not be able to come to Marble Cove right away, but you can talk to them, share your fears, and let them pray for you."

"I've done enough praying for all of us for nearly two weeks now, and what good has it done?"

Beverly winced, stunned by Diane's words. She was a big part of the reason Beverly had opened her heart to God. "We can't judge God."

"Why not? He made me struggle through some of the worst moments in my life the first time I had cancer."

"You were cured, Diane. Miraculously."

"That could have been a fluke. Some organism in my body grabbed hold of the cancer and...and, oh, I don't know. It just disappeared. Yes, it was a miracle, but was it one of God's miracles?"

"God's watching over you."

"He let Eric die. Totally out of the blue. He hadn't been sick. Then, with one snap of His fingers, God turned the lights out on my husband. I didn't even get a chance to say good-bye."

Beverly kept her eyes on the road. Diane was hurting. She didn't mean anything she was saying. All Beverly could do was to let Diane work through her fears, her bitterness, and her anger with God on her own. She, in turn, would stand by Diane's side and be there if she needed anyone or anything.

"Would you like me to go in to see the doctor with you?" Beverly asked an hour later when they sat down in the waiting room.

Diane picked up a magazine and stared at the front cover as if she hadn't heard Beverly's question. Slowly she turned her head. She shrugged. "I've been told that I'm one tough cookie. I can do it—" Beverly saw raw, stark fear in her dear friend's eyes. She reached out and took hold of Diane's hand, and at long last, Diane said, "Would you? Please? I might be a tough cookie, but there's nothing etched in stone that says I have to be tough today."

Beverly smiled and squeezed Diane's hand.

A little over ten minutes later they'd been ushered into Dr. Crowley's office and were sitting on one side of his desk, surrounded by pictures of his family—a pretty wife and three pretty redheaded daughters, all of their smiles as bright as Dr. Crowley's.

Beverly nervously checked her watch, keeping track of the seconds and minutes they had to wait, and finally Dr. Crowley walked into the room. He said hello to Diane, introduced himself to Beverly, and sat down on the far side of the desk.

"I wish so much that I could have called you myself to tell you that you're still cancer free, but"—he cleared his throat—"as I'm sure you've guessed by now, that isn't the case. The good news is, I believe we've caught it early."

"Cancer is never good news," Diane corrected, her usually calm voice laced with anger. "I've been through it once before. I already know what the chemo can do to you. I've experienced the nausea and vomiting. I've shaved my head rather than have my hair fall out here and there. I've—"

"Cancer is never fair," Dr. Crowley said softly, "and you have every right to be angry. I'd rather see you get that anger out of your system now than bottle it up and explode when you're in the midst of fighting the disease and need all your strength to get through each day."

"Five years ago you told me my cancer was so advanced that I might have only three months to live. What about this time around?"

"This time I believe it's fully curable. We have caught it early, Diane. But you will need treatment again."

"I'd like to get a second opinion."

Beverly frowned when she heard Diane's words. Last week she said she trusted Dr. Crowley without reservation. Why did she now want a second opinion?

"Do you have another doctor you'd like to see?" Dr. Crowley asked, as if Diane's statement was one he heard quite often. "I'd be happy to send him or her my reports and all of the lab work. I'd just like to do it now, as soon as humanly possible. I don't want to waste any time starting your treatments, and there are some more tests I'd like to have done before that."

Diane closed her eyes and Beverly reached for her hand, squeezing it tightly. She wanted to say "Stick with Dr. Crowley," but Diane had to make that decision on her own.

Diane was quiet for the longest time. She sat in her chair without moving an inch. She breathed deeply, over and over again. At long last, she opened her eyes. "Forget the other opinion." She swallowed hard. "I don't want to waste time. I just want to get this over with."

★ ★ ★

"Ask me some questions, Father?"

Mr. Wheeland looked up at Beverly when she strolled into his library Thursday evening, a stack of paper at least two inches thick and several books in her hands.

"Like what?"

"You know quite a lot about Marble Cove history, the past and the present, so just throw out any old question.

You know, who's the police chief? Fire chief? When will the potholes on upper Water Street be repaired? I'm sure you can come up with some great questions, Father, but on the off chance you're stumped, I've marked some pages in these books and papers." She set her collection on his lap. "I need to be prepared for any and all questions."

"I have a good one for you. Should the mayor and all town council members take a cut in pay, considering Marble Cove's current fiscal overload?"

If he thought he'd stumped her on that question, he was wrong. Beverly sat in one of the comfy leather chairs, crossed one leg over the other, knowing she looked very prim and proper, and offered up a thorough response.

Beverly's father nodded. "Good answer, my dear. Do you really have a plan of action ready?"

"It's in the works, and I'll have it completed and copied in time for the town hall."

"That's my girl."

They continued on for nearly an hour, Mr. Wheeland and Beverly batting questions and answers back and forth, and Beverly jotting down anything she was troubled by.

"Dennis the Menace and Lee Waters are both going to have coaches, you know that, don't you?" Mr. Wheeland asked.

"I imagined they would. Evelyn knows all the ins and outs of town business." Beverly grinned. "She's probably made up flash cards to use on Lee whenever he has a free moment. And Dennis, I'm afraid, has a lot of friends in high places. He's bound to have answers to most every question."

"Having answers and having the correct answers are two different things. You're on the right track, Beverly. You're going into this town hall meeting with your instincts and your gut on the line. People will see your sincerity. They'll see the spark in your eye when you talk about leading this town. That'll get you a long way."

"I certainly hope so, Father. If I don't win this election—"

"If you don't win, you'll attend every town council meeting and stand up for the rights of the people. That's what determined folks do, and I've always known you to be determined."

Beverly stood and flexed her shoulders to work out the tightness from long hours of studying, working at her consulting job, and worrying about Diane and Jeff. "Want some iced tea? A snack of some kind? Carrots, maybe?"

"Carrots, no. Iced tea would be nice. Thank you."

Beverly walked out of the library and before turning to go into the kitchen, caught a glimpse of Diane driving down the street, heading toward her cottage. She watched as Diane pulled into her driveway, got out of her car, removed a bag of groceries out of the trunk, and headed for the door. She'd been trying to get in touch with Diane ever since Wednesday morning, the day after they returned from the doctor's appointment, but her phone just rolled over to voice mail and no one answered the door. Now that Thursday had come around, she couldn't have been more worried about her friend.

Beverly poked her head back into the library, where her father seemed immersed in a book. "I just saw Diane. I'm going to run over to her place and—"

He peered over the top. "Leave her be...for now at least."

"She's worried sick. She shouldn't be alone."

"She's dealing with this in her own way," he said, setting the book in his lap. "If she needed you, or Margaret, or Shelley, she'd be knocking on doors asking for help. The way I see it, she needs some space right now. Leave well enough alone, and she'll come to you when she's ready."

Maybe her father was right. She might have a surefire way for solving Marble Cove's fiscal problems and making the town operate like a well-oiled machine, but she wasn't a counselor. She was merely a friend.

★ ★ ★

Diane strolled along the beach, kicking at sand and seaweed and the occasional shell. Rocky trotted along at her side, getting ahead of her, then turning back, usually with a stick in his mouth. He wanted to play. She didn't, and she won. It wasn't fair to Rocky. She supposed she wasn't being fair to anyone. Not her kids, who needed to be told. Not her sister-in-law, who still seemed fragile over Eric's death. Not even to Shelley and Margaret, who would try to mother her. And then there was Beverly. She'd called; she'd dropped by the house; and Diane had ignored her.

No, she wasn't being fair to anyone. But she simply wanted to be left alone.

Slowly she trudged up the stairs leading to Orlean Point Light. Rocky didn't care much for the stairs, but he went along anyway. The wind had picked up by the time they reached the top, whipping at her hair, drying out her lips and the tears she'd shed off and on since she saw Dr. Crowley on Tuesday. She and Rocky stood close to the edge of the cliff, looking out over the ocean. Waves crashed on the rocks below, touches of salty spray finding their way to her face, and then the wind dried it all over again.

At last she sat down on one of the benches where tourists often sat to get the best vista of Marble Cove, its harbor, and the Atlantic. It was stunningly beautiful and she never tired of it. Of course, she had no idea how much longer she'd be able to see this view. The last time she'd been given three months to live, but she'd miraculously survived; the cancer had magically disappeared. There was no possibility in her mind that she'd be that lucky a second time.

Why me? Her face was set into a frown when she looked up at the blue sky and the white puffy clouds. *Are You ignoring me, Lord? Have I done something wrong? Have You given up on me?*

She sighed heavily. I don't want to go through the chemo again. I don't want to see the pain in my daughter's eyes when she sits by my side for hours on end, doing everything possible to keep the nausea at bay. It's not fair to her, Lord. And I'm sorry, but it doesn't seem fair to me either. Haven't I been through enough?

Rocky plopped his head down on her lap and looked up at her with his sweet yet sad brown eyes. He whimpered, and Diane rubbed at the tears in her eyes, wishing she could stop crying, wishing she could just lie down, go to sleep, and find the nightmare was over when she woke.

The sound of the surf and the crashing waves had become a roar. The seagulls circling overhead, diving toward the rocks then soaring back up into the sky, screeched louder and louder, each one trying to outdo the other. The noise, mixed with her thoughts, had become so deafening she almost missed the ring of the cell phone she always carried with her. Grabbing it out of her pants pocket, she looked at the caller ID and saw her daughter's name.

Her heart beat hard and fast. If she answered, she'd have to tell Jessica the truth. Then she'd have to call Justin, then Jeanette, then her friends. Once she did all of that, she'd have to accept Dr. Crowley's diagnosis, have to stop denying it.

The phone continued to ring, and she realized she had no choice.

She pressed the button to speak to her daughter, cleared her throat, and said hello.

"Hey, Mom."

Diane forced a smile. She had to pretend that she was fine.

"I talked to Aunt Jeanette last night, not for our usual five minutes, but for nearly half an hour. She told me about the painting she'd found in the tower at Old First. Mom, I can't believe you didn't call me yourself to tell me the terrific news."

"I was going to wait until we knew if it really was a Joshua Reynolds."

"You have to stop waiting until everything's settled to tell me what's going on."

"I hate to bother you with trivialities. I know how busy you are."

"Fortunately I've learned how to juggle more than one person's good news and bad news at a time. It's all part of the job."

Tell her now.

Diane was just about ready to say something about the cancer when Jessica spoke up instead.

"Aunt Jeanette gave me an absolutely marvelous genealogical tour, telling me all about her great-great grandfather, the one who served in the Civil War, and about her grandmother—my great-grandmother—having tea parties with her when she was little."

That brought a soft smile to Diane's face, remembering the way Jeanette had lovingly caressed the old teapot in her display case.

"I told her that you had a teapot that great-grandmother had given you as a wedding present and she said the two of you had talked about it when she visited a couple of weeks ago."

"She seems to really love it," Diane said. "More than I ever have."

"You know, Mom, it just sits in your display case gathering dust—Well, it would, if you didn't dust once a week. But—"

"I know what you're going to say. I should give it to your aunt."

"It doesn't hold any sentimental value, not for you, Mom, but it seems to mean something more to Aunt Nettie."

Diane frowned. "Nettie? Why'd you call Aunt Jeanette that?"

"I don't know. It just slipped out. I seem to remember her telling me to call her that when I was little, but no one else ever did, so I stuck with Jeanette."

Diane's mind wandered back to the week after her honeymoon with her handsome new husband, to the stacks and stacks of gifts they'd received, to the hand-painted teapot and the card from Eric's grandmother. She remembered the lovely words she'd written, and at last she smiled.

"Are you okay, Mom?" Jessica asked. "I've talked up a storm and you've been deathly quiet for the past five minutes. Has something happened?"

A lot had happened lately. Good revelations and horrific ones. There was so much she needed to share with Jessica and Jeanette, with Justin and her friends, and not just the pleasant stuff, but the ugly as well.

Taking a deep breath, and with the warmth of the sun shining down upon her, Diane smiled softly, knowing it would make telling Jessica the truth a little easier to bear. "I am okay, honey, but there's something I need to tell you."

CHAPTER TWENTY-SIX

It had to be Shearwater Gallery's quietest Friday of all time, Margaret thought. So quiet that she sat in her office surfing the Internet, looking at everything she could find on Sir Joshua Reynolds. It wasn't in her course plan, but she thought she just might prepare a slide presentation over the weekend and show her students paintings done by some of the Old Masters.

The chimes on the front door rang and Margaret pushed away from the computer. At last. Here it was nearly two in the afternoon and her first customer of the day had come in. Of course, it could just be the mailman or Allan or Adelaide.

When she stepped around the corner she was more than a little surprised to see handstanding Jake Morris' mother in the middle of the gallery, looking at one of Margaret's more avant-garde paintings. There hadn't been a big rush to buy that work, but she was quite proud of her futuristic Puffin Island.

From all appearances, Mrs. Morris, in flip-flops, green-and-pink Bermuda shorts, and a green Boston Celtics T-shirt, didn't look all that interested in the abstract puffins, but when she saw Margaret, she smiled and waved.

"I was hoping to find you here."

"I'm here most every day," Margaret said.

"That's good to know. I was hoping you might begin another art class at the community center. Jake has accomplished so much with you as his teacher."

But he went home one night last week with paint in his hair, Margaret wanted to say. Instead she settled for, "Thank you. But I believe the original instructor will be teaching the next round of classes."

"That's too bad. She may be very good, but Jake's quite taken with you. He comes home every Monday and Wednesday evenings talking up a storm. Not that I ever believe he'll take up art. I think he'd rather join the circus." Mrs. Morris grinned uncomfortably. "His father and I are trying to steer him in another direction, of course."

"Well, we all find our way eventually," Margaret said, trying to sound reassuring.

"Listen, I know that Nicole Wharburton has talked with you about giving her private lessons. I suggested to her that it might be nice if those private lessons were semiprivate, and I'd join her. I've tinkered around with other crafts. Scrapbooking. Beading. Counted cross-stitch. None of those are the same as painting, but I believe I'd be a good student, and I'd love to learn."

"I did tell Mrs. Wharburton that teaching another class isn't currently on my to-do list."

"But surely you've given it some thought?"

Margaret thought about shaking her head, but that wouldn't be true. "I have given it some thought, but teaching another class isn't in my game plan at the present time."

"We wouldn't need to start until October."

October—the time she'd like to paint fall leaves and calm beaches and maybe a ripe apple or pumpkin or two.

"I'm just not ready to dive into another teaching assignment, Mrs. Morris."

"Oh, we don't need a decision right now. But please, would you give it some thought? It would mean the world to not only me but Nicole Wharburton as well. And I believe there might be other women in Marble Cove who'd love to have you as their instructor. Your work really is special."

Mrs. Morris smiled, shaking Margaret's hand before she said she had to go. She pushed through the door, the chimes tinkled, and she waved as the door closed behind her and she disappeared out of view.

Teacher? Me?

Margaret strolled around her gallery, looking at all the beauty on display. Jewelry, amazing glassware and pottery, and paintings: watercolors, oil, acrylics, most of them painted by her, because they were more and more in demand.

She thought about the portraits and the occasional landscape painted by Joshua Reynolds, and wondered if he had ever doubted his ability to paint. Probably not. She also wondered if anyone had ever asked him to teach or to be a mentor, and how that had made him feel. Good? Bad? Indifferent? Or maybe just not qualified.

She went back to her computer and studied another one of his paintings and chuckled. It was flattering to have two women ask for private—or semiprivate—lessons. She hadn't felt at all qualified, given the stress she felt in her Monday and Wednesday classes. But maybe she did have it in her after all—but as a teacher of adults, not children.

She was sure she could do it. Of course, then she'd have to give up the free time she desperately craved.

Oh well, she thought, as her telephone began to ring, *it isn't something I need to think about right now. Maybe in October.*

Rushing back to her office, Margaret grabbed the telephone and heard Diane on the other end.

"Hi there, Diane. Goodness, it seems like ages since I saw you. It's sad to live right next door to each other and end up wondering if your neighbor has gone on vacation."

"I've been around."

"Working on your book, I imagine."

"Trying to," Diane said.

"You haven't heard from Jeanette yet, have you?" Margaret asked. "I've been on pins and needles wondering what, if anything, she's found beneath that painting."

"I talked with her just a little while ago, but she still doesn't have any definite answer for us on whether or not it's a Joshua Reynolds. They're still trying to remove more of the oils that were painted over the original artwork."

"Well, I don't know how much research you've done on Joshua Reynolds, but I've read nearly everything I could find on the Internet. Did you know that one of his paintings, a portrait of a Tahitian youth named Omai, sold for 10.3 million pounds back in 2001? Ten-point-three million pounds! If our painting is a Joshua Reynolds, there's no telling what it will be worth."

"Hopefully enough to repair the roof at Old First."

Diane sounded tired. She'd probably been working extralong hours on her book. Margaret did that when she was caught up in a painting, obsessed with getting one particular feature right.

"Oh dear, I've been rambling on and on, when you're the one who called me. Is there something I can help you with? Do you need me to watch Rocky, or—"

"It's nothing like that, Margaret. I probably should have told you this in person..."

Diane hesitated, and Margaret suddenly feared the worst. Was Diane going to move away? She was such a dear friend and she'd hate to see her leave Marble Cove. But maybe she wanted to be near her daughter.

"You're not moving, are you?" Margaret asked.

"No." Diane sighed. "I just want you to know that I have cancer again. I'm fine though...Really..."

Margaret wasn't sure what else Diane said. All she'd heard was the word cancer, and all her own worries and cares flitted away in a heartbeat.

Cancer.

Again.

★ ★ ★

"I got three stars today. One for painting. One for playing quietly. One for...for...I forget."

"And one for cleaning up your mess as well as your friend Billy's." Shelley was all smiles as she pushed Emma's stroller down Main Street, with Aiden skipping along at her side. "Miss Davidson didn't tell me why you cleaned up Billy's mess."

"'Cause he told Teacher no! He wouldn't clean it up. Said he didn't have to."

"That's so sad. Maybe he was having a bad day."

"Yeah, maybe, so I cleaned it up for him. Miss Davidson said I didn't have to, but I told her I help you clean up your messes all the time, and I'm good at it."

Sometimes. Shelley grinned, but she didn't contradict Aiden's statement. She was happy that he was finally settling in at school. There were no fights getting him up in the morning, and he was usually ready to head out the door before she had her shoes on. She was even getting used to him being gone a few hours each day. Not that she was completely thrilled with the idea, but she was able to spend more time playing with Emma, reading to her, and letting her help around the kitchen. It was wonderful to have some time just with her daughter. It reminded her of the special time she and Aiden had had when he was a toddler. Those were years she could never get back, and she wanted to make the most of them.

Life was so sweet. Crossing Main Street, Shelley continued down Newport Avenue, looking at the calm ocean ahead of them. The waves lapped softly onto the shore. Far out on the water she could hear a ship's horn, and Mrs. Peabody waved down at Shelley, Aiden, and Emma, from her perch on her widow's walk.

"Afternoon, Shelley."

"Good afternoon, Mrs. Peabody. Isn't it lovely today? I'm going to take the little ones down to play on the beach for a little while. If you'd like to join us—"

"Looks to me like someone else is already joining you. There's been a strange car parked in your driveway for half an hour."

Shelley frowned. She wasn't expecting anyone. "Guess I'd better hurry on home and see who it is."

"I'll keep an eye out. If it's someone you don't want being there, let out a scream and I'll call the police."

"I'm sure there's no need to worry, Mrs. Peabody, but I'll definitely keep that scream in mind."

Shelley pushed the stroller a little faster, and Aiden had to run along at her side just to keep up. But when she was just one house away from her own, she stopped. She wasn't sure who the car belonged to, but she recognized the back of Susannah's head. Her sister leaned against the hood, staring off at the beach.

Shelley moved a little more slowly now. She couldn't miss Hailey sitting on the front steps. She had a brown paper bag, stuffed full of something, setting next to her. She had a battered backpack too, but nothing more.

All of her fears about "the pact" were, she imagined, on the verge of coming true.

"Hi, Suze." Shelley pushed the stroller around to the passenger side of Susannah's car, and smiled uncomfortably at her sister. "What a surprise."

"I would have called," Susannah said, "but I'm sure you would have told me not to come."

Shelley didn't know if she would have or not. She hoped that she would do the right thing and help her sister in her time of need. Now it looked like the matter had been taken completely out of her hands.

Shelley gave Susannah a hug, then waved at Hailey. "Hi, sweetheart!"

Hailey offered Shelley a halfhearted wave. She smiled faintly.

"Look, Shel," Susannah said. "I can't stay more than a minute or two, but I've got to leave Hailey with you. You promised. Remember?"

Shelley nodded. "I remember. This all has to do with the pact."

"I need you to take care of her."

"What's wrong, Susannah? Are you sick? Are you in trouble?"

"It doesn't matter, does it? You said you'd take care of her if I couldn't, and I can't."

"You've got to give me more of a reason than that."

"I can't give you any reason right now." Susannah reached through the open car door and pulled some papers off the passenger seat. "These are Hailey's school records. I've got her shot records here too."

Shelley touched her sister's arm, "Let's go inside and talk about this. I've got cold lemonade or soda, and I made cookies earlier today. Are you hungry?"

Susannah shook her head. "I'm not hungry. Hailey probably is. Maybe you can take her inside; then she won't have to see me leave."

"You can't just leave, Suze. I need to know where you're going. I need to know why. When will you be back?"

"I'm having some…money problems, that's all. As soon as I get everything straightened out, I'll come back for Hailey."

"You can't just take off. She's your daughter. You can't expect her to understand what's going on."

"I've told her I'll be back, and she knows she's going to stay here with you for a while."

Shelley ran her fingers through her hair. "I need to talk with Dan about this. Please, Suze, come inside. Maybe we can figure out a way to help you."

Susannah shook her head, then looked toward Hailey, still sitting on the steps. She blew her daughter a kiss and Hailey blew one back. "I've got to go, Shelley. Please, don't make this any worse than it already is. Just honor our pact. *Please.*"

What else could she say other than, "I will, Suze. You know I will. But—"

"I'll call. I promise." Again Susannah waved to her daughter. She blew her one more kiss, then dashed around to the driver's side, hopped into the car, cranked the engine a few times before it started, and backed out of the driveway.

Not more than thirty seconds later, Susannah was gone. In just a matter of minutes, the newer, happier life Shelley had dreamed of had changed. She looked toward the house, at Hailey sitting on the doorstep staring straight ahead. If someone wanted to paint a picture of shell shock, Hailey was probably a perfect model.

Shelley couldn't think about her own selfish worries any longer. She had to think of Hailey.

"Is Hailey gonna live with us now?" Aiden asked, tugging on Shelley's shirt.

"For a while, sweetheart."

"Where's she going to sleep?"

Shelley hadn't given that a thought, but there was really only one place. She wasn't about to put her niece on the sofa in the living room. "We'll get a bed for her and put it in Emma's room."

Hailey looked up, shaking her head. "I don't need a special place to sleep."

Shelley pushed the stroller toward the stairs, then sat down on the steps next to Hailey. "Of course you need a special place, and Emma's room is really pretty. Want to see it?"

Hailey shrugged. "You don't want me here, do you?"

Shelley took hold of Hailey's hand. "I want what's best for you, and right now, that's staying here with me and Uncle Dan and Aiden and Emma."

"You already have a family. You don't need me butting in."

"If I was a wicked stepmother, I might think you were butting in." Shelley smiled. "Fortunately, I'm not your stepmother and I'm definitely not wicked. Some people actually think I'm nice."

"That's what my mom said. That you're nice."

Shelley smiled. "You'll have to make your own bed, of course."

"I'm not very good at it."

"Then I'll teach you."

"I can teach her, Mom." Aiden plopped down next to Hailey. "Do you know how to read?" he asked her.

Hailey nodded. "I love to read."

"Aiden and Emma like story time," Shelley told her. "They also like to color and paint and go down to the beach to hunt for shells and sea glass. In fact, we were going to go down there in just a little while. You do want to go with us, don't you?"

"Is it okay? I don't want to be in the way."

Shelley's heart went out to Hailey. She was so lonely and forlorn and she'd been dumped on a near stranger's doorstep. How could Susannah do this?

"You won't be in the way at all. In fact, why don't we go in the house and you and Aiden can pack some fruit and cookies while I grab towels and buckets and shovels? We can be down on the beach in ten minutes."

"Can we build a sandcastle?" Hailey asked.

"I'm really good at building sandcastles," Aiden boasted. "I got a whole bucket full of sandcastle-making stuff. Can we take it, Mom?"

"Of course you can. In fact, why don't you take Hailey inside and show her around."

"Okay." Aiden popped up from the stairs and took hold of Hailey's hand. "Come on. I'll show you my bathroom. It's really cool, with trains on the walls. Mom says she's going to have to change the bathroom someday, since Emma needs girl stuff, but for now, it still has trains. But you can put some pretty girl stuff in it, if you want. I won't mind too much."

Just fifteen minutes later, when they were on the beach, Emma dug in the sand, and Aiden and Hailey laughed while trying to build a castle with turrets and a moat and a tower. "For Rapunzel," Hailey said. "Have you ever heard the story of Rapunzel?" she asked Aiden.

Aiden shook his head. "Did she turn straw into gold?"

"No, that's Rumpelstiltskin. Rapunzel had long blonde hair, so long that she dropped it out of the tower window so the prince could climb up to the very top and save her."

Aiden's eyes widened. "That must've hurt."

Hailey shrugged. "I don't think there's anything in the book about her head hurting, but if I read it to you, we can add that in. I like changing the stories sometimes."

Shelley smiled, surprised at how quickly Hailey had fit in and how comfortable she was feeling already: not that she expected that comfort level to last for long. Tonight there would probably be tears, and that might continue for countless nights to come. They'd make it work, though. God had smiled down on them, and already Hailey was feeling like a part of the family.

Shelley grabbed her cell phone when it rang, hoping it was Dan, so she could tell him the news, but it was Diane. "Hi there," Shelley said, and without skipping a breath, continued on. "You'll never guess what happened."

Shelley told Diane everything, then Diane said, "I have a rollaway bed that I've used for company. It's not the greatest, but it'll work for a little while, until you can get something better."

"Oh, that would be wonderful. We're down at the beach right now, but I'll come by for it right after dinner, if that's okay."

"I'll roll it over to your place now and leave it out by the garage."

"Are you sure?"

"Of course. I have extra sheets and blankets and a pillow too. I'll put them in a bag and leave them with the bed."

"You're a lifesaver. Thank you so much. You know without me saying this, of course, but if there's anything at all that I can do for you, just let me know."

"Actually, Shelley, there is." Diane hesitated a moment. Her voice sounded weary. "I'd appreciate it if you could say a prayer or two for me."

"You know me, Diane. Praying's never a problem. Is there something special you want me to say?"

"You always know the right words, especially when someone's in need or hurt or sick. And, well"—Diane took a deep breath—"I have cancer again. God doesn't seem to be smiling down on me these days, but maybe He'll smile down on you."

CHAPTER TWENTY-SEVEN

I wish I knew what I could do to help her," Margaret said, walking through the house like a zombie, without purpose or focus. "I've called. I went over there last night and here it is Saturday, and she won't answer the door or the phone and she hasn't come outside to clip her roses or anything."

"We all deal with grief and fear in different ways," Allan said, standing at the kitchen counter alongside Adelaide, helping her mix up a batch of cookies. "I know it doesn't seem like Diane to shut herself up behind closed doors, but she has, and I think we should leave her alone for now."

"What if—"

"There are no what ifs," Allan said, gently. "Her curtains have been open during the day and they're closed by sunset. We've seen Rocky in the yard, and he seems happy as a clam. So please, Margaret, no more worrying about that. Diane's a resilient person. She'll work through this in her own good time."

"I could take her some cookies," Adelaide said. "Diane likes chocolate chip. She says Dad and I make them better than anyone. 'Cept maybe Shelley."

"That's a great idea." Margaret was sure Diane would open the door for Adelaide. "When they're all done and cooled off, we can put a bunch on one of my pretty plates and you can take them over to her."

"I'd better take some oatmeal cookies too. For Rocky, since dogs shouldn't eat chocolate."

Allan shook his head. "You two are determined to interfere with Diane, aren't you?"

"It's not interference, sweetheart. It's being a good friend."

Margaret grabbed a pair of kitchen shears. "I'm going to clip a few roses for her too."

"She has a million roses already."

"You can never have too many roses." Adelaide dropped a healthy spoonful of batter on the cookie sheet. "I heard Diane say that once. Mom and I agree."

Margaret wriggled her eyebrows at her husband and went out and cut nearly two dozen of her prettiest long-stemmed roses. She looked next door at Diane's. The curtains were open and she stared for the longest time, hoping to see some movement, but there was no hint at all of Diane inside the house.

Slowly she walked back into the kitchen and found a pretty vase for the flowers.

"Any word yet on the painting you ladies found in the Old First bell tower?" Allan asked.

Margaret shook her head. "Not a one. Of course, I know it can take a long time to authenticate a painting. To restore one to its original glory can take months."

"Mom's so smart. I heard her telling people at church how artists fix old paintings and clean them and stuff like that. She should be a teacher. But not for kids, though."

Margaret's shoulders stiffened. Even though she knew Adelaide was right, it still rankled her to know that she'd done a lousy job with her preteen art students. "Why do you say that?"

Adelaide's face fell. "I'm sorry, Mom."

"No, Adelaide. It's okay. It's just that I trust your judgment. Why do you think I shouldn't teach kids?"

Allan turned toward his daughter, interested in her assessment.

Adelaide thought for a moment. "No patience. My teacher says you have to have patience to teach kids. She says that's why I'll be good at it."

"Do I have patience with adults?"

"Not all the time." Allan grinned. "On the other hand, I think adults would be far more interested in hearing about art techniques, which is something you can teach them easily. And let's face it, most adults who attend art classes do it because they want to. Kids, on the other hand, usually do it because their parents want them to. There's a big difference."

"So you really don't think I'm a lousy teacher?"

"You're a good teacher, Mom."

"I agree," Allan said. "Painting is your passion. That isn't necessarily something you can teach people, but people certainly learn more when they know the instructors enjoy what they're teaching."

"You know, I've been asked by a couple of my students' parents to teach an adult painting class—private or semiprivate."

Allan cocked one eyebrow. "Do you want to?"

Margaret shrugged. "I'm not sure. I'm flattered that they asked, but deep inside, I've been worried sick that I couldn't do it, that I'd get as frustrated as I have with my preteen class."

"They've given you a vote of confidence," Allan said, wrapping an arm around her waist and holding her close to him. "Maybe you should accept that and tell yourself 'I can do it.'"

"All right, I can do it." Margaret smiled. "And I can do it really well. The big question is, do I want to do it?"

"Only you know the answer to that."

★ ★ ★

"I'm home!"

"Daddy! Daddy!"

Shelley stuck her head out of the kitchen and smiled at the sight of Aiden and Emma caught up in their dad's arms. He was kissing them and they were kissing him back. One whole week away from home was way too long. She'd missed him terribly. Of course, he would have come home when she'd called to tell him about Hailey's arrival, but she told him she could handle the situation on her own. He needed to work; he couldn't start taking off for every little emergency.

With both kids still in his arms, Dan strolled toward the kitchen and gave Shelley a big, nice, long kiss. Aiden and

Emma giggled, and out of the corner of her eye, Shelley saw Hailey climb up from the spot in the living room where she'd been playing with the little ones.

"Oops! Looks like I need an extra arm or two." Dan slid Emma into Shelley's arms, set Aiden on the floor, and headed Hailey off at the hallway. "Do I get a hug from you too, Hailey?"

She shook her head.

"Then why don't we just shake hands for now?" Dan stuck out a big paw. "Hi there. I'm Uncle Dan. You must be Hailey?"

She nodded and slowly put her hand in his.

"He doesn't bite." Aiden ran toward Hailey and hugged her. "My Dad is a good hugger. But it's okay if you don't hug him. He won't be mad."

"All right kids, it's bedtime," Shelley called out. "Go brush your teeth, get into your pj's, and Daddy and I will come tuck you in."

"Do I have to?" Aiden asked, and Dan gave his son a one-eyed stare, which meant *I'll brook no arguments from you, young man. Not tonight!* In a heartbeat, the children were off at a tear.

"I'll get Emma ready," Hailey said. "Is that okay?"

"Of course it is," Shelley told her. "Thank you, sweetheart."

When the hallway was silent and the noise was coming from the bedrooms and bath, Shelley stepped into Dan's arms and relished his hug. "I've missed you."

"I can imagine. It can't have been easy with an extra kid around."

"She's been a piece of cake. She never argues. Never whines. Never cries."

"*Hmm.* Doesn't sound normal."

"She's had it tough, Dan. I don't know how tough. I don't know much of anything, and she doesn't seem to want to divulge all that much."

"I guess you—we—just have to give her time."

"The thing is, I don't know how much time we'll have with her. It could be a couple more days; it might be a month or longer."

Dan frowned. "You still haven't been able to get hold of Susannah?"

Shelley shook her head. "She left me a phone number, but the service has been cut off."

"That's not good."

"I've talked with my dad and Maggie, but neither one of them has heard from her. She seems to have dropped off the face of the earth. But I'm guessing by the fact that she left Hailey's school and shot records with me, and her birth certificate, that she must have planned to be gone for a while."

"We'll make the best of it."

"I have to enroll her in school. I've got to see if we can get her on our medical insurance, just in case." Shelley sighed. "None of that matters, though. I've enjoyed having her around. And Aiden loves her."

Dan smiled. "Come on, let's go say good night."

Shelley kissed Aiden on his forehead, and as she did so often, she swept his blond hair away from his face. Dan kissed his cheek and gave him another big hug. "I love you, son."

"Me too, Daddy."

"Thank you for being extraspecial nice to Hailey."

"She reads to me and Emma and she tells stories. I gave her some of my sea glass, 'cause she said she'd never seen anything so pretty in all her life."

"Then we'll have to take her down to the beach to see if we can help her find her own," Dan added. "Why don't we do that after church tomorrow?"

"Can she bring a friend?"

Dan looked up at Shelley. "A friend? Already?"

Shelley shrugged, then looked down at Aiden. "Who's Hailey's friend?"

Aiden grinned. "She was scared the first night she was here, so I gave her my guardian angel to watch over her. She told me she was going to take her everywhere, if that was okay with me." Aiden frowned. "I didn't know there were girl guardian angels. I always thought mine was a boy, but Hailey says no, she's a girl."

"That was kind of you," Dan said. "I'm sure if God hasn't already sent down another guardian angel to watch over you, He will soon."

"Oh, good." Aiden rolled over on his side and tucked his hands under his pillow, and Shelley thanked God again for blessing her with such a precious son.

★ ★ ★

Beverly's knuckles were on the verge of growing calluses from knocking so many times on Diane's door. Of course, how she could hear the knocks through Rocky's insistent barking was anybody's guess. The poor dog wanted to let company in; Diane wanted to keep them out. But Beverly wasn't going anywhere.

"I'm not leaving, Diane," Beverly called through the door. "So you'd better let me in before I wear a hole in your door."

She knocked again. And again. And again.

Finally, the door flew open. "I know you mean well," Diane said, "but I'm dealing with this cancer thing in my own way, and while I'm at it, I'm trying to write. Unfortunately I'm not making much headway because too many of my neighbors have been knocking on my door and ringing my telephone."

Beverly's eyes narrowed on her friend. "Are you going to let me in or not?"

Diane sighed heavily and stepped aside. "It doesn't appear I have much choice. If I don't let you in, you might rent a Sherman tank and mow my door down."

"Or hire the Big Bad Wolf to huff and puff."

Diane grinned. "You do know that's only a fairy tale."

"Yeah, but at least you cracked a smile."

"I've done that once or twice in the past week."

Beverly stared Diane up and down. "Have you gotten out of your pajamas in the past week?"

"Why bother? I wasn't expecting company."

"I hear Adelaide brought cookies and roses over to you and ended up leaving them on the doorstep. Do you really think it was appropriate not to invite her in?"

"I might have been in the shower at the time."

"I suppose that's a good excuse."

Diane turned, walking toward the kitchen. "Do you want some coffee or tea or—"

"No. What I want is for you to tell me how much longer you're going to keep this up?"

"Until I need someone to take me to my first chemo appointment."

"I'm surprised you haven't canceled or backed out."

Diane's eyes widened. "I'm angry; I'm not out of my mind. If I want to tackle the cancer, I've got to put up with all the horrid stuff that goes with it."

Diane walked back into the living room and collapsed on the sofa. "How's the campaign coming along?"

"Pretty good. Of course, I'd been counting on you to help out. Being down one volunteer is rather daunting."

"I'm sure you have a ton of volunteers."

"I have quite a few, but I only have one best friend. I'd rather have her working with me than an army of volunteers."

"Are you trying to butter me up?"

Beverly laughed. "Is it working?"

"Some. Besides, this is my last pair of clean pajamas and I've run out of laundry detergent and fabric softener. I might need you to run to the store for me."

"I'd rather we went together."

Beverly sat on the sofa next to Diane and put a hand on her friend's knee. "Your friends miss you. They're worried too."

"I'm coming out of this funk. It's just taking awhile."

"Have you and God made up?"

"We're back on speaking terms again."

"No more ranting?"

Diane shook her head. "We were both getting tired of that bad attitude of mine."

"That's what I like to hear."

"When I had my talk with Jessica, she cried—at first. Actually, I think she cried for a couple of days. When she called me on Saturday she told me it was high time I had a little heart-to-heart with God. She told me I needed to stop asking Him why I had cancer again, and ask Him to hold my hand a little tighter while I battle this thing."

"I always thought you had a pretty smart daughter."

"I'm still not the happiest camper on the face of the earth."

"But you're smiling, Diane. That's good for starters. But I need more out of you."

"Like what?"

"I need you to knock on doors or make phone calls, and if you don't want to do either of those things, I just need you to walk around town wearing your Vote for Beverly button."

"I can do that."

Beverly grinned. "I figured you could."

The telephone rang, the shrill sound making Diane tense. "I am so tired of listening to this thing ring. I was almost ready to cancel my service."

"Do you even bother to see who's calling?"

"On occasion."

"Are you going to look now?"

Diane rolled her eyes. Even from where Beverly sat, she could see Jeanette's name on the phone. "Are you going to answer it?" Beverly asked. "She could have news for us about the painting."

Diane answered with her normal hello.

Beverly wished she could hear the other side of the conversation, but all she heard was Diane's steady stream of "Uh-huh." "Yes." "I see." "Really?"

The call lasted for a good five minutes. Diane was smiling when she hung up.

"Well, good news. It looks like there's a real Joshua Reynolds painting hidden beneath some other artist's attempt at a landscape."

"I heard a Joshua Reynolds sold at auction for ten million pounds back in 2001. Does Jeanette think—"

"That was a special painting. Joshua Reynolds normally brings in somewhere in the fifty to a hundred thousand–dollar range."

"We could repair the roof with that kind of money. That's our most important goal."

"We might know even more come Friday."

"How? Why?" Beverly wished Diane would give her all the details in one fell swoop.

"Jeanette has an appointment with an expert at Sotheby's in New York. She's meeting with him Friday afternoon. And you'll never believe this, but Reverend Locke is going to meet Jeanette in New York. They're going to Sotheby's together."

"He must be feeling so relieved."

"Jeanette said he was remaining stoic. You know, the typical—" Diane broke off.

Beverly frowned. "What's wrong?"

Diane walked toward the window. "You'll never believe this."

"Good grief, Diane. Do you have to put me through the suspense yet again?"

"All right, no suspense. Jeff's SUV just pulled up in front of your house."

Chapter Twenty-Eight

What on earth are you doing here?"

Jeff laughed, wrapped his arms around Beverly's waist, and spun her around. "You're supposed to be excited to see me, not miffed that I showed up without calling first."

"I'm not miffed, I'm just...Oh, I don't know what I am. You've been gone for weeks on end, we've only communicated by text message, and your messages have been—"

"Short. I know." Jeff grabbed hold of her hand. "Come on, let's go down to the beach. We need to talk."

"About what?"

"About you and me."

She wasn't so sure she wanted to go, but she let him tug her along. They walked side by side and completely silent, as if neither one had anything to say to the other. This was what she feared. It was over, and he was merely trying to break it to her in a nice way.

When they reached the sand, Beverly slipped off her heels and Jeff kicked off the flip-flops he'd been wearing. They kept on walking until they reached an old sandcastle. He let go of her hand; she steeled her heart for the worst.

He drew in a deep breath and looked out toward the ocean. If he wasn't going to get this over with, she was.

"Look, Jeff, if you're going to break up with me, please, do it now, do it fast, and get it over with. You've been stringing me along for weeks, talking about my taking a trip to Jordan, as if I'd really want to go there all by myself. You've cut off your text messages in midsentence. To tell you the honest truth, you've just about driven me out of my mind. So please, get on with it."

Jeff frowned. "What are you talking about? Why would I want to call it quits between you and me, when it took me months to come even somewhere close to winning your heart?"

"And then you went off to Russia and then to Jordan with barely a how-do-you-do in between trips."

"I admit that wasn't the smartest thing to do."

"You think?"

Jeff chuckled. "While I was in Russia, I got to thinking about our relationship. I thought it might be progressing too fast. I kept thinking I had nothing to offer you. No home. No steady income."

"I have no home either. I definitely don't have a steady income. But who cares? We're both doing quite well."

"I care, and the more I thought about it, the more scared I got."

"Did you ever think about sharing your thoughts with me?"

"That's not the way I operate."

"Then it's time to change."

Jeff laughed. "And then I got to thinking that you might laugh at me—"

"About what? I've got news for you, Jeff. I find you almost perfect, not just in the looks department, but in the personality department too. We get along great, and—"

"Would you stop talking for a minute and let me ask you my question?"

Beverly rolled her eyes. "All right, go ahead. I'm waiting."

Jeff sighed, not once, but twice. She was just about ready to turn around and walk away, when he knelt down on bended knee. This couldn't possibly be what she thought it was, could it?

Jeff reached out and took her hands. "Beverly Wheeland, I had a lot of time for soul-searching in Russia and in Jordan. You know what they say about absence making the heart grow fonder? It's true. It's even more true when you send your girl text messages and she doesn't text back. It makes you realize that you've done something wrong, that you've made a huge mistake by not asking this question earlier, or stating your true feelings. So, Beverly, I've got to tell you, I've never loved anyone the way I love you. I want you beside me now and always. And"—he took yet another deep breath—"will you marry me?"

Beverly smiled. She loved him desperately. She wanted to be with him...but—"Shouldn't you be in Turkey right now?"

"That's not an answer to my question. Couldn't you give me a yes or no before we move on to another topic?"

"I could, but what happened to your Turkey trip? Is it canceled? Did you cancel it?" She smiled suddenly. That had to be it. He backed out of the Turkey trip so he could come back to Marble Cove to be with her.

"I had to see you." He stood, her hands still in his. He moved in close. "I couldn't wait any longer, so I told my editor I'd be in Turkey a day later than planned, and I used my own money to fly home."

"And you're only going to be a day late getting to Turkey? Weren't you supposed to be there today?"

He nodded slowly. "I have to catch a plane tonight."

"You tell me you don't want to be away from me, and then you propose, and as soon as I give you an answer you hop back on a plane and take off for Istanbul."

"That's about the size of it."

Beverly laughed. "And I suppose you want an answer right now?"

"It would give me something great to hang on to while I'm in Turkey."

"You'll have the ruins of Ephesus. Isn't that enough?"

"Enough would be having you there with me."

"I'm not going anywhere with you without a ring on my finger."

"Then say yes. We can hop on a plane—"

"I have a town hall meeting in a week. I have campaigning to do."

"But you could go to Turkey instead."

"I could, or you could stay here and campaign with me."

"But my job—"

"Don't say another word, Jeff. I'm not giving up my plans to run for mayor, and I doubt you want to give up your travel plans."

"So you're telling me 'No'? You won't marry me?"

"I'm telling you I'll think about it."

Jeff sighed heavily. And then he laughed, shaking his head. "As much as I'd hoped for an answer tonight, in the past year I've learned that you don't jump into anything without giving it a lot of thought."

"No, I don't."

"Well, go ahead and give my proposal a lot of thought. Remember that I love you." He pulled her close and kissed her. Right then and there she wanted to give him an answer, but she couldn't. "And please, Beverly, I'm not one for begging, but I hope that your long, drawn-out thoughts will lead you toward me, not away."

This from a man who was going to fly off to Turkey at any moment, leaving her alone...again.

★ ★ ★

The first text message came late Tuesday night. *Arrived Istanbul, not Constantinople. There's a song by that name, or something close. Recorded back in the fifties, when life was simpler, and men proposed with flowers and the lady, well, she rarely ever said, "I'll think about it." Have you?*

Beverly sent her text message back without any hesitation. *Think about you constantly. And the town hall meeting. No time to think about anything else.*

The next message came Wednesday night. *How about a honeymoon in Jordan? As I mentioned before, you'd love it. Petra's gorgeous by night. So are you.*

Beverly had given Petra a lot of thought. She'd loved Jeff's photos. She loved Jeff. But she also loved Marble Cove. Could she leave here to make him happy? Would he live here and stay by her side, or hop on a plane several times a month and take off to the four corners of the world?

She wished her mind wasn't filled with such confusion, especially now, when she had the town hall meeting to think about.

While she hesitated to answer, another text came through. *I'm falling in love with Ephesus. You would too. Will have to put it on the honeymoon grand tour. Thank God I'm making good money and will be able to afford our special trip.*

It didn't take her but a moment to tap out her response. *I've always heard sailing down the Nile is thrilling. Crocodiles and pyramids. What more could a girl want? I know—to be mayor.* She ended with a smiley face.

★ ★ ★

By Thursday, Diane's voice was hoarse from making so many calls on Beverly's behalf. It wasn't always easy convincing the citizens of Marble Cove that a relative newcomer to town could do a better job as mayor than lifelong residents, but by the time she hung up, she was fairly sure she'd won over another vote.

Making all of these calls was good for her nerves. They kept the depression she'd sunk into last week at bay. Praying with her friends had been a godsend too. She'd hated the thought of having them hover, but that hovering had given her courage.

All of a sudden, as if he'd sensed something special about to happen, Rocky sprang out from under Diane's desk and ran to the front door, barking wildly. Just then, Diane saw Jeanette's old Volkswagen pull up beside the picket fence. She wasn't expecting her, but the sight of her sister-in-law made her smile.

And she couldn't wait to see Jeanette's smile when she gave her the gift.

"I thought you were headed to New York!" Diane said when she opened the door. "What's happened to your meeting at Sotheby's?"

"I am. The meeting's tomorrow. Reverend Locke and I decided to drive down together. The leaves on the trees are starting to turn, and who can resist taking in the sights, something neither of us would see if we flew?"

"Then I imagine you can't stay long?" Diane asked.

"Ten or fifteen minutes at the most." Jeanette wrapped Diane in her arms. "How are you doing?"

"Much better than last week." Diane swallowed hard, trying not to think about what the next months held in store. "Actually, I'm feeling pretty good. Keeping a positive outlook."

"You amaze me, Diane. I wish I had just an ounce of your strength."

"We make quite a pair. You amaze me too with all your talent..." Diane smiled. "We could pat each other on the back all day long, but I'd rather chat awhile before you have to run off. Would you like some lemonade or iced tea? Anything?"

Jeanette shook her head as she sat down on the sofa, and Diane sat across from her.

"Jessica told me that the two of you had had a lovely chat last week. She said you'd mentioned the tea parties you and your grandmother used to have."

"I'm sure I must have told you about them at one time or another."

Diane shook her head. "I don't think so. I'm surprised you didn't mention them the last couple of times you were here, especially when you were admiring the teapot she gave Eric and me for a wedding gift."

Jeanette took a deep breath. "She was always so sweet when I was little; always so delicate and proper, setting her dining room table with her best china and crystal, with crisp white linen napkins and...and with that teapot she gave you. I always thought it was one of the prettiest things I'd ever seen.

"She taught me how to hold my pinkie finger when I drank from a delicate cup, or any cup for that matter, and she told me that someday I'd make someone a good wife and hostess."

Diane chuckled. "That seems to have been the dream of every woman older than we are, that her children should marry and have children and live happily ever after."

"She told me that when I got married..." Jeanette shrugged. "It doesn't matter. Not really."

"What? You can't get my curiosity up, then forget the punch line."

"All right, she told me that when I got married, she'd give me that teapot. Other than her husband, the teapot was the most precious thing she owned. It had belonged to her mother and her mother before that. I was never upset that she'd given it to you. I have to admit, though, that I was always a little jealous."

Diane went to the display cabinet and took out the teapot. Walking back to the sofa, she handed it to Jeanette. "It's yours."

Jeanette shook her head. "I can't take it, Diane. Grandmother gave it to you, and—"

"No, she didn't. Not on purpose, anyway." Diane removed the lid, took the card from inside, and handed it to Jeanette. "Read this."

There was nothing at all written on the envelope, but there was a wedding card inside. Jeanette opened it slowly, and read the words out loud. "'For my darling Nettie, for tea parties past, present, and future. I love you. Grandma.'"

Jeanette looked up at Diane, a questioning frown on her face. "Why did you keep it if you knew it was for me?"

"I'd never heard of anyone named Nettie before I saw what your grandmother had written in the card, and I really didn't give it all that much thought. There were so many wedding gifts to open and send out thank you notes for, and we just assumed your grandmother had forgotten my name and wrote someone else's. After all, it was wrapped in wedding paper, with the card tucked under the ribbon."

Jeanette laughed, a lone tear slipping down the side of her nose. "Grandmother did go downhill fast, once the dementia took hold. But really, Diane, I'm sure she meant it for you. After all, I never did get married."

"You're being a bit too cavalier, Jeanette. I want you to have it, with my blessings."

★ ★ ★

Beverly's stomach was in knots for days leading up to the town hall. She'd given speeches so many times in her life that they usually came second nature. But this was different. She had to prove to the citizens of Marble Cove that she had what it took to run the town. That she knew its history, its laws, its people.

She rubbed her right hand. Her knuckles were sore from knocking on so many doors, but it had been worth it.

At last it was early Saturday evening. She stood in the wings and watched people file into the auditorium. It was just a trickle at first, but finally the seats began to fill up.

"Nervous?" Diane asked, sliding her arm around Beverly's waist.

"A little. It's hard not to be when this is all you've thought about for nearly a month. I can tell you that I'm not half as nervous as I was when I played piano for Easter at Old First."

Diane laughed. "You've had a lot of other things on your mind too. Me. Cancer. Jeff. I believe you've proved that you can multitask."

Beverly laughed and peeked around the corner to see if there were any people that she knew. "Mrs. Peabody's in the very front row, sitting next to my father."

"Anyone else?"

"Edward Maker and Celia Patterson are walking down the aisle. And I think everyone who lives on Newport Avenue is out there."

"Even Mr. Calder?"

Beverly nodded. "But I imagine he'll be cheering his grandson on, not me."

"Hi there." Shelley gave Beverly a quick hug and Margaret followed suit. "Is it okay if the three of us stick around up here on the stage to watch, or would you prefer having us down in front?"

"Wherever you're comfortable. I doubt I'll notice anyone while I'm out there on the stage. We did a rehearsal earlier, and the lights are awfully bright."

"What about Jeff?" Margaret asked. "Have you heard from him? Is he going to make it?"

Beverly shrugged. "I've been busy; I know he's been busy. And it's an awfully long way from Turkey to Marble Cove."

"You two haven't called it quits, have you?" Shelley asked, in her normal straightforward way.

"No, in fact—and you have to promise to keep this a secret, since I haven't even told my father—" She had her friends' full attention. They seemed to anticipate what she was about to say, and since it was only minutes before the meeting was to begin, she couldn't keep them in suspense much longer. "Jeff proposed."

There was a long, deathly silence. At last, Diane asked, "And you said yes?"

"I said I'd have to think about it."

"You didn't!" Margaret was aghast.

"How could you?" Shelley asked, frowning. "You love each other. If you can't see it, I sure can."

"There's so much more than just being in love," Beverly rationalized.

"Such as?" Beverly was sure Diane would have been on her side, but she looked disapproving when she asked, "When do you plan to make your decision? Doomsday?"

"After the election. Maybe. Maybe sooner. I just don't know."

Pastor Carl walked up before Beverly could add any more of an explanation. "One minute until we get this show rolling. Would you mind taking your place, Beverly?"

"I'd be happy to, Reverend."

Shelley and Margaret both blew Beverly a kiss. Diane gave her a quick hug, took out a tissue, and wiped a speck of lipstick from the edge of her mouth. "There now. You're perfect. Go out there and knock 'em dead."

The noise was almost deafening, a mixture of applause and multiple conversations. Except for his sneer when he looked at Beverly, Dennis looked like a million bucks in an expensive suit.

Poor Lee. He was visibly shaking.

At long last the commotion died down and Pastor Carl introduced the candidates, told everyone how the meeting would be run, then looked out at the audience and called on the first person, a face Beverly vaguely remembered as living on the north side of town. She'd knocked on his door, offered him her campaign pitch, and he slammed the door in her face.

"Mr. Calder. There are those of us in Marble Cove who were devastated when the plans for your resort were tabled by the town council and mayor. If or when you become mayor, will you try, once again, to get those plans approved?"

"Thank you, Gene," Dennis said. He obviously knew the questioner. "Building that resort has been a lifelong ambition of mine. Like you, I was also devastated when the plans were turned down. The resort could have brought significant revenues into our town…"

Beverly's mind drifted away while Dennis droned on, all charm and sophistication, reminding Beverly of Jeff's advice. *Don't shoot for charming. Forget sophistication.*

The next question was directed at Lee and had to do with the businesses on Main Street. "There's talk of closing Main to automobile traffic to make it more touristy. Do you support this plan?"

Lee looked as if he'd been blindsided; the same thing could happen to her. She knew it. Someone had pulled a question not only out of left field, but out of the clear blue sky. Was there really a plan to close off Main Street?

Lee shuddered in his boots. His mother, Evelyn Waters, was sitting in the front row and on the edge of her seat. She looked as if she wanted to hold up cheat sheets so Lee would know the answers. But was there really an answer to this question?

"I'm sorry." He looked from Beverly, to Dennis, to Pastor Carl. "Could I have another question?"

Beverly spoke up then. "Mind if I answer?"

"Not at all, Ms. Wheeland."

"As we all know, Main Street is a beloved part of Marble Cove. I've often wanted to count the cobbles, and I try to imagine the founders of our town picking out each stone, trying to find ones that were close in size and shape, and laying them, stone by stone, thousands upon thousands of them, their backs aching as they toiled. But the fruits of their labor were beyond compare. For well over a hundred years people have walked over those stones. They've ridden horses there, driven buggies and wagons, herded sheep and cattle, and in our last century, opened the road to the automobile.

"Our shops on Main Street have changed over time. We no longer have a butcher or a baker or even a candlestick maker on Main, but we have an outstanding variety of shops that cater to locals and tourists alike. They park their cars on the cobbled street. They go to the wharf and haunt our gift shops, galleries, cafes, and even the Pet Place has been a favorite of many for nearly twenty years now.

"It would be a shame to close down Main Street to automobile traffic. Unfortunately, time is getting the better of the cobbles. If we want to secure the future of our beautiful town and its Main Street, we will—one day in the near future—have to come up with a way to move traffic around without harming either the street or the businesses on Main.

"I must say, until tonight, I hadn't heard of any such plan, but we may have to look into the feasibility of such an idea in the near future. But it will not be done without input, not only from engineers, but most importantly, from the businesses on Main and citizens of our community." Beverly smiled. "I hope I've answered your question."

Beverly was afraid she might turn red when the applause began and didn't die down for quite some time. Dennis was fit to be tied; Lee looked like he wanted to run and hide; and Beverly just smiled, listening to more and more questions, answering when it was her turn, and feeling as though she'd nailed each answer.

An hour later, it was over. People began to file out. Others came up to the stage to shake her hand and to ask how they could get a campaign button or sign for the front of their house. They asked questions they weren't able to ask during the town hall, and Beverly was more than happy to answer.

She didn't see Dennis Calder or Lee Waters anywhere around. They couldn't have left already, could they? Not when there were still so many people to meet and greet.

She tried to get to everyone who wanted to talk, but that was near to impossible. She'd have to plan a few more meetings, at restaurants, coffee shops, anywhere that a group of people could form.

She couldn't remember ever getting so many hugs and kisses. Her father beamed, wearing his pride on his sleeve. Mr. Maker, who'd come all the way from Augusta, wrapped her in a bear hug, then slipped his hand back around Celia's.

If only Jeff were here—

"I've never witnessed such an incredible town hall meeting."

Beverly whipped around at the sound of the familiar voice. Jeff stood mere inches away. His smile was broad, and she thought he was the most beautiful sight in the world. She wanted to tell him she'd missed him, that she was glad he'd come, but any words she could have said were cut short when Margaret, Shelley, and Diane surrounded them.

There were more congratulations, pats on the back, hugs—and when she thought she couldn't take any more, Reverend Locke appeared out of nowhere.

"I thought you were in New York," Beverly said, holding out her hand. He took hers and held it warmly.

"I was there yesterday for the meeting and flew home this morning."

"And?" Diane asked.

"It appears all of our hopes are ringing true." Reverend Locke smiled. "The painting's definitely a Joshua Reynolds. Better yet, it appears it's the portrait of Reverend Thorpe's wife Evangeline, the painting he brought with him from London." His eyes twinkled as he quoted Psalm 17:15. "'I will behold thy face in righteousness: I shall be satisfied, when I awake, with thy likeness.'"

"That's incredible!" Margaret could barely contain her excitement. "And its value? Could Sotheby's give you an estimate?"

Reverend Locke grinned from ear to ear. "Conservatively... three million."

Beverly was sure her mouth dropped open. Never in her wildest dreams had she imagined that much.

"That portrait is the answer to our prayers," Reverend Locke said. "I hate to part with it, but perhaps it's time to share a piece of Reverend Thorpe with the rest of the world."

"It's an amazing treasure," Diane said.

"An amazing treasure, all right." Beverly looked into Jeff's eyes, holding his hands tight. "Sometimes the greatest treasures are not where we expect to find them."

Before she could utter another word, she was swept away by several members of the audience, who had questions, lots and lots of questions.

For now, all she could do was blow Jeff a kiss. Later, she just might give him her answer.

About the Author

USA Today best-selling author Patti Berg began penning stories while in elementary school, when she wrote the script for a puppet show that she and her friends put on at a local hospital. Thirty years later, one of her dreams came true when the first of her many warm and lighthearted novels appeared in bookstores.

Scared of dogs until the age of fifty, Patti now goes out of her way to pet every dog she gets close to and would happily bring home all of the puppies in the pound if her less impulsive husband would only let her. He's had less success keeping her from saying yes when family, friends, and others ask her to volunteer. A past president, secretary, and newsletter editor of the Sacramento Valley Rose chapter of Romance Writers of America as well as past president, Web site and conference coordinator for RWA's Published Authors' Special Interest Chapter, Patti is currently volunteering with the Ada County Idaho Sheriff's Department.

She lives in southwestern Idaho with her husband of thirty-three years and a huggable Bernese mountain dog named Barkley. To learn more about Patti, go to pattiberg.com.

A Conversation with Patti Berg

Q: When you're not writing, what sort of activities do you enjoy most?

A: Lunching with my friends! Going to the movies with the girls. Long countryside drives with my husband. Buying girly things for my granddaughters, and video games and adventure books for my grandson; they all live way too far away! Being an active member of the Friends of the Star, Idaho, Library—the best library ever—and helping to make sure there is money for summer reading programs and other activities for our small community. Volunteering with the Ada County Sheriff's Office and Eagle, Idaho, Police Department. Life is good!

Q: What are some of the things in your bucket list?

A: In addition to a trip to England, I'd love to ride a camel across the hot Egyptian sands to visit the pyramids; sail along the Nile to visit Karnak, Luxor, and the Valley of the Kings; marvel at the city of Petra, carved out of rose-red rock, in Jordan; tour the holy sites of Jerusalem; stand beneath Michelangelo's masterpiece on the ceiling in the Vatican's Sistine Chapel; and spend long hours in front of Leonardo da Vinci's *Last Supper*, marveling at his work and the holy event he depicted. As you can tell, traveling far and wide is pretty much my entire bucket list.

Q: What makes a story great?

A: To me, it's the characters. They don't have to be heroic or larger than life; they simply have to come alive on the written page. When readers can feel a character's emotions, when they can laugh or cry right along with the character, or cringe with fear or take a deep breath, throw back their shoulders and chase after the bad guy, just as the character in the book is doing, then the author has succeeded in creating a great story. I want to step inside the pages of a book when I'm reading. I want to become the main character and forget everything else going on around me. If you're going to write—concentrate on your characters: give them a past and a present; give them emotional conflict, something to fight for, something to achieve. Do that and you'll create a great story.

BAKING WITH SHELLEY

Shelley's Gingerbread Cookies

3 cups all-purpose flour

1 teaspoon baking soda

¾ teaspoon ground cinnamon

¾ teaspoon ground ginger

½ teaspoon ground allspice

½ teaspoon ground cloves

½ teaspoon salt

1 stick unsalted butter (at room temperature)

¼ cup vegetable shortening, at room temperature

½ cup tightly packed brown sugar (light)

⅔ cup molasses

1 egg

Preheat oven to 350 degrees.

In a medium bowl, sift the flour, baking soda, cinnamon, ginger, allspice, cloves, and salt. Set aside.

In a large bowl, use an electric mixer to beat the butter and vegetable shortening until well-combined (about one minute). Add brown sugar and beat until the mixture is light in texture (about two minutes), then blend in the molasses and egg. Gradually mix in the flour mixture to make a stiff dough. Divide the dough in half, wrapping each half in plastic wrap, and refrigerate until chilled, three to four hours.

To roll out the cookies, take out half the chilled dough and let stand at room temperature about ten minutes, or until warm enough to roll out without cracking. Place the dough on a lightly floured surface and sprinkle the top with flour. Roll out the dough ⅛ inch thick. For softer cookies, roll out slightly thicker. Use cookie cutters to cut out the cookies and transfer to nonstick baking sheets, leaving one inch between cookies. Rechill scraps of dough, while using second half of chilled dough to cut more cookies.

Bake ten to twelve minutes at 350 degrees until the edges are set and crisp. Cool on the sheets for two minutes, then transfer to wire racks to finish cooling.

Decorate with royal icing (below).

> 3¾ to 4 cups confectioners' sugar
> 3 tablespoons meringue powder
> 5 to 6 tablespoons warm water

Combine all ingredients in large mixing bowl. Beat with hand-held mixer for ten to twelve minutes or until peaks form. Makes three cups.

FROM THE
GUIDEPOSTS ARCHIVES

This story by Judy H. Armstrong of
Headland, Alabama, originally appeared in
the January 1992 issue of *Guideposts*.

Mrs. Webb was blind and frail and her health had been declining for many months. She and her husband lived in the shadow of our church, Headland First Baptist.

On New Year's Eve she went to bed early as usual while Mr. Webb watched TV. Then unexpectedly at 10:30, she came into the living room and announced, "Honey, I think we should stay up until midnight and hear the church bells ring."

In all the years they had lived in town, Mr. Webb could not remember hearing church bells at midnight on New Year's Eve. As far as he could recall, the bell at First Baptist had not been rung in over seventeen years. Nevertheless Mr. Webb replied, "Of course, dear, come and sit beside me. We'll see the new year in together."

And so they sat and talked, waiting. Midnight came and with it the unmistakable sound of a church bell. "There it is," Mrs. Webb said, and indeed, the bell high in the steeple at First Baptist was ringing.

That was to be the last night that this old married couple was to spend together, for in the morning Mrs. Webb died peacefully in her sleep.

Mr. Webb did not know that the bell at First Baptist had only recently been fixed. Nor did he know that a youth group was spending the night in the church in a "lock in," or that on the spur of the moment the young people would decide to ring in the New Year. His wife knew none of these things either, but she knew the bell would toll.

Read on for a sneak peek of the next exciting book in
Miracles of Marble Cove!

Steps of Faith
by Camy Tang

A sudden thumping at the front door made Diane jump in her seat at the breakfast table.

"Diane!" She heard Beverly's voice, muffled from the door and the distance from the kitchen. A cup of cold coffee and a bowl of soggy cereal sat untouched on the table.

For a moment, Diane considered not answering it. She felt so tired and listless. But she remembered Beverly's words about not giving in, not letting the diagnosis of cancer defeat her. She rose and hurried to the front door, although it felt almost as if she were slogging through knee-high water.

Beverly's concerned face broke into a smile when she saw Diane. "Did you get my message?"

Next door, Margaret's minivan backed out of her driveway, then drove up in front of Diane's house and came to a stop. Margaret rolled the window down and grinned. "Are you ready?"

"Ready for what?"

"I hope I'm not too late." Shelley ran across the street, a stuffed-full cloth tote bag over her arm and a picnic basket sagging between her hands. "I had to wait for Frances to pick the kids up."

"Late for what?" Diane looked in bewilderment from Shelley to Margaret and then to Beverly.

"We planned a surprise for you." Beverly ducked into the house and grabbed Diane's jacket, hanging near the front door. "Put this on. It'll be chilly."

"Wait a minute. I have work to do—" Diane began.

"It'll still be there when we get back." Beverly gave her a calm smile and shook Diane's coat insistently.

With a little grumbling, Diane slipped her arms into her coat. "Let me get my shoes on."

"Put on your hiking boots," Beverly said. "There's a nice trail."

"Where in the world are we going?" Diane laced up her boots.

"A new park." Margaret appeared at the open front door.

"Why today?" Diane straightened.

"Because you didn't answer your phone all last night. We knew you must need some cheering up." Beverly held the front door open, and Shelley walked out ahead of them. "So we planned this little holiday. Margaret's the one who suggested the new park."

Margaret spoke over her shoulder as she led the way to her idling minivan. "The entire time I've lived here, it's been overgrown and unusable. I can't wait to see what they've done to improve it."

Diane allowed herself to be bundled into the car, and she realized that the tiredness that had seemed to permeate her limbs earlier was lifting.

It took about ten minutes to reach the park, which was on the west side of Marble Cove. It was somewhat inland but not too far, because Diane could still smell the ocean as she got out of the minivan in the dirt-packed parking lot.

It was delightfully sunny for October, and the crisp brightness of the day made it seem warmer than it actually was. The four friends crossed the park, colorful leaves and sparse gray grass crunching under their feet, and set up on a wide wooden table nestled under a towering oak tree. Shelley unloaded the cloth tote bag and flipped open a tablecloth that they spread over the table. While Beverly continued to unpack the bag, Shelley began taking food out of the picnic basket.

"Gracious, what army are you feeding?" Diane peeked inside a bowl filled with chocolate chip cookies and other desserts. She reached in and snagged a pecan bar.

Shelley grinned. "I wanted to perk you up a little and wasn't entirely sure what would do it, so I went for the full spectrum."

"Here's the coffee." Margaret set down a large thermos and reached in for a snapdragon cookie.

Diane felt tears gather behind her eyes, but she blinked to keep them back. They'd done all this for her.

"I saw some roofers on top of Old First yesterday," Beverly said. "They were hard at work on it."

Diane smiled. "Oh, good. I'm so glad Old First now has the funds to be restored."

"Thanks to us." Shelley held her coffee cup out, and they all toasted. "Here's to determination to recognize mysteries and follow clues until they pay off."

"Hear, hear!" Margaret laughed. "Allan said that it was stubborn single-mindedness, but I think I like 'determination' better."

"Even though it was stressful for a while there when we thought Old First would have to close down," Shelley said, "it drew us even closer together for the past eight months, don't you think?"

"That's why we wanted to surprise you with this outing." Margaret reached over to touch Diane's hand. "We're your friends and we're here for you during this hard time. We *want* to help you through this."

Diane appreciated the words and Margaret's gentle squeeze of her fingers, but she was relieved when Margaret let go of her hand. She knew she couldn't battle her cancer alone, but at the same time, she didn't want to burden any of her friends. They all had so much on their own plates.

Beverly had told her to fight. She could do that. She missed having Eric with her, but she had fought cancer before. She could do it again.

"I appreciate your concern for me, but part of my fear the last time this happened was not knowing what to expect from the treatments." Diane still didn't like hospitals, but they didn't inspire terror like they had the first time she'd gone in for her chemo treatments. "The doctor called and said he's sending my blood samples for additional tests. He wants to see if I'll be a good candidate for a new clinical trial drug."

"That's a good thing, right?" Shelley asked.

"I think so. I have an appointment with in him two weeks and then hopefully I'll start treatment. It will help knowing you're all praying for me."

Shelley nodded eagerly, but Margaret's expression was concerned, and Beverly looked apprehensive. Diane changed the subject. "Anyway, you all have things going on in your own lives. Shelley, how are things with Hailey?"

A shadow of anxiety crossed Shelley's face. "She's been fine, especially considering I don't think she understands why she's staying with us and not with her mom."

"Have you been able to get in contact with Susannah?" Beverly asked.

"I tried calling every number I can think of, and I can't get hold of her. It seems that her phones have been out of service."

"Do you think she's all right?" Margaret asked.

"I..." Shelley swallowed. "I hope so."

"What did she say when she dropped Hailey off at your house?"

Shelley recounted the conversation, including how cryptic her sister had been.

"What have you told Hailey about her mom?"

"That's just it." Shelley shrugged. "I don't know what to tell her. I don't know what Susannah's doing."

"She didn't say anything to you, maybe in the weeks before she dropped Hailey off?" Beverly asked.

Shelley paused. "I have this feeling that when she called me this past month, it was to prepare me. She reminded me that I promised I'd take care of Hailey if needed. Something tells me we'll be taking care of her for more than just a few weeks, or even a few months."

"Why would Susannah abandon her daughter for so long?" Margaret asked gently. "You know your sister. She wouldn't do that, would she?"

"Not if she had a choice. But I think this time, she doesn't. I just can't think of any explanation why." A line of worry creased Shelley's forehead.

Diane could imagine how she must feel. Shelley already had her hands full with two young children, and it must be overwhelming to suddenly have a nine-year-old added to the mix.

"How does Dan feel about all this?" Margaret asked.

Shelley gave a slightly watery smile. "He's been such a trooper. He's been helping out as much as he can."

"Be sure to let us know when you need help," Margaret said.

"Or before you go stark raving mad." Beverly smiled.

Shelley gave a short laugh, but it sounded almost reluctant. "Let's not talk about gloomy things. What we all want to know, Beverly, is have you decided whether you're going to marry Jeff?"

Beverly blushed, but her eyes shone. "I haven't told him yet, but yes, I will."

Margaret whooped and Shelley's tense expression dissolved into a joyous smile. Diane felt a bubble of happiness in her chest that replaced the buzzing anxiety that had lain just under the surface for the past week.

"When will you tell him?" Shelley's voice was a high-pitched squeal.

Beverly laughed. "We're having dinner tomorrow."

"Do you know when you want the wedding to be?" Margaret asked.

"Not yet. It'll depend on his work schedule and also if I win the campaign for mayor."

"Are you nervous about the election?" Shelley asked.

"Not so much right now, but I'll probably feel it more nearer the end of the month, closer to the election date."

"I'm sure you'll win," Shelley said.

"I'm not quite that confident, but I'm sure the residents of Marble Cove will pick the person who will make their town the kind of place they want it to be."

"Anything new with you?" Shelley asked, turning to Margaret.

Margaret tilted her head. "Matt Beauregard called and asked me to do a few more paintings for greeting cards, but he asked if I could do them without lighthouses this time."

Shelley frowned. "I'd think that since your lighthouse paintings sell so well, he'd want you to keep doing those."

Margaret smiled. "Well, the last six paintings he bought from me were lighthouses, so maybe he's lighthoused out."

Shelley gasped in mock horror and said in lofty tones, "You can *never* be lighthoused out."

Everyone laughed. Margaret stood slowly patted her stomach. "Shelley, those treats were wonderful, but now I need a walk."

"That sounds good." Shelley jumped to her feet.

They stowed everything in Margaret's minivan and then headed to the far end of the park, where a trailhead awaited them.

"Is the trail dirt?" Diane glanced at her hiking boots. "Or mud?"

"It looks like it's been packed down and covered with gravel," Margaret said. "Good thing it hasn't rained recently or it would be a river of mud."

"My mother-in-law talked to some of the people who fixed up the park," Shelley said as they started down the trail. "In the spring, when the ground's dry again, they're going to pave the trail so bikes and strollers can use it."

They wound their way between rambling blackberry bushes, stripped of greenery by the autumn coolness, and tall trees with branches clothed in red, gold, and brown leaves. The sunlight dappled down through the branches and tickled Diane's eyes as they walked. "I've been in Marble Cove for over a year and I've never been here before," Diane said.

"This whole forest area has been mainly inaccessible for as long as I've lived here," Margaret said.

"Dan's mom said that when the local residents cleaned up the park, they also started to open up these old trails,"

Shelley said. "She told me that these were once shortcut paths that people took through the woods. Until recently, they hadn't been used for decades."

"What used to be around here?" Diane asked.

"Houses?" Shelley guessed. "We're not too far from the ocean, although it's mostly rocks and cliffs on this part of Marble Cove's shoreline."

Diane grinned. "Are we going to stumble onto some decrepit old vacation house?"

Shelley giggled. "With ghosts of tourists past."

But as she spoke, Diane suddenly heard a high, airy toot. It lingered in the air almost like the last note of a song. "Did you hear that?"

Her friends had also paused. Beverly nodded. "It sounded like...a train whistle."